Last Wish

by
Connor Black

Last Wish
Copyright © 2020 Connor Black

Editing by The Pro Book Editor

ISBN: 9798647218551

Main category—FIC019000 FICTION / Literary
Other category—FIC000000 FICTION / General

First Edition

He who is outside his door has the hardest part of his journey behind him.

–Flemish proverb

1

Cancer comes like an arrow, unexpected and silent, from a cruel enemy hiding in the shadows. The expectation is that you'll fight, you'll counter the damage from that arrow with every tool, treatment, and hope.

Hope is the most difficult. It's hard to hold. Some days, it's hard to find. But still, you stay positive, which is what I did for my wife every day.

"Hello, my love!" I gently moved a tube on Lauren's cheek aside and gave her a kiss before lifting the insulated bag off my shoulder. "A bit chilly tonight, so I thought chicken soup would be best." I opened the zipper and withdrew a large cup, setting it down with a spoon and napkin. "But before that, I have good news to share. You're looking at the new accounts payable manager!"

I knew Lauren would be pleased. She'd always encouraged me, no matter what the occasion. In fact, it was through her positive support that we'd met. Not much more than two years ago, I'd reluctantly joined some colleagues for drinks after work. As the night went on, the music in the bar was turned up and, before long, everyone was dancing. Everyone but me. I'd been too shy to make my way to the dance floor.

One of the boys from sales had come over and given me a hard time for not joining everyone, the drinks having given him a bullish tone. "C'mon, John! Stop being a baby and get out there with us!" he'd said.

A hand had wrapped around my own as a beautiful woman with flowing blonde hair appeared out of nowhere to save me. She'd said, "He's just asked me to dance, so I hope you'll take a rain check?" Her disarming smile had sent him off with a sneer, and then she'd led me to the opposite side of the dance floor.

I'd done my best to find the beat and move to it, thankful for her help but also worried about appearing terribly awkward.

She'd looked me in the eye and, as if reading my thoughts, said, "You're doing great. Relax. Let your body enjoy the music."

She'd put me instantly at ease. That day and every day since.

Lauren's enthusiasm for life had helped me break out of my careful, structured shell. Well, perhaps not entirely as I was more of a lifelong project. But she certainly gave it her all. I remembered her laughter at my closet of white shirts and gray suits and her eyes sparkling when I headed off to work in one of the bright ties she'd convinced me to try. And her poking fun at my squished face when she'd first suggested we leave the bed unmade on Sundays. She was full of such joy and energy every moment that together, our happiness was unstoppable.

Our courtship had lasted a year before we married and escaped on a beautiful honeymoon to Key West. Soon after, we'd found a cute little house in a perfect suburb. It had needed some work, for sure, but as we were only twenty-six, we had plenty of energy to put in the elbow grease and stay on budget. We'd loved every minute, from installing new sinks to painting. Each room was, of course, a different color, because that was just how vibrant she was.

She'd always said her love of life came from a semester abroad in college. She'd arranged to take a term of design classes in London and, like many other students who study there, loved the idea of weekends away in continental Europe. The first trip planned was to Paris. Lauren told me the story as only she could, barefoot on the bed, her arms around a colorful pillow, and her blonde hair wild and askew.

"It was my first time, John. My first time going to a country where everyone spoke a different language, where history was measured in centuries, not decades. It was magical! A story through every doorway, around every corner. And in every delicious bite!" she'd said.

"I can imagine," I'd replied, even though I couldn't imagine it at all.

"Sophie, a friend from my art history class, went with me. We had an absolute riot rushing around to all of the museums and cafés. We tried to act like the French girls did, pretending to be aloof yet totally full of style. We knew we were terrible impersonators but couldn't care less!"

"So, what happened?"

"A mistake, of course. The best things in life always come from mistakes!"

I remembered she leaned forward spontaneously to give me a kiss. After her lips had left mine, she'd touched my nose. It was a fun little quirk of hers that I loved. She said it made sure the person you loved, loved you just as much back, because who else would let you touch their nose?

I'd smiled and asked, "What was the mistake?"

"Our return tickets said one o'clock. Midday departure, so no problem, right? It turns out they were for one *AM* because

Europeans use the twenty-four-hour clock. We were twelve hours late!" She'd given the pillow a big squeeze before opening her eyes wide and saying, "Whoops! Life lesson, that one."

"So what did you do?"

"It turns out Sunday afternoon is the worst time to go from Paris to London on a train, or a plane, for that matter. But there was one spot left on the last train that night."

"So you made it back for class the next day," I'd resolved, feeling at ease that she'd figured it out.

"Nope! I told Sophie to take the seat!"

"Uh-oh. What did you do?"

"I played hooky, John! Something every nineteen-year-old needs to do!"

I remembered her jumping up and down on the bed when she said this, bouncing around in a circle. I'd laughed at the carefree way she knew everything would simply work out for her. It almost always did. Almost.

She'd flopped back down on the bed and told me about how she'd switched the classes from being graded to 'pass/no pass' and trained around Europe on her own for two weeks. "It was amazing, John! I just let the trip take me away! Backpackers shared meals and stories, even a few clothes in the crazy hostels we stayed in. I laughed and roamed, completely free!"

I remembered being floored but at the same time captivated by her sense of adventure.

She'd thrown her hands down on the comforter and opened her blue eyes wide before exclaiming, "We should do it!"

I'd hoped she didn't mean what I thought she did. "Do what?" I asked.

"A trip. A *big* trip! Weeks and weeks!"

"Play hooky and become vagabonds? We can't do that!"

"I know, I know. We can't exactly cut class anymore," she'd said. "But we could still do a big trip! We could go to Europe, or even farther!"

Even swept up by the energy of the moment, I'd been nothing if not a careful, calculating sort. I had my accounting job, and she'd recently started working with a great interior design studio. We had modest incomes, bills to pay, and a detailed plan for our life together. She was going to work for a couple of years longer as we saved up for her to become a stay-at-home mother, and I was going to work as hard as I could to make sure she realized that dream. Our future was to have the white picket fence, two beautiful children, a dog, and smiles all around. The spreadsheet in my mind shuffled as she spoke, trying to calculate how this would change the timing of our plans. I remembered, now with great regret, how I'd explained that our future was carefully budgeted. How we were saving for her to be home with our eventual children. Reluctantly, I suggested we could possibly sock away a small portion of our salaries to maybe go someday.

Maybe. Someday. The words had just slipped out. They fell on the conversation like cold water on a fire.

She bounced back after a time, and rather definitively at that. A Lonely Planet book appeared in the hallway. Instead of it being their guide to Italy or France or even Europe, the one she'd chosen was Lonely Planet's *World*, which was even more frightening.

And then there was the jar that appeared on the kitchen counter a week later. Partially filled with worn bills, it had been labeled with a piece of tape declaring its purpose: *BIG TRIP*, complete with several exclamation points and a smiley face. All of our savings had been done on a computer through the bank's web site, so the gesture was purely symbolic. But symbols work, especially if they stare at you while you're making coffee every morning. She'd certainly been resilient, my wonderful wife.

And she'd been equally strong when the headaches came a year—almost to the day—after our wedding. They'd spike suddenly and last for hours. Then came nausea, imbalance, and a constant need to rest. The cancer required all manners of surgeries and treatments. She'd gone through them more positive than any one person could ever be, joking with doctors and laughing with nurses. But still, she never improved. It consumed her, eventually leading to a coma that had gone on for months now.

I spent every day with her, leaving for work only when I absolutely had to. I ate every meal at her bedside table, telling stories heard in the hospital halls. I read books to her. Her favorites, but only the ones with happy endings. I slept in the chair right next to her at night, praying for her to wake up.

She never did.

Late one night, a chorus of beeps drew in nurses and doctors. In the gentlest of voices, they told me she was gone. They did their best to comfort me, but the reality of saying goodbye to Lauren left behind the darkest emptiness one could ever feel. Threads of her happiness and light were consumed by the sadness of a life without her. She'd been the one person in the world who'd given me the gift of love. The gift of happiness.

***

Our neighbor, Mrs. Garland, took care of all the arrangements. The retired executive assistant who'd only recently lost her husband was like an angel with a clipboard. She arranged a beautiful service at the local church and held a wake at her house. Neighbors and friends were all there, as Lauren was adored by everyone.

A few days after the service, she brought a man to the house. He was a skinny, elderly lawyer with a gentle way about him. He took me through Lauren's will and explained the ugly, tedious matters of life insurance and contracts that needed to be tended to. It didn't feel right, removing Lauren from titles and accounts. It didn't feel real, and as he turned page after page, I fell into a haze. It all seemed so insignificant.

At some point, he declared that we were finished. The papers were stacked carefully and placed in his briefcase. Before closing it, he removed an envelope from a pocket and handed it to me. The outside read simply, *JOHN*.

Seeing her handwriting was like a spark that brought my attention back in an instant. It contained a letter from Lauren dated several months ago, before her first surgery.

> *My darling,*
>
> *As I write this, you're sleeping next to me, your breathing as steady as your wonderful character. If you're reading this, I am sorry to have left you, my love. While the doctors continue to run tests, I think I know what's inevitable…what the tests can't see yet. But I want you to know it's OK! My life has been a blessing because of you!*
>
> *I know this is hard, and there's nothing I'd like to do more than just hold you, but you will need to move on. And knowing you as I do, my little planner, moving on is not going to be easy.*
>
> *So I have one last wish…one wish I know will help.*

Take the trip we dreamed of! I want you to go...to go and see the world!

You're so wonderfully cautious that it will be difficult. But please go! Just go! Take a step forward. It only takes one step, and the rest will come. Explore faraway places. Feel every moment, soak everything in, and let it fill you with life.

And while you will miss me, I only want you to miss me for a little bit. Don't carry any sadness! Use this journey to heal, to smile and laugh. Use it to love again, John. There's a lot of it in you, and I want you to share it. Let people see how wonderful you are and feel what I do! There's nothing that would make me happier.

With my love and my hugs forever,

L

I looked up from the letter gutted, my eyes awash in tears. "She knew," I said.

The attorney nodded. "Yes, Mr. Winter, she did. And I have to say that there has not been a more impressive woman to walk into my office. She wasn't just putting on a brave face; she *was* brave and more positive than anyone should have been in her circumstances."

"She always saw the silver lining," I said trying to manage a smile through the tears.

"If there's nothing else, Mr. Winter?"

There wasn't. There was only the letter and the pain in my heart.

I'm not sure how long I sat at the dining room table after he left, but the sun had long since set and I found myself in complete darkness. In a blurry trance, I went to the hall closet and pulled the chain to turn on the light. On the shelf above our jackets and coats was a shoebox labeled *TRAVEL* in Lauren's handwriting. She'd always written in all capital letters, their heights varying large and small in a completely random pattern that made even the most boring of words lively. I pulled the box down and sat on the floor in front of the closet door.

I must have stared at it for an hour before lifting the lid and looking inside. It was nearly empty. Just two passports. I withdrew the one on top and flipped to the second page. It was mine. Lauren had insisted I get it when we were engaged. The pages were stiff and blank. Beneath it was Lauren's. I flipped to her picture. You weren't supposed to smile for your passport photograph, but she couldn't help it. Her happiness shone through the laminate, the hologram, and probably right through the camera in the post office. Seeing that smile in a blank passport that would never be used on the trip she'd dreamed of brought a huge wave of sadness. I wept, letting the tears come like a river.

Days went by, all hazy and most with little sleep. I tried to occupy myself with tasks but didn't know where to start. Everything I touched reminded me of her. Her favorite mug, the one with a monkey on the side. What was I supposed to do with it? If I used it, it wouldn't be hers any longer. But if I donated it, it would be as if I was cleaning her out of my life. The same with her favorite winter coat. Her heart-shaped paperweight. I was paralyzed. Worried about everything that needed to be done, yet starting not a single thing.

The days became weeks. Weeks in a dark cloud, numb and detached. I withdrew into my own shell, taking indefinite leave from work and rarely venturing out. Every time I thought I was getting better, something would trigger a memory. A to-do list in a drawer, her lavender shampoo in the shower, even a blonde hair falling off the collar of her coat in the hall would send me to the floor. The stages of grief, I learned, weren't linear. They'd sneak up, out of order and scattered. They'd linger sometimes for days, sometimes ripping through one after the other in a matter of minutes. Nights were the most difficult, getting lost in the tangle of memories and what-ifs.

Mrs. Garland, my personal saint, became the only contact with the world around me. She brought food over every day, meals that still poured in from neighbors. One early afternoon, she stopped by, her arms full.

"Hello, Mrs. Garland. Let me get that for you," I said, taking the dishes and leading us into the kitchen.

"Tonight appears to be turkey tetrazzini, along with a salad and some bread, courtesy of the Blacks," she said.

"That is very nice of them. Thank you again for looking after me."

"Say nothing of it." Looking at me carefully, she said, "John, I know this is hard. Believe me, I know."

I put my arms around her. Our shared experience had put us long past the need to explain why.

"There, there now, dear. I think it's time."

"Time?" I asked, breaking away.

"For you to pull up your britches."

"I know. Just not ready yet," I replied, a little ashamed at the mess I'd become. "And I wouldn't know where to start."

"We'll figure it out. But I know she would want you to go on and start your life again."

I hesitated, thinking of the letter that had sat untouched on the dining room table since the lawyer left. I led her into the dining room and picked it up. "Perhaps I should let you read this," I said.

Mrs. Garland took a seat at the table and brought glasses up from the chain around her neck. She read in silence. When finished, she let the glasses fall back down and dabbed a corner of her eye. I passed her a tissue from one of the many boxes that had been needed around the house lately.

She nodded her thanks and wiped her eyes. Still holding the tissue, she said, "She was a wonderful girl."

"She sure was."

"You know this is a gift, John. It's a gift from her to you."

"Her last wish," I said.

"You can think of it as a wish. But really, it's a gift. She's given you the chance to be happy. She's given you a way to start."

"I'd been thinking of it as a wish. But I see what you mean, and that makes it even more precious, doesn't it?"

"It does. Precious is the perfect word." She set the letter down and turned to me. "You have to honor her request."

I looked down at the letter.

She let the silence between us grow uncomfortable before finally saying, "Look at yourself, John."

I was in old sweatpants and a dingy T-shirt, complete with dirty hair and stubbly face.

"You need to do this now. It's time."

"I can't just leave. I need to remember her. Here, in this house. I need to take care of her things. To honor her."

"She wants you to remember her out there, John. Out in the world, with open eyes. Her things here are just that. Things."

"And there's the house. Utilities, the mortgage, the lawn—"

"John, I was the assistant to the CEO of a Fortune 500 company. I will manage the house and take care of everything. Retirement never suited me anyway, so I am taking charge. You're going to do this, and you're going to start right now."

"Mrs. Garland, before I met Lauren, I was one of those people terrified to go anywhere. She was the spark, the energy in us as a couple. And if I couldn't even go overseas *with* her, there's no way I can do it *without* her."

"You're going to do this. And you are going to do this now. How much longer are you going to hide here? I know something about grief, John, and this is something you need to do. For her, *and* for you. Now."

"Now?"

"Now. Get yourself in the shower."

"But—"

"Shower. Now. I am going to get a notepad, and you are going to get yourself cleaned up."

I did as she asked, trusting that she understood loss and realizing that I was fortunate to have her by my side. Standing in the shower, running shampoo through my hair, I knew I should listen to her. She knew the mourning process, and I needed to do as she, just like Lauren, asked. I needed to pull my shoulders back and move forward.

Committed now, I went to work with Mrs. Garland, handing over files, phone numbers, passwords, and countless other details. Her executive assistant skills went into high gear instantly, and I imagined her old bosses had thanked their lucky stars every time she came through the door. Her questions were concise, her decisions brisk, and by the time the day was done, she had everything she needed. She closed the leather folio of notes and instructed me to get my laptop.

"Mrs. Garland, you can go. I will book the tickets, I promise."

"I am sure you will. But humor me, please."

She wasn't giving an inch, and I knew she was right not to. While my commitment was there, it was fresh and still fragile. I returned to the table, laptop open and ready. "Where should I go?"

"Where did she want to go with you, John?"

"Everywhere. She wanted to see Europe, Asia, Africa, and more. Why didn't I ever take her? Why did I have to be so careful about saving and waiting?"

"John, you're going to ask yourself questions like this every day. And let me tell you, the what-ifs are toxic. Absolutely toxic. Don't let them win, ok? You will need from this day on to look forward, not back. Keep your memories of her, every single one of them. But don't regret anything. There's no sense in it. None."

I closed my eyes, knowing this was one of those bits of advice that hurt and seemed impossible.

"Ok," she said. "Let's start with someplace easy."

"England?" That would be a good place to start. The food would be safe, and since I only spoke English, language wouldn't be a concern. They'd have chain hotels too, which would give some familiarity.

"England it is," she replied. "Pull up the British Airways web site."

I did as she suggested and was presented with the form to make a reservation. I entered London as the destination. The cursor advanced to the departure date field.

"Tomorrow," she said.

"Mrs. Garland, that's too soon. A week or two would be better, so I can plan things out."

"Tomorrow, John," she said sternly. "You need to do this now."

I hesitated, my fingers frozen. Everything in life I'd planned and weighed carefully. Every flight I'd taken, though there hadn't been too many, had been carefully calculated for the best schedule and price. Wasn't I supposed to make a spreadsheet for this to make a clear decision? I did that for the espresso machine, and that had worked perfectly. Surely this was a more significant decision.

"John?" she asked, nodding her head toward the screen.

I had to listen to her. To Lauren. I selected tomorrow and was immediately presented with a more terrifying question: Return or One-Way?

"How long should I stay?" I asked.

"This is a journey, John. And going to London is only the first step. There will be another destination after that. It's what she wants."

"Just go," the letter had said.

I moved my mouse from the return date box to the little circle next to One-Way. I'd never made a one-way ticket. Never done something without thought to what would happen afterward. My anxiety built, forming a wall to protect me from doing something unplanned. Something unknown, my greatest fear.

"Take a step forward."

I clicked the One-Way circle. The return date field disappeared. It was simply gone just like that. Mrs. Garland put her hand on my shoulder, and through her touch, Lauren encouraged me further. She was proud. Happy. Excited. Before I knew it, I'd entered my credit card. Mrs. Garland's hand didn't move the entire time, but squeezed gently as I clicked the purchase button.

Next came lodging. I booked three nights at a Marriott, feeling that it would be safe to start with a known hotel chain and use the points I'd accrued visiting the main office in Boston a few times.

"Now then, you'll need to head out and pick up a few things and pack. I'll go book a taxi for you." Checking her watch, she continued, "I will see you off at two o'clock tomorrow, ok?"

"Thank you, Mrs. Garland."

"You are welcome, my dear. Now get going!"

After she left, I began with energy and a purpose. I could pack for London. We'd watched some travel shows and knew people looked nice there. Going into the closet, I pulled out our large suitcase and added shirts and slacks along with a pair of loafers and a light jacket. But I'd be going to other places as well and found my closet severely lacking in things other than work clothes. I hopped in the car and drove to an REI intending to stock up.

And stock up I did. Before I knew it, the whole staff was treating me like an honored guest. They dashed back and forth, piling everything up at the front register. Pants made of some sort of nylon with zippered legs that allowed them to become shorts. Shirts to block rain. Different shirts to block sun. A hat in case there was more sun, and mosquito spray. A bear whistle. Water bottle. Water purifier.

I began to wonder if the salespeople had actually ever been to England. But they carried on, getting more targeted on a twenty-something male traveling to Europe. Wool socks appeared. Essential, apparently, due to their ability to wick sweat I didn't even know my feet had. Trail running shoes with some form of magical ability to provide both support and flexibility. Base layers and top layers, short sleeves and long. A Gore-Tex jacket with windproof zippers. An assortment of little packing bags in which to keep various odds and ends. A Black Hole backpack for day outings that would also serve as a carry-on. A huge rolling-suitcase-duffel contraption to hold the bulk of the gear. A wallet that hung in my pants to protect against pickpockets. A travel neck pillow that looked like the thing the guy in the cubicle next to mine sat on after his hemorrhoid surgery.

I came home with five bags of supplies and spent the rest of the night sorting, packing, and repacking. By the time Mrs. Garland arrived the next day, everything was neatly folded and organized. We hugged, and I knew I couldn't have taken this step without her. She was truly a blessing. It was one of those times in life when two people found in each other just what the other needed. After one last hug, she set me into the taxi and sent me off into the unknown.

2

I joined the masses lining up beneath the electric blue UK Border signs at Heathrow cloudy from lack of sleep and very nervous.

I've taken the first step, Lauren. But it is terrifying without you by my side.

The winding queues were crowded with businesspeople, families, tour groups, and solo backpackers. Most of the passports they held were blue like mine, but there were plenty in colors I didn't even know existed. They came in red, green, and black, each stamped in foil with varying crests and letterforms. Before long, I was at the front of the line where a glass turnstile opened and I took my turn in front of a border control officer. I handed him my passport and arrival card.

The officer gave me a brief glare before taking my papers. As he entered information into his computer, he said, "Purpose of your visit?"

"Um, tourism," I replied.

He forced a cautious smile in return. After a moment, he said, "Sir, you don't have a departure date on your arrival card." The glare returned.

"I'm not sure when I will be leaving," I replied.

He looked up from his computer, still stern. "There is a ninety-day limit to the amount of time you can stay on a tourist visa."

"I can't imagine I will be here that long," I said.

He looked down at my passport and flipped through the pages. "Is this your first time out of America?" he asked.

"It is," I said. "My first stop on an agenda that is frighteningly open at the moment."

This response passed some form of test, because he smiled genuinely this time. He placed the arrival card back on the counter with a pen. "Why don't you give your best estimate on a departure date so that we can get you sorted."

I entered a date and passed it back.

He had me place my fingers on a fingerprint reader while he finished entering something into the computer. Afterward, he raised his stamp and said, "Mr. Winter, here's to your first port of entry." With a bit of flourish for emphasis, he stamped my passport and bid me good day.

I was quite relieved at clearing that first test as I made my way to baggage claim. Finding the carousel the pilot had said would contain our bags, I went to an open space and waited. Gradually, the bags came out. One by one, my fellow passengers took their suitcases off and loaded them onto trolleys. The metal belt thinned until there were no bags left. Mine never came. I continued to wait, but still, nothing.

I was terrified. After all of the packing and careful consideration that had gone into everything I might need, I had nothing. For someone who plans every step in life, it was a devastating blow.

Defeated, I found the British Airways lost baggage counter only to learn that the bag wasn't even in their system. I filled out the form they provided and left. While they promised to track it down and send it to the hotel, they didn't sound terribly optimistic.

I spent the day reluctantly playing tourist and doing my best to stay awake. At the hotel concierge's suggestion, I purchased a ticket for the London Hop-On Hop-Off bus. I saw Big Ben and joined the lines to see Westminster Abbey, St Paul's Cathedral, and many of the places I'd seen only photographs of before. Eventually, the bus loop brought me back to the hotel where I promptly collapsed. I slept like a rock, completely through until well past breakfast the next day.

While room service prepared lunch and a large pot of coffee, I emptied my backpack on the bed to take inventory. The pile was meager: one change of clothes just for this eventuality, phone, charger, and the silly neck pillow that I hadn't even used. The hotel was kind enough to give me a converter for the charger and a small toilet kit. That was it. John Winter off to see the world, carrying practically nothing, completely unprepared.

Feeling dejected, especially after a lengthy call where British Airways explained that my suitcase had entirely vanished, I headed off to the local American Express office to file a claim. A nice, slim young man named Ashton explained that American Express would be happy to reimburse me. He had me fill out a form to describe the contents of the suitcase, which I completed and handed back to him.

"Wow, that's quite a list," he said. "Where were you headed?"

"To be honest, I'm not exactly sure. This is my first stop on the way to see the world."

"See the world? Doesn't get broader than that."

"I know. Probably need to rethink things at this rate."

"Not at all," he said. "I'm doing it myself right now."

"Really?"

"Yes. This is a replenishing job. I left New Zealand two years ago to see the world, and every once in a while, I pick up jobs to fund the next leg of the journey. Iceland next!"

A lifestyle like this was utterly foreign to me. Not having a home base and working at different places around the world was simply too nebulous to comprehend. But then again, I was frighteningly close to that myself.

He leaned forward and spoke quietly, with the hint of a smile. "John, do you mind if I give you a little advice?"

"Ashton, at this moment, I would welcome any advice you might have."

"This list?" he said, showing the form I'd just filled out. "You don't need any of this shit."

"What?"

"If you're going out to see the world, you just need a little curiosity."

"Right, but I also need some practical things. Sturdy running shoes, a raincoat, travel pants, things like that."

"First off, mate, you don't need running shoes unless you're running. Those trainers with fluorescent laces and stripes only serve as a flag to say, 'Look at me! I'm an American on holiday!' As for a raincoat, it's a good idea. But better is simply finding an old church or a farmer's house. Because in those places, you meet the people. And it's through *people* that you experience the world."

"Isn't seeing the world visiting cities and famous monuments?"

He shrugged. "To people going on holiday it is. Sounds like you're after a little more."

"I think I am," I said quietly.

He lowered his voice to match my own. "What do you want to get out of your travels?"

I didn't have a simple answer for him and was hesitant to share the truth with a stranger. My mind cycled through several responses that avoided the truth, each entirely disingenuous. Lauren would have taken one look at Ashton's kind face and told him everything he wanted to know. I was going to have to learn to trust people as she always had.

I pulled her note from my pocket and slowly unfolded it. "My wife passed away recently. She left me this note."

He accepted the paper and after reading, said, "Jesus, mate. I am so sorry." He was genuinely touched. Opening a drawer in his desk, he grabbed a pen and paper and wrote a name and address. "My mates and I are meeting at this pub tonight. Why don't you join us? We'll help sort you out as best we can. Places to go and the like."

"That would be great, Ashton. Thank you."

He handed me the paper. "Half-six, ok?"

"Half-six?"

"How the Poms say six-thirty," he explained. "And I'll be sure to take care of your claim before I leave."

***

The pub Ashton had chosen was difficult to find. Down a narrow alley off a small side street, the name was not much more than faded yellow lettering on a window. It was clearly a locals' place, filled with an interesting mixture of workers and businesspeople. Ashton stood at a table with an attractive, professional blonde woman who he introduced as his girlfriend, Hailey.

"So, you're traveling?" she asked.

"Not off to the best start," I replied.

"John told me about your suitcase. Don't worry, you'll figure it out."

Noticing her accent, I asked, "Where are you from?"

"Holland, but it's been years since I've lived there."

"Where have you lived?"

Ashton gave a laugh. "Don't ask her that, mate. A better question is where *hasn't* she lived!"

Hailey held her hand over her mouth in a way to hide a chuckle. I wasn't sure if it was a gesture of shyness or modesty, but it was a pleasant contrast to the roaring, open laughs I was used to at home.

"A bit of everywhere, I guess. South Africa, Courchevel, Prague, Bali, Paris—"

"Oh, Paris, where I met my looooove!" came a mocking voice from behind me as a friend of theirs arrived.

"I did, indeed!" Hailey said, squeezing her arm around Ashton.

"I'm Grant," the newcomer said. "From Oz."

"John," I replied, shaking his hand. "Oz?"

"Australia. Ashton told us about your troubles. Sorry to hear, mate. Beer?"

I said yes, and Grant headed to the bar. By the time he came back, an Indian woman named Anika had joined the group carrying a worn paper shopping bag. Her arrival must have been anticipated because Grant had a drink for her as well.

"To our new traveler!" Ashton said.

We touched glasses over the table, and all took a sip. The beer was nice, smoother and less bitter than I was used to.

Grant must have noticed me licking my lips. "Too warm?" he asked.

"A little different flavor than I expected. But it's delicious, thank you."

"Don't forget that everything is going to be different. What separates the good travelers from the bad ones is not thinking that the way they're used to is better."

"Like cheese on everything!" said Anika.

"Or not having milk in your coffee after noon. I still have a hard time with that one!" added Grant.

"And zipper trousers," added Hailey.

I embarrassingly remembered the zipper pants I'd packed. Sure, they weren't the most attractive, but they sounded practical at the time. Just as well they were gone.

"And trainers with jeans!" said Anika.

Grant chimed in once again. "That one stumps me too! Just don't get why it's bad."

"Trainers?" I asked.

"Sorry, 'sneakers,'" she said.

"Well, mine are gone anyway. These'll just have to do," I said pointing to my penny loafers, the only shoes I had left.

"Not necessarily," Anika said. She bent down to the bag at her feet, returning with a pair of brogue boots. They were handsome and sturdy, like a halfway point between a nice pair of oxfords and a work boot.

"Ashton told me about your suitcase and thought you were about the same size as my old boyfriend. Give these a try. They'll hold up a lot better than yours."

I bent down to put them on and asked, "What happened to your boyfriend?"

"Bloody fool pissed off to Southeast Asia. No use for them there," Grant added.

"How are they?" Anika asked.

I finished tying the laces and stood up. "They fit perfectly! Lighter than they look, and these soles are really comfortable."

She smiled. "There are a couple of other things he left behind in there. Shirts, a jumper, and a nice jacket he bought in France."

"Thank you so much, Anika."

"They should work for a while. And when they don't, just pass them along to another traveler," she said.

"Alright, everyone. We need to come up with some ideas for John," Ashton declared as he raised his glass. "He's got a blank passport, and our job is to set him about filling it!"

"Being as I'm here, could we start with the UK?"

"Fair enough," Grant said. "Ashton here will tell you to go out to a fishing village and live in some old codger's bilge, working the nets for a pound a day."

"C'mon, mate! It was twenty, plus all the cod I could eat!"

Everyone laughed.

"But my suggestion would be to get out into the countryside. London is a blast, but it's a big city and becoming a little too similar to America these days."

"What about the sights here? I went to Tower Bridge and the Eye today. What about Windsor Castle?" I asked.

Hailey answered, "See some of those places in every city. The ones you really want to see, the ones that have some meaning to you. But don't make them your mission, John. You want the feel of a city, and you don't get that running through a checklist."

It was a perspective I hadn't really considered. European vacations were often discussed at work, but in precisely that form:

a checklist. And I'd always thought of travel being a process of checking places off a list. It suddenly became clear that my whole life was full of checklists. They held me together, gave me purpose.

"How do you know if you saw everything you have to see, then?" I asked.

"Don't worry about what you see and what you don't, John. You have to fill your heart with experiences." Placing a hand on my chest, she said, "Now, what's it telling you?"

"Lauren talked about going to Stonehenge. She wanted to see what the mystery was about."

"Then go to Stonehenge, John. One idea, one little reason, is all you need to start. And then you're off," she replied.

Anika said, "And everywhere you go, talk to people. Ask questions. Listen. *Really* listen, and you'll be filled with wonder."

"And eat!" came a new, colorful voice laced with an unusual accent I couldn't place. A jovial man with long, dark hair joined us. "Eat everywhere!"

"And here we have Matia, our very own Basque chef blessing the United Kingdom with his presence," Grant said by way of introduction.

Matia took a theatrical bow.

"Nice to meet you, Matia," I said.

"I am sure Ashton has told you to meet the people as you travel, John. But don't believe him! People are full of shit! It is the food that will tell you everything you need to know about a place!"

"And drink," Ashton said, heading off to the bar for another round.

"He is right, drink as well. But the food, that is what you want. Where are you headed?"

"At the moment, Stonehenge. After that, I have no idea."

"My friend, there is no food at Stonehenge! There's literally *nothing* at Stonehenge but bloody fields and sheep!" he said, laughing loudly. "But there is a little pub out that way that serves a wonderful butcher's plate and makes an amazing black pudding Scotch egg." He patted his pockets. Not finding what he was looking for, he turned to Hailey, who pulled a pen from her purse. He turned one of the cardboard coasters over and wrote *The Pheasant, Shefford Woodlands* on the back. "Tell them Matia sent you."

"I will."

"But after that, you will need to taste the world. Food is the true story of a region. In every town, go first to the market, always early in the morning. It's there you'll see what the region is known for, what brought life! And happiness!"

"Where is your favorite food?" I asked.

My question started an avalanche. All five of them began a rapid-fire dialog of foods they'd tried around the world. From the best to the strangest. The talk of food eventually led us to an Indian restaurant, where we switched to wine, and the table was soon filled with more curries than we could ever handle. Some were mild and rich with flavor, others hot enough to cause my brow to sweat and eyes to water. The drinks flowed, as did the ideas. They took turns adding to the coaster Matia had written on earlier. A café in Paris, the name of a guide in Tanzania, the specific week to be in Tokyo for the cherry blossoms, the best *bun cha* in Hanoi. The list went on an on until every little edge was filled.

My phone was seized, and they added apps I would need. Apps for purchasing plane tickets, booking trains, and several more for apartments, hostels, and room shares. At one point, Anika looked confused and asked why I didn't have one of the more popular photo-sharing apps.

I shrugged. "Never had the need."

"You will now, John. And we'll want to see where you go! It's how all of us stay in touch, how we get ideas, and how we meet up in corners of the world." She tapped away and then held the phone as far as her arm would reach and shouted, "Everyone! A photo for the start of John's adventure!"

We crushed together, and glasses were raised, and cheers were made. She tapped a few buttons and handed the phone back. Our photo was there, *The first step* written beneath.

As I stumbled back to the hotel later that night, I knew I was fortunate. Not just for the list of ideas that they'd given, but for the passion they'd shared and the warmth and friendship they'd shown, even knowing I was only passing through.

Lauren would have loved them.

***

With the small pack on my shoulders and new boots on my feet, I entered Paddington Station and was instantly overwhelmed. The confidence they'd given me the night before had been replaced by panic and fear. Bright light from the translucent roof illuminated a mass of Londoners and tourists busily heading here and there. Everyone knew exactly where they were going and was doing so with speed, efficiency, and little care for anyone in their path. The sounds and volume were overwhelming. Pings and pongs followed by mechanical voices calling trains and platform numbers. The voices of hundreds of travelers echoed up from the marble floor and down from the ceiling, the two banging together, adding to the stress that overcame me.

I saw a row of ticket machines and, after waiting in the queue for a minute, stood dumbfounded before one. I pressed button after button, trying to find some Stonehenge reference while feeling the pressure of impatient people behind me. Finally, I pressed a red X button a few times to cancel and stepped away.

These were the things I'd need to handle. So, taking a deep breath, I tried to calm myself. I remembered the 'how to get anywhere' app they'd mentioned last night. I tapped the icon on my phone and eventually found the train and bus combination that would get me there. Looking back to the ticket machine disparagingly, I remembered the train ticketing app they'd added. A few taps more, and I was booked on a departing train ten minutes from now.

Searching the electronic boards mounted high above a seating area, I found the platform number and made my way through the turnstiles.

***

"Amazing, isn't it?" asked an older man who had stopped next to me with his wife on the circular path surrounding Stonehenge.

"It is," I replied. "And here, just in the middle of a field."

"Can you believe it?" he exclaimed. "Just fantastic!" And with a broad smile, they carried on, catching up with their tour group.

I'd always imagined things to see around the world were in cities. The Smithsonian, Louvre, Sistine Chapel. But here we were, just as Matia had promised, in the middle of the English countryside with literally nothing around.

Lauren had always wanted to know whether it was a clock or a stage for some form of primitive worship. Flipping through the brochure, I learned that it was thought both were likely. I tried to imagine people placing these tremendous stones according to the movement of the sun some 4,000 years ago. There would have been hundreds of them pulling the stones on log rollers. There would have been camps for them to sleep, troughs of water, fires cooking food, and holes in the ground for bathrooms. There would have been arguments and love, even children born during the years this would have taken. The winds of time had blown away every hint of their presence other than the stones. Years of work, toiling, calculating. Yet all that was left were questions and the legends that sought to answer them.

A cloud had come in. It wasn't really raining, though you could see and feel minuscule drops of water swirling. I used my phone to find the best way to get to Shefford Woodlands and sadly found the public transit route was by bus and would take five hours and four transfers. Upset for not seeing this earlier, I went into a bit of a panic. I looked around the parking lot, trying to calm myself. In the center of the lot, a man closed the rear door of one of the smaller tour buses. I jogged over and caught him just as he was settling into the driver's seat.

"Might you be heading to Shefford Woodlands?" I asked.

"Near enough. But I am afraid this is a private tour," the driver said.

As he went to close his door, a woman's voice from inside said, "Wait, that's our son!"

"Is he now, Mrs. Brown? Funny how I don't remember him joining us this morning."

"Oh, be a good sport, George. Aren't we going his way?"

"Indeed," the driver grumbled. He gave me a steady gaze, then gestured with his thumb to the other side of the van with the slight hint of a smile.

I opened the door to find three couples and one woman by herself, all clearly in their 70s or more, occupying the three rows of seats.

"Thank you!" I said to the couple I'd met on the path. "Thank you all," I added. One of the men moved to the second row, and I settled in between two elderly women, one of whom was on her own.

"You can be my date," she said in a gentle voice, patting my leg.

"I can take you as far as the M4 junction," the driver said. "Easy walk from there. Should take us a bit more than an hour, I'd expect, so settle in."

The woman next to me said, "That will give you enough time to tell us your story, young man."

And so I did.

Ethel, as I learned my date's name was, asked to see Lauren's note. After reading it, she removed her reading glasses and dabbed her eyes with a tissue. With a shaking hand, she passed it on. It was apparently to be shared as part of the trip. Through glistening eyes, she grabbed my hand with both of hers. "Thank you for sharing, John."

I smiled back. "Tell me about yourself," I said.

"We're more alike than you might know," she replied. "I lost my husband in a factory fire years ago."

"I am sorry," I said gently.

"Don't be, darling. He was a wonderful man, dashing in his Sunday best." She looked away, staring out the window to the countryside.

I remained silent until she turned back, then quietly asked, "Does it get any easier?"

"I am afraid not. But you carry on. And over time, those holes in your life will be filled. The scars stay, but if you open yourself up, you'll find that the hurt can be warmed away."

It was a profound way of looking ahead, one that gave both sadness and hope.

"You'll be fine, John. I just know it," she said, placing her gloved hand on my leg again. "Now, I am sure the others have stories to share."

And with that the page turned and the others told me about their hometowns and villages, their children and grandchildren, their successes and challenges. They'd never met before this tour, but each found common threads. They opened up, sharing support and kind words along with a few tears and plenty of laughter.

The trip became a mobile group therapy session that I was sad to see end when they dropped me off at the motorway junction with warm wishes. I felt peaceful and thankful as I waved them goodbye.

It was dinnertime by the time I made it to the Pheasant, and I was happy to see it was also an inn. There was no desk at the entrance, but to the right, happy sounds came from the pub. I approached the bar, and a well-dressed young man asked what I would like.

"I came for the black pudding Scotch egg, not that I know what black pudding is," I said. "But might you have a room as well?"

He smiled and reached a hand across the bar. "I'm Jack," he said. "And black pudding is blood sausage. Pig blood mixed with oatmeal. Delicious!"

"John Winter," I replied. "And I am certainly not bold enough to try that!"

"Well, there are plenty of other things on the menu."

"A chef in London named Matia said you have wonderful food here."

His face widened into a smile. "That's nice coming from the crazy Basque. How many nights might you be with us?"

"Just one for now. I am rather lacking plans at the moment."

He smiled and said, "Just a moment." After going into a small alcove and retrieving a key, he said, "Let's get you settled in."

Every time I'd checked into a hotel before, a clerk would spend several minutes typing into a computer. There would be forms to fill out and a credit card taken for payment. It was suspicious that none of this was being done.

"But won't you need a card?" I asked.

"You look like you've had a long day, John. We'll sort it all out in the morning," he said with a genuine smile.

We crossed a vestibule just outside the pub door and went up some stairs where he unlocked a door for me.

"Would this room be alright?"

I'd expected a room in a country pub to be dark and drafty and was surprised to see it was colorful, bright, and warm. "It's perfect," I replied.

He smiled, seeming genuinely pleased. "Excellent," he said. "You've got a kettle for tea or plunger coffee here, and there's fresh milk in the fridge under the stairs. Please let me know if there's anything else you need."

"Thank you, Jack."

"We'll see you for dinner later, then."

I set my bag down and ducked slightly to look out the windows. The sun had set not long ago, leaving the vast expanse of fields cast in a warm glow. Turning, I scanned the room. Lauren would have loved the pastel colors and variety of patterns on each fabric. She would have adored the idea of winding down the country roads and finding this cute little inn.

I lay back on the bed, thinking only of her, here with me. As the room darkened, thoughts of dinner were forgotten. My eyes closed, moist with loneliness.

***

After finally trying black pudding with my breakfast—and finding it to be strangely nice with eggs—I wandered into the village of Shefford Woodlands. Without much more than a church and two dozen cottages centered around a large brick house, it was easy to imagine its history. Workers would have lived in the small homes nestled side by side, looking after the fields and livestock. Horse-drawn carriages would have creaked and bumped down worn paths carrying grain and lamb and wool. They'd have dressed in their most formal clothes to pray at the tiny church on Sundays. The air would have been filled with the scents of woodsmoke and dung and sweat born from hard, honest work.

I took a left at the only intersection and walked down the short, narrow lane to see if I could have a look over the wall at the main house. I'd learned it was the heart of the village, where the primary landowner would have lived centuries ago. As I went down the gentle slope, I came across an elderly woman in her dressing gown staring at a pile of bricks. It was clear a section of wall had fallen down, leaving a gaping hole and a rather significant number of bricks reaching from the grass out to the middle of the road.

"Good morning," I said gently, so as not to startle her.

"Hardly," she replied quite sternly.

"This doesn't look good," I said gesturing to the bricks.

"I don't imagine it does. Do you think you'll have it sorted today?"

"Excuse me?" I asked.

"We can't leave such a mess out here."

"Well, I, ah…" I stammered, really not knowing what to say.

"You'd best get a move on," she said. And with that, she turned and walked slowly and carefully back through the gate.

I'd apparently just been instructed to tidy up hundreds of bricks. I stood there, both perplexed and amused. This situation called for a departure. I'd obviously been mistaken for a worker due at any moment, and it would be best to leave. But my feet stayed where they were. I looked around and wondered what if there wasn't someone coming to help this old woman after all. I didn't have any plans for the day. Nor for any day, in fact. So, thinking a little exercise might do some good, I put down my pack and set about moving bricks.

I'd just started when a stern voice called out, "Just what do you think you're doing?"

I looked up to see a man marching toward me with a wheelbarrow that he was steering directly for my knees. I dropped the two bricks I'd just picked up and put my hands up in a primitive reflex to show I meant no harm.

"Sorry! A woman who was just here asked me to help!"

"Oh, bollocks," he said, and then he ran briskly back through the gate.

Again, I saw it was time to leave. But still, I thought why not see this through and began placing bricks in the wheelbarrow. By the time I'd filled it to the point it would still be maneuverable, the man returned.

"I am sorry about that. I think what happened is that you were mistaken for me. Mrs. B doesn't see too well these days."

He offered his hand and said, "Name's Colin." His grip was firm, his fingers tough with callouses.

"Nice to meet you, Colin. I'm John."

"Well, John, I should clean this mess up. Sorry about the mix-up."

"Want a little help? I've got nothing else to do at the moment."

He looked at the bricks and then back to me, weighing his natural suspicions against the amount of back-breaking work he had before him. "Can't pay you," he said.

"I'm not after a paycheck."

"Might have an extra sandwich is all."

I smiled. "A sandwich after this, I'm sure will be welcome."

"Alright, then," he said. "Let's get to it."

He took the wheelbarrow, and while walking it to the barn explained that the winter had been unusually brutal. The soil had heaved considerably this spring, and with little foundation set when the wall was built two hundred years ago, the bricks finally gave up during this season's shift. He planned to put the bricks by an old barn, to be replaced later by a tradesman after a new foundation had been laid.

Through the course of the morning, we went back and forth and back and forth, loading bricks into the wheelbarrow, moving them just outside an old barn and neatly stacking them. Colin was quiet at first, but after the first few loads, his suspicions began to ease. We chatted about the weather, then about the maintenance old homes like Woodlands House require. Safe subjects. Eventually, he asked me what I was doing in Shefford Woodlands. I told the story of Lauren once again.

"Oh, mate. I am so sorry."

Despite hearing so many similar expressions of sympathy, I still didn't know precisely how to reply. But thankfully, there were still bricks to move, so I simply shrugged and got back to work. Colin was kind enough to let it go, working silently alongside me for a few moments before changing the subject.

When we were most of the way through, a woman appeared with a plate of sandwiches and a bottle of water with cups nested on top. Colin introduced her as Klara and then proceeded to explain why I'd appeared in Shefford Woodlands from America.

"My poor thing," she said. "Please, have something to eat."

We sat down on a short retaining wall that separated areas of the gardens, the plate between Colin and me. To my surprise, Klara sat next to me, her hand on my shoulder while we ate. I was thankful for the meal, but even more so for the comfort.

As Klara spoke with an accent, I asked where she was from and learned she'd come from Poland to work as a carer, something not entirely uncommon in the UK. The owner of the estate, whom they referred to only as Mrs. B, had dementia. When they talked about her, they did so in a beautifully loving way. It was plain to see they were fierce protectors of her dignity in the little village.

With only crumbs left on the plate, I thanked Klara.

"Where will you go next?" she asked.

"I don't really know," I replied. "I suppose Paris. She'd been once before, and I know she wanted to go back. I read that it's easy to get there via train?"

"Paris is lovely, John. And yes, you can take the train. Colin will need to take you to Newbury, and from there you'll go into London to get on the Eurostar. It's simple, but too late now. Tomorrow."

"Tomorrow?" I asked.

Colin looked at his watch, a dusty Casio with a few drops of paint on the case. "It's coming on two now. By the time we get into Newbury, you wouldn't be in Paris until quite late."

"We have an extra bed in the annex. It would be much better to go tomorrow," Klara said.

Colin nodded and said, "We've still got the rest of those bricks. Might as well tackle them while you're still dirty!"

I looked down at my shirt and pants, seeing I was a bit of a mess.

"We'll take care of those tonight, John," Klara said.

I patted my thighs, sending up a small puff of dust, and said, "Guess we better get back to work then!"

Colin, as it turned out, appreciated having a little help after years of tending to the grounds on his own. He enlisted me into some jobs that required two people, and by dinner time, we'd replaced some slate roof tiles on the main house, patched a gutter on the barn, and used the tractor to pull out a stubborn tree stump. At dusk, we arrived at the door of the annex—their name for a wing of the main house that had been sectioned off to be a living area for caretakers—filthy dirty and tired.

Klara met us at the door. Dropping a hamper at our feet, she said, "Don't you two dare come in like that! Drop your clothes in here and get up to the showers!"

Colin and I looked at one another and laughed. But when a Polish woman points at you and puts on her tough voice, it's in your best interest to do what you're told.

I emerged from the shower thoroughly clean to see that Klara had placed my backpack inside the bathroom and set some fresh clothes on a stool. A pair of chinos and a wonderfully soft shirt along with boxers and socks. I checked the shirt and pants to see if they were my size, but the label only showed a tailor's name, leading me to believe they'd been custom made for someone. I gave them a try anyway and found they fit rather well. I hung my towel on the rack and went down the stairs, following the sound of voices and laughter. I found a small doorway that led into the main house's kitchen where Colin and Klara were preparing dinner.

"Don't you look nice, John!" Klara exclaimed.

"Thank you very much, Klara! But these aren't Colin's, are they?" I asked.

"No, no. They belonged to Mrs. B's husband. From the photos I've seen of him, I thought they might fit." She gave a tug on my sleeves and smoothed the shirt at my shoulders. "I'd say they're perfect."

"He passed away several years ago," Colin said. "Klara told Mrs. B you didn't have much, and she said we should give you something proper to wear."

I looked around the room, noticing Mrs. B wasn't in the large kitchen. "Please tell her thank you," I said.

Just then, another woman came through the door. She was blonde like Klara, but with touches of gray. With a kind, modest smile, she introduced herself. "You must be John. I am Jada." Her voice was soft and gentle as she shyly extended her hand. "I also take care of Mrs. B, and I am glad to see that Mr. B's clothes fit you very well."

"Thank you," I replied, shaking her hand.

"Please, have a seat," she said, ushering me to a table in the kitchen that had been set for four.

I sat down and realized this humble table in the kitchen was for the help. I couldn't see into any other rooms beyond a pantry and suspected behind that would be a dining room, complete with a bell in the floor that would ring here when plates needed to be cleared or the next course served. Yet despite the fact that we were eating in the kitchen, the table had been set with silver and the water glasses were crystal. The napkins were cloth with hand embroidering, and the bread plates were bone china with wildflowers hand painted around the rims. It was such a contrast to my home, where everything was new and whisked to your doorstep in twenty-four hours or less.

Jada sat opposite me, her back straight and shoulders back, and quietly said, "Klara has told me about your wife. I am very sorry." Despite her posture, she was terribly shy and hesitant with her English.

"Thank you," I replied sincerely. "Tell me about yourself, Jada."

"I am from Poland as well, and also care for Mrs. B. She is wonderful lady. Very kind."

"It sounds like you all take very good care of her."

"Being carer is very hard. But with Mrs. B, it is not a job. We love her very much."

"I am sure she feels the same way. I got to know the nurses that looked after my wife, and have to say, it is a special trait to care and share your love with someone. It helps them more than you know."

She looked down at her hands, and a little color came to her cheeks.

Returning her eyes to mine, she changed the subject. "I like to travel to interesting places. You will go to interesting places?"

It was my turn to be shy. Or more accurately, embarrassed not to have really planned my journey. "I hope so, but I am afraid I don't know exactly where I am going. Paris was just the first thing that came to mind."

"This is ok. You will find your way. Paris is good start. It is not adventurous. But is good start for you, I think."

I loved both her sincerity and frankness. She was absolutely lovely. "What would be adventurous, do you think?" I asked.

She pursed her lips and replied, "Africa and Asia. I very much like both. Cambodia and Laos are adventurous. So is Africa."

"You've been to these places?"

"Many times," she said matter-of-factly. "I go sometimes myself, sometimes with my daughter. Her husband is diplomat, so is very easy for her to travel. We have been to many interesting places."

I was barely making my way through one small portion of England and terrified at the thought of going to a country where I didn't speak the language. I couldn't imagine going to Asia or Africa, continents where all of the most frightening news stories came from. Yet here was a shy and conservative woman, in her long skirt and sweater set, who had gone out of her way to visit places that scared me.

"This is what your wife wanted, no?" she said.

"I'm not sure."

She reached her hand across the table and put it on my own. "This, I am sure." Her dark brown eyes, reflecting both gentle sincerity and stern determination, locked with mine. "You will see."

I was suddenly warm with emotion. I'd known this woman only for as long as we sat at that old table, yet she felt like an aunt who'd looked after me for ages and would always make sure I was safe. Before I could reply, Colin announced that dinner was ready.

He and Klara had poached a salmon on a massive stove they explained was an Aga. The brown monstrosity was big as a car, had no knobs, and was apparently always on. They opened some of the many doors on the front of the stove to reveal potatoes as well as some asparagus and bread that was being kept warm. While Colin plated, Klara put the finishing touches on a salad and set it on the table.

We ate happily together, the conversation weaving effortlessly through weather, the history of horse racing in West Berkshire, current Hollywood dramas, and politics. After dinner, Jada took a plate upstairs for Mrs. B while we washed and dried the dishes. Later, Klara showed me to a small bedroom in the annex. The clothes I'd worn had been cleaned and were neatly folded at the end of the bed. She smiled and said Colin had taken care of it as she left.

I couldn't help but be in awe of how kind they'd been after only a chance meeting on the road outside. They were all lovely, and for the first time in a long while, I fell asleep with a glimmer of happiness.

3

Happiness, I've learned, can be rather fleeting and didn't appear to have made it all the way to Paris with me. While I was happy to have figured out the train (or more accurately, followed Klara's detailed instructions) and made it to Paris, I was a more than a little anxious. Like the station in London, Gare du Nord was vast and full of noise. I could only read the occasional English translations below the signs, and there wasn't a chance I could understand the robotic voice coming through the speakers. It could be telling me there was a tsunami on the way for all I knew. I made it outside to the dirty cobblestone pickup area, a little weary of the edgy characters in their tracksuits loitering about. Finding a taxi parked next to a bollard, I had my first French interaction.

The taxi driver shouted at me as if I had violated a human right. "*Non, non, NON!*" he said, complete with dismissive facial expressions and wild gesticulating to the light atop his dented Renault. It was break time, apparently, and he wasn't to be disturbed. Thankfully, another taxi driver saw this and came in to help. I was undoubtedly easy prey. But he delivered me, after some time and excess expense, to the Marriott on the Champs Elysées.

Still rattled by the first taxi driver, I was relieved to enter the familiar surrounds of a chain hotel. The desk clerk explained that I had enough points for three nights and then handed me a keycard. My phone pinged as I sat down on the bed—Klara had tagged me in a photo. It showed Colin and me next to our stacks of bricks, sharing a laugh. I smiled and remembered I'd promised them I would post pictures. I found a nice one from Stonehenge, added it, and then set out to see Paris and post a few more.

I visited the sights I felt Lauren would want me to see: the Eiffel Tower, Pont Alexandre III, Musée d'Orsay, and the Tuileries Garden before visiting the Notre Dame reconstruction effort. The next day, I joined the masses of tourists from around the world in the Louvre, all of us in awe of the history on display.

Despite the presence and proximity of so many people, I was alone, lonely and sad. I knew it was my fault for not engaging. I'd fallen into a pattern of walking all day to see the sights and ordering dinner in the room. My spirits spiraled downward. By the end of the third day, I hit bottom. Wrapped in a numbing fog, I couldn't see how to carry on. I couldn't even see *why* to carry on. I'd started this trip for Lauren, and while I was nervous, there had been a few moments of excitement those first days. I'd formed a map in my mind then, with a line showing a journey from the UK across Europe and then around the world before coming home. But as my outlook dimmed, the line became a loop through Europe and back home. It was contracting even more now, and I found myself ready to head straight home from Paris.

Tomorrow.

I was ashamed by my failure. Of failing Lauren. But I couldn't see another way.

Curled in the corner of the dim hotel room, my eyes swollen and cloudy, I launched a travel app to see if there was space on a flight home.

A notification pinged, and a message from Ashton covered the top of the screen. *Still in Paris?*

Yes, I replied, not yet wanting to admit I was leaving.

Dinner tomorrow night at 9? A link to a bistro followed his message.

I hesitated, thinking I probably should tell him I might not be here after all. He would be disappointed and try to convince me to stay. But less than a week ago, he'd been so helpful, so maybe his positive nature was what I needed.

Before I could second guess myself, I tapped a reply. *Sure.*

Lovely! Pack your bag and bring it with you. We have a surprise!

I suddenly felt anxious. *Are you sure? I am fine at the hotel. What surprise?*

A wink emoji was all that came back. But that wink was enough. It kept me in Paris for another day; it gave me hope. It was a wink that I would only come to learn years later had changed the course of my life.

***

I was happy to see Hailey had taken the train down with Ashton. They both gave warm hugs and, through our dinner, asked questions about my trip so far. They were quite impressed that I'd taken a ride with the elderly tour group and were strangely excited about my brick stacking in Shefford Woodlands.

"And since then, John?" asked Hailey.

"I've seen it all. The Eiffel Tower, the Louvre, the—"

"We saw your pictures, John. They're actually why we took the train down to see you," said Ashton.

"You weren't coming for work? Or fun?" I asked.

"No, John. For you," Hailey replied.

"Your pictures the last few days, John. They have one thing in common," Ashton said. "There are no people in them."

"If there is some social media etiquette I'm breaking, I'm sorry. This is all new to me."

"That's not it," Hailey said. "Tell me, how did you feel in that little West Berkshire town?"

"Like I had a little purpose for the day, which was nice."

"And how did that really make you feel?" she asked.

"A little happy, I guess."

"And how have you felt here in Paris?"

"Well, I, ah—"

"John, it's us. We've been there, so be honest," Ashton said.

"A bit lonely." Feeling ashamed, I quietly added, "Maybe a little depressed."

"That's what we thought, John. So we're here to help."

"You have already done so much."

"Nonsense," Hailey said. "This will be fun. But you have to trust us, ok?"

Before I could reply, Ashton hopped up and said to Hailey, "Let's get going before he can answer!"

Hailey gave a happy shriek. Quickly chasing after him, she said, "Come on, John!"

Their excitement truly touched me.

"Ok, what's this about?" I asked.

"Our own travelers' rite of passage!" Ashton said.

We walked to a neighborhood Ashton explained was called the Marais, eventually stopping at a beautiful old apartment building. Hailey opened a small door set within an even larger set of red double doors, and we stepped into a cobblestone courtyard filled with small trees and potted plants. We crossed the peaceful enclosure and entered the building, heading up the stairs until we stopped at a landing with a solid black door fitted with a lion's head carving. With a smile and a wink, Ashton pressed a buzzer off to the side.

The door was eventually opened by a burly, older man with short salt-and-pepper hair and a joint balancing precariously on his lower lip. He ignored Ashton and Hailey and instead stared directly at me. He took a deep inhale, then slowly let out a cloud of smoke.

Turning to Ashton and Hailey, he said, "Him? Are you fucking kidding me?"

What a wonderful start. Could I please go back to the old house in England with the friendly people?

"Lovely to see you too, Omri," Ashton said, waving the smoke away as he crossed the threshold to embrace the grumpy man.

"I see you're as charming as always, darling!" Hailey said, taking her turn with a hug.

The man's eyes instantly softened, and he returned her embrace with genuine affection. "It is so wonderful to see you, *habibi*," he said. "How is Ashton treating you? Are you ready to leave him for me yet?"

"Not a chance, you old perv!" she replied, removing the joint from his hand and taking a puff before handing it back.

"One must always be hopeful," he grumbled. "Come in. Introduce me to my next victim."

Victim?

But Hailey and Ashton just smiled and walked in as if the apartment was their own. As I later learned, it really had been their home for a time, much as it would soon become mine.

We wound through expansive hallways and ornate rooms with tall ceilings and towering doors and windows. To say it was eclectic would have been an understatement. A sitting room appeared to be straight out of the 1800s. Thick, dark curtains framed towering windows. Fine antiques glimmered in soft light, their beeswax polish heavy in the air. The parquet floor squeaked as we passed through what must have once been a ballroom, complete with massive chandeliers hanging below an intricately sculpted ceiling. The sides of the vast space were littered with lights, stands, and open cases of what looked to be photography gear. Next was a dining room, the centuries-old table in the center surrounded by a hodgepodge of mismatched, strikingly modern chairs in every color.

Lauren, you would love this beautiful place!

Finally, we entered a large room that had been stripped down to the structural stone and wood, giving it the feeling of a hip loft. Half of the space had been converted into a modern kitchen, glistening in white marble and stainless steel. The other half was a living area, complete with soft leather couches and sheepskin-covered chairs. Despite the room's large size, the space was inviting and comfortable and clearly the heart of the home.

Hailey waved me over to a couch while Ashton and our strange host continued to the kitchen area.

I leaned to her and quietly said, "I don't know what you're up to, Hailey, but your friend sure doesn't like me."

"Relax, John. Omri is a sweetheart. You'll see."

"I heard that, *habibi*! I am not a sweetheart!"

"Yes, you are!"

"And I am not a halfway house for any more of you vagrants!"

"You love it, Omri!"

"I do not!" he shouted.

Hailey fixed him with a stare and a wicked smile.

Omri took another puff of his joint. As he exhaled, the corner of his mouth turned up just the slightest bit. "But tell him how this works in case I change my mind."

"See?" Hailey said.

Omri Uziel was raised in Tel Aviv, the son of a painter and a soldier. Upon retirement from his career in the Israeli Defense Force as a paratrooper, he moved to Paris to pursue his love of photography. His eye and technique proved legendary, and he quickly became one of the most sought-after fashion photographers in Paris and eventually, the world. This apartment, a bequest from a particularly affectionate heiress some years ago, spanned a full floor of a classic 16th-century French Gothic building in the heart of the Marais. Hailey explained that it served as his studio, his home, and an informal school.

"A school? This is a school?" I asked, gesturing towards the vast expanse of the beautiful apartment.

Hailey said, "Well, there's not really a single word to explain this place. It's a little bit photography studio, a little bit hostel, and a little bit orphanage."

"And what does one learn at this school?"

Just then, Omri and Ashton returned. Ashton handed a glass to Hailey, and Omri gave me one as he sat down on the couch next to me.

He stared directly at me in his very intimidating way. "You will learn to live, John. To live," he said.

I readied a jovial reply, but the look in Omri's eyes told me his statement was entirely serious.

He leaned towards me, still staring. His face intense, he asked, "Do you want to learn to live again, John?"

At that very moment, I realized that living—living without Lauren—was precisely what I needed to learn. But could an eccentric Israeli in bare feet, jeans, and a T-shirt sprinkled with flecks of marijuana ash teach me to live without Lauren? I strongly doubted it. Then I remembered that the few precious moments on this journey so far had evolved entirely on their own.

Quietly, I said, "I think that's what I need, Omri."

His eyes transformed instantly, turning warm and inviting. He smiled and touched his glass to mine. "I know it is what you need, John," he said. With a nod to my drink, he said, "Now that that's settled, tell me what you think."

I took a sip and enjoyed the taste and warmth. "Brandy?" I asked.

"Almost," Omri replied. "It is Armagnac, the sister of brandy and cognac. Those two evil bitches keep her hidden in the shadows because they are jealous of her beauty. Afraid she will steal all of their suitors!"

Ashton and Hailey laughed.

I joined in, then asked, "Is this how the school works? Through metaphors?"

"In actual fact, John," Hailey said between giggles, "it does!"

This realization only caused them to laugh even louder.

Ashton caught his breath and said, "What you will do, John, is live here and help Omri as an assistant. He's a great teacher, and you will learn absolutely everything about photography."

"But he will also give you some assignments," Hailey continued, "and there's nothing easy about them. But leave your fears behind and trust the process, ok?"

A leap of faith. "Ok, Hailey. I'll trust you and do just as you say," I replied.

"I said the same thing to her once, John. But the gorgeous tease never gave me the instructions I hoped for," Omri said.

Ashton rolled his eyes, and Hailey threw a pillow at him. I laughed at this banter between friends, bewildered by the curious intersection of circumstances that had landed me here.

We talked late into the night, drinking and laughing, enjoying ourselves as if we had not a care in the world. Omri and I said goodbye to Ashton and Hailey, and he showed me to a bedroom that would be mine.

I woke the next day to gentle light filtering through linen curtains and the rustle of some fabric. I turned toward the noise to find a young woman standing at the foot of my bed, completely undressed.

She gave me a huge smile and, without a care in the world that she wore nothing at all, said, "*Bonjour!*" She bent over and picked up a pair of jeans she'd just removed and tossed them on the bed next to a leather jacket, T-shirt, and her unmentionables.

"Good morning," I replied, averting my eyes.

"*Ah, anglais!*" she exclaimed. "Good morning."

Even looking away, I could tell she'd made no effort to cover up. "Miss, I am afraid…"

"*Pas de problème.* I will just check my face before I see the makeup artist." She pulled a chair to the small makeup table and sat down after turning on a circular lamp. "*Lanvin aujourd'hui.* Ah, sorry. Today."

I flopped back down and rubbed my eyes. *Oh, Lauren, I'm not sure this was what you meant!*

I extracted myself as discreetly as possible and made my way to a bathroom down the hall to shower and dress. Voices could be heard echoing from a distant hall as I went to the kitchen in search of coffee. Two men in black slacks, white shirts, and aprons stood at the large island, which was now covered with plates of chopped fruit and pastries.

Seeing me enter, one of the men turned and said, "*Bonjour, monsieur. Café?*"

"*Bonjour,*" I replied. "Coffee would be very nice, thank you."

"*Ah, Américain,*" he said and began making a café crème from a large machine. After frothing the milk and drawing espresso, he placed the cup on a saucer before me. In precise English, he said, "If I may, sir, it is very nice in France to say *Bonjour, monsieur*. Or *madame*, or *mademoiselle*, as the situation requires, rather than only *bonjour.*"

"Thank you for the tip," I said, smiling.

"*Je vous en prie.*"

"What is your name?"

"Etienne," he replied.

"Etienne, I am afraid I know only a few words in French and appreciate your help."

He smiled and bowed his head slightly. "It is my pleasure."

The coffee was delicious, and I said as much before asking where I could find Omri.

"I believe they are in the studio. Just down the hall." He gestured just beyond the kitchen, to a part of the vast apartment I hadn't seen last night.

Thanking him, I took my coffee and headed that way. Following voices, I entered a large room filled with soft light. Masses of white muslin sheets hung high in the ceiling, cascading over the tall windows, and spilling across the floor. In the center was a large white chair with a woman in a white dress nestled in a mass of pillows. A small, fluffy white dog rested in her lap, and a second woman kneeled beside her. It appeared as if they sat on a cloud. Omri knelt in front of the set, behind a camera mounted on a low tripod. He spoke to the models gently, instructing them on subtle adjustments to their positions. As he spoke, lights on metal stands fired like lightening into huge white boxes. The models moved with grace, following his instructions until their positions came together in a beautiful S-shape. The lights fired more quickly now, and Omri unclipped the camera from the tripod and moved slightly to one side. After more bursts of light, he stopped and said, "*Merveilleux, mes filles. C'est fini!*"

Omri handed his camera off to a young man and saw I'd entered the room. "Good morning, John!"

"Good morning, Omri," I replied. "This is stunning!"

"Thank you. It was your idea, you know."

I was puzzled. "How is that?"

"Last night, when you were speaking of your wife, you said you were sure she was in heaven sharing her love with everyone there. So I decided for this shot, I would use the whites and make the set look like they had traveled to heaven for you!"

I was touched and entirely surprised.

Omri turned and gave a lengthy set of instructions in French to the young men and women surrounding the set. As they moved back and forth, adjusting camera equipment and pulling down the miles of fabric, he introduced me to each one. There were five of them, not including the models. As they shook my hand, Omri told a little story about each and how they were essential to his success. He knew them well, and it was clear respect for one another ran both ways.

"Now come. I need coffee."

Etienne once again went to work. While we took our time selecting from the vast assortment of pastries, Omri explained how each day was different in the studio. Today was to create a set of four photographs celebrating Lanvin, one of France's oldest couture houses. *Vogue* was writing a story on their second rebirth under the vision of a new creative director. Tomorrow would be a portrait of a politician.

As Omri used a tiny spoon to scoop the foam left in his cup, I asked, "What would you like me to do today?"

He licked the spoon and set it on the saucer. "What did you notice about the photographs we just took?"

"It was amazing. The whole setup was theatrical."

"Tell me one thing you saw."

"Omri, I am an accountant. I don't know a thing about art, and don't even know the right words to use."

"I'm not asking the accountant. I'm asking you, as a person, here with me right now. A blank canvas. The words we use are tribal, simply dramatic to make us feel better about ourselves. Now tell me one specific thing you noticed, in your own words."

"Well, I noticed that you gave some instructions to the models, and after they moved their arms and legs and adjusted one of the dresses, they sort of came together."

"Together how?"

"In an organic shape, like a wave or an S."

He clapped his hands together. "See? This is not hard! That is part of composition, and organic was a good word. The man-made world is full of hard angles. Nature uses soft shapes, and I wanted their bodies to flow like the clouds of fabric around them. I wanted the curves and shadows to drive the eye to Amélie on the chair. Composition is about the arrangement of light and shadow drawing your eye to the heart of the story you want to tell."

"Okay," I said, not actually understanding at all.

But he was patient. He went to a side table, grabbed a magazine from the top, and rummaged in the drawer below. Finally extracting a marker, he brought both to the counter. For nearly an hour, he flipped through the magazine. On each photo, he drew lines, explaining to me where the photographer wanted your eye to move. After going through almost all of the images, he went back to the beginning and started again. This time through, he drew gridlines, telling me about the rule of thirds and how points of interest should be at one of the four intersection points.

"So today, I want you to watch. Look through the camera and think about composition. Think about the shapes and shadows and the point of interest."

The young woman who'd been in my room earlier entered and Omri smiled. "Camille, *ma chérie!*" he said.

She went straight to Omri, and he air-kissed her cheeks so as not to touch her makeup. Holding her hand, he raised it up and said, "Let me see!"

She pirouetted beneath his arm, showing a dress covered in a print reminiscent of Roman times.

"*Tu es ravissante!*" he said. "Now, let me introduce our friend John."

She giggled and nestled into the crook of Omri's arm.

I said, "We met this morning rather, ah, intimately. It seems my bedroom is also Camille's dressing room."

Omri gave a laugh. "Truer than you know. But, John, you're not in America anymore. Time to let go of your prudish ways!"

"I am sorry to frighten you today, John," Camille said, using the French pronunciation of my name, *Jean*.

Omri hopped off the stool and, with Camille in his arm, said, "Let's see how things are coming along."

We returned to the studio, where I was surprised to see the room had changed entirely. Where it had been light and completely bright before, now blackout curtains covered the windows. A large, mottled gray sheet hung at one end of the room and extended halfway across the parquet floor. Scattered in front of the backdrop was an arrangement of ancient statues large and small, along with an assortment of fractured columns both standing and laying on their sides. Two models stood in the center, and Camille left Omri to join them. Their dresses each differed significantly, but I could now see the set was designed to support the resemblance of their patterns to ancient times. As Gabriel, one of Omri's colleagues, directed the models into place, Omri explained. Madame Lanvin was a constant traveler and heavily influenced by what she saw visiting Roman ruins in North Africa. Their new designer had followed one of her itineraries from over one hundred years ago and was trying to bring the brand back with his own perspective on her original route.

"*On est prêts,*" Gabriel said.

"They are ready," Omri translated for me.

To Gabriel, he said, "Tell me what you have."

Gabriel looked at me, knowing Omri had used English for my benefit, and switched to English himself. "Camille's dress should be the centerpiece. Chloe and Amélie will frame her. With

Amélie's outfit so dark, I think she has to take the front and Chloe the back."

Omri nodded his agreement. Pointing at the camera, he said, "Please show John."

"*Oui.*" Gabriel waved me over and had me look through the viewfinder.

I took care not to touch the camera as it had several cords plugged into it and was undoubtedly positioned precisely. Moving my eye to the viewfinder, I was surprised to see how different the scene looked. The background fell away to darkness, and the statues looked older and more damaged than they did with the naked eye. A grid like the one Omri had drawn overlaid the screen, and I could see that Camille's face was at one intersection and a dramatic spray of fabric at the bottom of her dress was on the opposite intersection of lines.

"Amazing, Gabriel," I said.

He smiled and then waved Omri to the camera.

"No," Omri said. "This is your shot."

"*Vraiment?*"

"*Oui.*" Omri stood behind Gabriel as he snapped the shutter.

The two spoke together quietly, which resulted in Omri eventually going in between the models and adjusting their dresses and poses slightly. Gabriel directed a few more changes, and it was interesting to see the famous photographer acting as an assistant. They worked nicely together as a team, without ego or hierarchy. After a while, Gabriel had the shots he wanted and went through the images on a laptop before the scene was to be reset for the next shot. Again, Omri took time to talk to me about composition and light while his colleagues transformed the room once more.

When the final shot of the day was complete, the models went to change and Gabriel sat with Omri to select the best images on one of the computers. The rest of us set about putting the equipment away. Monique managed the gear, and as we worked, she explained how each piece was to be packed. Once everything was loaded in wheeled cases, she led me farther around the apartment to a storage room. I was shocked at the amount of equipment. There were cases of cameras, lenses, and video equipment all surrounded by lights on stands large and small. Each item had its place, and I listened carefully as she explained how everything was labeled and organized.

Walking back to the atrium, I saw it was completely empty. A blank slate ready for the next transformation. Omri's colleagues had scattered to different rooms in the apartment for some quiet time. Some were on their phones, and two lay on the couches in the kitchen, their eyes closed as they wound down from the day. The only noise came from two new people in the kitchen, and by the beautiful smells, they were busy preparing dinner.

I decided I would lay down for a minute myself and headed back to my room. I opened the door to see Camille towel-drying her hair, once again wearing absolutely nothing.

"John!" she said excitedly.

I backed out of the doorway quickly, and said, "Honestly, Camille, do you have to always be undressed in my room?"

"Oh, John. *Je suis désolée. Un moment!*" After a moment, she said, "Ok, you may come in now." She wore only a dark gray oversized sweatshirt. But it was a start.

"*Merci*, Camille," I said, sitting down on the bed. I took off my boots and put my feet up on the bed, tired from standing all day.

She hopped on the bed and stretched out right in the middle, somewhat too close for comfort. "Omri said to us about your wife," she said. "I am sorry."

"Thank you," I replied. "She was wonderful, and I miss her every day."

"We will help you," she said. "Omri is a very nice person. He likes you, you know?"

"He has been very nice. I know he has helped some of my friends too."

"I know. Ashton and Hailey. But this is not what I mean. He likes you in a different way."

Well, that's something that will wake you up even more than a half-naked model in your bed. "What do you mean?" I asked, trying not to sound like I was considering packing my bag and scrambling out of the apartment.

But Camille was close enough to have sensed my reaction and gave a hearty laugh. "This is not what I mean!" she said, still laughing. "Omri does not like boys! He likes the models very much. And sometimes the woman assistants. But no boys. You are very silly, John!"

"Phew," I said. "That is a relief."

"What I try to say is that he was married before. In Israel. His wife has died too, a long time ago."

It explained why he was so intense with me the previous night and so gentle today. It also explained why Ashton and Hailey brought me here to begin with, the sneaky bastards.

"Thank you, Camille, for telling me," I said.

"Of course."

We lay in silence for a long time before I finally said, "Camille?"

"Yes?"

"Can you please put on some pants?"

She laughed and hopped off the bed. Rummaging around in a bag, she pulled out a pair of jeans and waved them at me. Making quite a production out of it, she pulled them on. Then, in a sarcastic but friendly tone, she asked, "Does this make you happy now?"

"It does, thank you."

"*Bon*," she said, jumping right back onto the bed and taking her spot in the middle once more.

At this point, I could only laugh. She laughed too, knowing she'd made good fun of my "prudish ways" as Omri had called them. I understood then that she wasn't flirty or forward. She wasn't teasing. She was simply a person happy to make a friend. Happy to have someone to talk to today.

After spending weeks mourning, locked away almost entirely alone, I was quite aware that since leaving, I cherished sharing conversations with the people I'd met. Most of them were people I would have never thought I would have a thing in common with. But it turned out we did have things in common. We were curious. We wanted to listen and tell, learn and contribute. I appreciated every time on this trip someone had reached out to me and recognized that's all this young woman wanted right now. Maybe life's only more complicated if you make it so.

"Tell me about yourself," I said.

"What would you like to know? About my work? Modeling and fashion?"

"No, not about work. Work isn't who we are; it's what we do. Tell me about something you love, something you're scared of, or even just the color of your childhood house."

She was silent and still for long enough that I turned to look at her.

"You have good questions," she finally said. "But when you are a model, work *is* who you are. It is your face; it is your body. Everyone has something to say about it. Sometimes what they say is not very nice."

Problems that are entirely unknown to accountants. But I did understand what she meant. "When I was in college, a friend of mine was on the basketball team. He was quite good, and so we would sometimes see him on the sports news channel. As you said, commentators would sometimes be nice and sometimes mean. When they were mean, he didn't worry and said they were only judging the one small part of him they could see. He said what matters is your character. What you value and feel inside is something protected by the love of friends and family, and no television critic could ever change it."

"Hmm," she said. "I like your friend."

"So, tell me something you love."

"Puppies and chocolate."

"Those aren't real answers. Everyone loves puppies and chocolate."

"Ok, then. I love flowers."

"That might be a little better," I said. "Why?"

"My mother was a florist. She used to have a cart here in Paris. She used to wake me up very early and take me with her to the market to buy flowers she would make into arrangements and sell. I remember how her eyes would be delighted every time we went into the market. She said it was the most colorful place in the world."

"I like that answer. So, tell me the color of your house growing up."

"It was an apartment in Paris. When you ask a Parisian this question, the answer will always be gray."

"Ok, then. Favorite thing to draw when your parents gave you a piece of paper."

"A cat."

"Why a cat?"

"Our apartment was very small, very close to another. Through the window, I could only see the building next to ours. And the neighbor across had a big, fat cat sleeping on the window every day. We used to have... What do you call the contest with looking?"

"A staring contest."

"Yes, this!"

"Who would win?"

"The cat, John. A person cannot beat a cat in a staring contest."

"I should have known. Now tell me something that scares you."

Again, she didn't answer right away. After a moment, she said, "You tell me this first."

This was a pretty easy one for me. "My biggest fear is the unknown. Doing something unplanned, where I don't know what to do or what will happen next."

"I think what you are doing now is unknown."

"It is. And I am scared. But I decided last night to be as strong as I can and just take it one day at a time." After waiting a moment, I turned to see if she was still listening.

She'd propped her head on her arm and was staring at me rather intensely.

"Your turn," I prompted.

She held my gaze for a second longer before tucking her hair behind her ear and saying, "Tell me one more. One more thing you are scared of."

I closed my eyes, hesitant to answer.

In a soft, kind voice, she said, "It is ok to tell me."

I turned back and looked up toward the ceiling. "I am afraid of living without my wife."

"You will find a way, John. Omri is ok now, yes? You will remember your wife every day, but you will live happy."

"I hope."

"Ok. I will tell you mine now," she said. "I am afraid of being old and alone."

"You are a model. You'll never be alone."

"But you said my job is not all who I am."

"You're right, I did. Sorry, that was petty of me."

"But it is a part of who I am. And now, this means I meet only people who are wanting my picture for their business. Or sex. Or money."

"There are good people out there, Camille. Stay away from the bad ones. Just the fact that you can tell what people really want means you will know who is bad and who is good. Be patient and good people will come when you least expect it."

We lay there silently, each lost in our thoughts. The door opened, and Omri came in. Whereas one might usually poke a little fun at two of his friends lying in bed together, he didn't. He clearly had a sense of people and only asked if we were ok.

We nodded yes, and he gently told us that dinner was ready whenever we were and left the room.

We got up, and I tucked in my shirt while Camille ran a brush through her hair.

As we left the room, she grabbed my hand. Squeezing tightly, she said, "*Merci*, John," and headed for the dining room.

We arrived to find a festive atmosphere. Everyone from the shoot was seated around the table, engaged in lively conversation. I took a seat next to Monique, who was kind enough to pour me a glass of wine. The center of the table was filled with serving dishes, and everyone's plates were half full. I took a few things from a nearby bowl and had more passed to me. There were salads and meats, bread, and vegetables. Everything was delicious, and Monique was especially kind in explaining each.

"Is every night like this?" I asked.

"Not every night. But after a long shoot, Omri likes to feed everyone and make sure we are happy."

"It's like a family here."

"It is," she said. "Some will come and some will go, but the feeling is always the same."

"I liked that he allowed others to shoot the photographs today and didn't do it all himself."

She nodded. "He is like this and has allowed us all to grow as photographers. Give me your phone, and we will add our names so that you can see some of our work."

I unlocked my phone and handed it to her. "Have you worked with Omri long?" I asked as she typed.

"I have," she said. "He is a very organized person, probably from the army. But he wants to focus on the photographs. So I help him schedule and take care of the equipment."

"Given the scale of today, that sounds like a lot."

"Some days," she said. She turned and handed the phone to the assistant next to her, Jaques. It appeared my phone was going to make the rounds and everyone was going to enter their names.

There was a tap on my shoulder, and I turned to see it was one of the other models, Chloe. "*Il commence,*" she said, which I guessed meant something along the lines of *time to start.*

I didn't know what was starting, but she pointed to Gabriel, who was wheeling in a large television monitor on a stand.

"We see the photographs now," Chloe said.

Monique explained, "Most photographers send you home after a shoot. But Omri wants everyone to see the result of their work for the day, even if it's just a rough edit."

Gabriel sat at the end of the table and connected his laptop to the monitor. "*Prêt?*" he asked.

"*On devrait parler en anglais pour John,*" Omri said.

"Sorry. Ready everyone?"

"*Oui, oui!*" said the third model, Amélie, who sat wrapped in Omri's arms.

Gabriel put the first image up on the screen, the one in all white, and the room erupted in applause. The photograph was incredible. I'd seen the set, with all of the white fabric and models in their interesting dresses, but to see it cropped as it would appear in a magazine was staggering. The highlights and shadows were more prominent than I remembered and created the sense that the women were floating in heaven, just as Omri had said.

Gabriel clicked to the photo with the statues, and again, I was amazed at the richness of the image. Omri hopped up and pointed at different parts, complimenting Gabriel on his arrangement. He went on to praise Chloe's expression and pose and the warmth of Amélie's eyes.

Gabriel moved to the next image, filled with tans and lines of golden sun slicing through. I remembered how they'd created the effect with lights and no real sun at all. Again, Omri went to great lengths to compliment others at the table for their contribution.

The screen changed again, and a stunning image of Camille appeared in a yellow suit. She stood defiantly, a bag in her hand and sunglasses on top of her head, looking just beyond the camera. Even as an accountant, I could appreciate the strength and confidence in her stance and expression.

Omri went to Camille, put his hands on her shoulders, and said, "This is what we will recommend for the cover."

Gabriel tapped once again, and the photo reappeared. This time, it was cropped differently and the *Vogue* masthead had been inserted along with some dummy copy to simulate what the magazine would look like. It was wonderful to see it that way and hear the cheering everyone gave to one another.

We carried on for a while after that, talking and drinking. Eventually, the plates were cleared and as the caterers cleaned up and most everyone said their goodbyes, only Omri, Amélie, and Camille remained. Amélie was wrapped in Omri's arms, and it looked like she would be wrapped in him for the night. Camille sat alone on the opposite couch, her knees to the side and feet beneath her.

After tapping out a text on her phone, Camille said, "I must go. The car is here." She said goodbye to Omri and kissed cheeks with him and Amélie.

I stood up and said, "It's time for me to go to bed. I'll walk you down."

She looked over to Omri and Amélie, her eyebrows rising slightly.

"He's going to see it someday," Omri said with a shrug.

I was tired and didn't give much thought to what he meant.

Camille tapped another message onto her phone, and we walked downstairs and through the courtyard. I opened the door set into the large gate only to have a flash go off in my face. I saw stars for a second as more went off.

A half dozen paparazzi shouted to her and came closer. A burly man in a suit pushed them back a few feet, giving us room to get to a long, dark sedan. Another man held the door for her while casting stern looks at the photographers. Before getting in, she stopped and turned her head to the side in what I thought would be the start of the French cheek-kissing routine. But all she did was rest her head against my shoulder and hug me. I returned the embrace and said goodnight. The burly men gave me a nod and jumped into the car themselves. The paparazzi began shouting questions to me.

I simply turned and went back into the relative peace of the courtyard.

In the kitchen, Omri and Amélie were smiling.

"What the hell was that?" I asked.

They broke into laughter.

When Omri finally caught his breath, he said, "You still don't know who she is, do you?"

"Camille? By all appearances today, she's a model."

Still laughing, Omri said, "Camille Amari is a *super*model, John. And she is *the* supermodel right now."

"She likes you, you know," said Amélie.

I frowned at her. "I'm not really on the market."

Omri laughed again. "Oh, I think you made that very clear! You are the only man in the world to want her to put clothes *on*!"

This brought another round of laughter.

Taking a few breaths to calm himself, Omri added, "But really, John, she appreciated you talking to her today. She liked that you asked questions and listened. She liked that you cared about who she is. Who she is inside."

I shook my head at them and turned to go to bed.

"I will put my clothes on for you any day!" Amélie shouted as I walked away.

They both laughed once again, and I held my middle finger high up in the air as I left the room.

Which, of course, only had them laughing more.

***

The next morning, I went into the kitchen to find Amélie sitting at the counter drinking coffee. We exchanged the Parisian double-cheek kiss, and I went to make a coffee but was somewhat dumbfounded by the large, chrome espresso machine. Amélie gave some instruction from her side of the counter, and my first coffee was at least passable.

I rummaged through the cupboards a bit, and then the fridge, finally deciding I would make an omelet.

"Can I make you an omelet, Amélie?" I asked.

"*Non*," she replied. "I cannot eat too much. I will just have a bite of yours."

A bite of my eventual omelet turned out to be half, so I went to make another as Omri joined us. He gave Amélie a kiss that was not exactly the double-cheek variety. I just smiled, and after sliding the omelet onto a plate, passed it over to him.

Amélie went to a side table to remove her phone from a charger. Something caught her attention, and she turned to show Omri.

"*Mazel tov*, John!" he said. "You're famous."

Amélie turned her phone so that I could see. It was a news app showing a picture of Camille and I that the paparazzi had taken the night before.

"Hooray. That's just what I wanted," I said, waving the spatula in mock celebration.

"If you are not busy being famous today, we are going to learn some basics," he said once Amélie had gone back to bed.

"Don't you have a politician to shoot?" I asked.

"Yes, but that is not until later. I want to shoot from the roof, and the evening sun is wonderful there. The day is about you."

And he was true to his word. He taught me as he would a class, going through principles with a marker on large sheets of paper, followed by practical application on a camera he'd selected for me to use as my own. He talked about focus points and focal lengths, followed by white balance and how it can be used to warm or cool an image. He explained exposure, and how ISO, aperture, and shutter speed work together. For each topic, he had something for me to experiment with. By midday, the kitchen counter looked like a preschool had visited. Various fruits were scattered about, along with bottle caps we'd spun to try shutter speed. There was even a stuffed animal and a small statuette the rental company had forgotten to take back the day before.

When he'd handed me the camera that morning, I was intimidated by all the dials and buttons on the top and back. But now, I understood what most of them did and told him as much.

"Yes! I am glad you feel it is clear now. But remember, the camera is a tool. You need practice. Adjusting based on light and composition needs to come like second nature. This will allow you to focus on the story you're trying to tell. That story, that feeling you want to create, is the part that matters."

"So with your politician coming today, what story do you want to tell?"

"That is a good question. This man is not my favorite, but I am not that involved in politics to care much. What I know about him is that his intentions are good, even if his methods aren't always successful. I know he usually appears sincere, and I hope he proves to be so."

"So how will you decide how you will photograph him?"

Omri shrugged and said, "I will talk with him and try to understand him a little. I will look at the light and the city we will use as a background and see what happens."

"That's it?"

"Sure, why make it so complicated? Want to try yourself?"

"Well, I…"

"Come with me. Bring your camera with the fifty."

As we walked around to his bedroom, he called ahead, "Amélie, can John take some portrait shots of you?"

"Of course!" she replied. "Would he like me to put clothes on?"

"*Non, non, habibi!* He is an artist now and will only take nudes!"

"*Ah, parfait!*" she squealed.

When we came in, I saw they'd both been having me on. Amélie was fully dressed, wearing jeans and an oversized sweater.

Omri explained what he'd been teaching so that she understood, then had her pose at different places in the room and helped me with both the camera settings and the composition. He explained the difference that could be created when the light came from the front, the side, and the back. Amélie remained patient throughout and even showed how dramatically her body position would impact a photograph.

"Always talk to the subject, John. Ask questions or give them prompts. You will learn about them, see new expressions, and the ideas for a photograph will come."

I checked my camera settings and set up for a shot of her from the shoulders up. I said with all sincerity, "Amélie, can you take your clothes off for me?"

She burst into a laugh, and I pressed the shutter.

"I think you have the idea, John!" Omri said, laughing. "Let me see if you caught the right moment. Instant reactions like that are difficult."

I pressed the replay button to show the image. It was a straight-on shot with the background blown out, and her expression was priceless. Her eyes had just squeezed shut and her mouth was at the perfect point of her laugh to look purely joyful.

"Well done!" he said, turning the camera for Amélie to see.

"Ah, you got me! That is a great one, John. Can you send it to me later?"

"Of course."

"I must go now, *mes chéris*. You have fun!" She kissed us both and then hurried out the door.

We had a light lunch and then Omri spent the afternoon on the computer showing me how to crop and edit the photos to fix mistakes or enhance points of interest. It was fascinating how much you could do, and I was surprised to learn there was a mobile version of the tool.

Omri excused himself to get ready for the afternoon shoot, so I went back to my room and dug out my phone to try the photo editor. There were a few notifications, comments on a picture someone must have posted when my phone was passed around the night before. It was actually quite a fun image of everyone at the table, laughing and carrying on amidst a sea of food and wine. The comments were from Ashton and his friends, words of encouragement and happiness that I was having a good time. A few were from strangers, mostly remarking on Camille, Chloe, and Amélie. There were also a few hundred new people apparently following me, which was rather strange. I thumbed through to see that everyone from the table last night must have added themselves to the feed. There were a few pictures from the shoot and more from dinner. I had been tagged in some, which must have been why I had new followers. I was a little surprised by this but shrugged it off and went to read a text that had come in from Hailey.

It was a screenshot from the news app Amélie had shown that morning with the message, *So happy we knew you before you were famous!*

What have you gotten me into?! I replied.

Now, now, you will love it! she said.

I do already. Omri and his friends are all wonderful. Thank you. For everything.

Her reply was a series of hearts.

I used a dongle to load some of today's pictures and sent Amélie her funny photo. I decided to post it, figuring it would make Ashton and Hailey happy to see that I was making the most of their little Shanghai.

After a while, Monique came to my room. "Ah, John. I am glad you are here. Will you please come and help Gabriel and me?" she asked.

"Of course, Monique. Sorry, but this apartment is so large, I didn't even know you were here."

She smiled, but weakly, and I could tell she was under some pressure. I'd only known her for two days but could tell she was a professional and not the type to stress easily. I got up from the desk and followed her out and to the staircase.

At the top floor, a policeman stopped us.

"This man will need to wand you for security," she said.

I held my hands out.

The officer ran his device across my front and arms and motioned for me to turn around.

Now facing Monique, I asked, "Monique, what sort of politician are you shooting today?"

"John, today, when we are using English, we will say 'photograph.' Omri used the word you just said earlier today, and one of the policemen became very nervous."

I rolled my eyes a bit but understood.

The policeman was done with me and indicated I could leave, so Monique led the way up the stairs, opening a metal door where we were greeted by another policeman. While he looked me over, I scanned the roof to see three more policemen spread about. We walked across the gritty surface to the corner, where Gabriel was in a heated argument with a woman in a suit. A police badge hung around her neck. Given the others were in uniforms, I realized she must be in charge.

While their French was frighteningly fast, I could tell by the tone of their voices that Gabriel was frustrated and losing this argument badly. His face was red, and I could see he was at the end of his rope. When I saw his hands ball into fists, it was time to interrupt.

"What seems to be the problem, Gabriel?" I kept my voice calm and steady.

"This woman will not allow us to photograph on this corner!"

"Ok," I said. "Why is that a problem?"

He thrust his hand out and said, "Because the sun sets here and this position allows us to try light from two different directions. This way, we have the best light when the sun is still up and when it turns gold at the horizon. It is the way we shoot outdoor portraits!"

I turned to the policewoman and said, "*Bonjour, madame. Parlez-vous anglais?*"

"Of course," she replied tersely.

"If I could ask, what is the problem with this corner?" I said.

She looked at Monique and asked, "Who is this man?"

"John Winter. Our Director of Facilities," Monique replied.

This morning I was just a homeless widower, so the day was certainly taking a turn for the better. But it was clear Monique was just giving me some weight in the game.

The sour female officer turned her attention back to me. "Why were you not here last week for the walkthrough?" she asked.

"I was needed in London, I'm afraid." Never lie to the police. Unless you are Monique. For her, it's ok.

"Very well. I am Commissaire Divisionnaire Reynard, and I lead the president's security detail."

The president? I tried not to show my surprise. Keeping my voice steady, I said, "Commissaire, what is the problem with this location? Are you worried about snipers? Or something else?"

"Ah, Mr. Winter, I see you are American. No, we are not worried about snipers here as you are with your president. This is France. No, we are worried about this wall. It is too low, and we will not allow the president to stand where it is so easy to fall."

"So the height of the wall is the problem?"

"*Oui.*"

Gabriel came back to the conversation, still fired up. "The short wall is why we get the rooftops in the picture! Over there," he said, again rather dramatically thrusting his arm out to the center of the roof, "you will not see the rooftops!"

Monique said to me, "As you remember, John, 'classic Parisian rooftops' were in the agreement sent over by the president's office."

"Yes, of course." I wasn't lying to the police, just following Monique's lead. In my book, that's ok.

I walked over to the wall that ran around the perimeter of the roof and looked over the side, finding that six stories was high enough to make me feel a little wobbly. But stepping back and looking at the wall, it didn't seem low enough to be dangerous.

The policewoman noticed me sizing up the height and said, "We have measured the wall, *monsieur*. The photo will not be taken there."

Gabriel threw his arms up in the air.

"Commissaire," I asked. "How far from the wall will he need to be?"

"At least three meters," she replied.

I paced off three meters from one side and moved Monique to act as a marker, then measured from the other side of the corner and shifted her slightly to stand at the intersection.

Gabriel came over and made a camera shape with his hand. He held it high above his head and said, "This is the angle I would need to catch the rooftops. But when we are this far back, half of the shot will be the ugly wall!"

"Commissaire, I am going to discuss this with my colleagues for a moment, if you don't mind."

She gestured that it would be fine, so I led Monique and Gabriel a few steps away.

"Thank you for coming up, John," Gabriel said. "This woman was so rude. She made me very upset!"

I grabbed his hand and said, "Gabriel, I know you're upset, but this is easy to fix. If you both weren't so flustered, you would have solved it in less than a second. It's the angle you need, right? So let's get a platform that raises everyone up a foot or two. You get on it with him, and your angle should be high enough to be above the wall."

Gabriel closed his eyes and let out a breath. "I let this woman get to me for no reason! Of course, that is an easy solution."

I walked back to the policewoman and said, "I am sorry for the trouble, Commissaire. We have a solution that will keep him three meters from the sides. Would it be ok if the president stood on a low platform? Maybe only a foot or two?" I bent down and showed her how much I thought we'd need.

She hesitated, thinking.

"It will be very wide, and we will make sure he is in the center." I had a suspicion. It didn't really need to be proven, but I wanted to make a point that I knew. To avenge Gabriel. I asked not with words, but with the tiniest hint of a smirk and a raised eyebrow.

She replied, "Yes, this will be fine." In a lower, more direct tone, she continued, "And you will be discreet."

"We will, thank you."

I stood and extended my hand. As she shook it, I decided to press my luck. "As this whole discussion has set us behind schedule, could a few of your officers come help me carry up the gear we'll need?"

"*Oui*," she said, waving three men over and instructing them to follow me.

We went back downstairs and wove our way to the equipment room.

Monique heard me coming down the hall and said, "John, we're going to need your help carrying the portable stage up there."

"Don't worry," I said just coming to the doorway. "I am as strong as three men."

She looked up from the equipment as the officers arrived. "Yes, you are!"

The policemen gathered the portable stage parts and headed back to the roof, leaving only Gabriel, Monique, and I in the storage room.

"Thank you, John," Gabriel said.

Monique added her thanks as well.

I smiled mischievously.

"What?" Gabriel asked.

"He's afraid of heights," I said, and the three of us erupted in laughter.

***

"John, set the other ladder next to mine and come up," Omri said. "With your camera," he added.

The shoot was nearly done. Omri had what he said was a winner but was taking a few extra shots to round out the set. As it turned out, the French president could not have been kinder. He was approachable and gracious, if not a bit cautious on the stage. Even the commissaire had softened, likely because we knew her secret.

Omri was two steps up a small ladder, giving him just enough angle to frame the subject and the Parisian rooftops. I climbed up next to him, and he instructed me quietly to take some photos. I dialed in what I guessed were the right settings and took a few pictures simultaneously with Omri.

At one point, one of the president's advisors came up on the low stage.

"*Un moment s'il vous plaît?*" he asked.

He handed a leather folio to the president, who turned to his side and opened it to read something. I was too far away to see what it was, but it looked like a letter of some sort. The last bit of sunlight bounced off a gold foil crest at the top of the sheet of paper. I brought the camera to my eye and took a quick photo.

"*Sera-ce tout, messieurs?*"

"*Oui, Monsieur le Président.* I think we have everything we need. Thank you," Omri said.

With that, the president reached up to shake Omri's hand. I grabbed a picture of that as well before stepping off the ladder to shake his hand.

As we shook hands, he leaned forward conspiringly. "My security director said you were very understanding," he said quietly. "Thank you."

"Of course, Mr. President," I said.

When the last of his entourage left the rooftop, I turned to Omri. Raising my arms in the air, I said, "The president? Really? You couldn't tell me?"

He laughed. "It was part of the contract to keep it confidential."

I understood but asked, "Why so little security?"

"The woman was right," Monique said. "You are used to a large secret service with thousands of officers and their planes and cars. The threats here are less, and it's a smaller country, so our president has only dozens of officers. I think less than one hundred, perhaps."

The low number caused my eyebrows to rise.

"But it only took one man to discover their secret!" Omri said. "Monique told me how you helped today, John. You listened and heard something we did not."

"That's what a Director of Facilities does, boss. Now, where are my business cards?"

Everyone laughed, the atmosphere once again friendly and relaxed.

4

The next morning, I went into the kitchen to see a young woman sitting at the counter, drinking a glass of water. I introduced myself to learn her name was Hélène, and she was quite clearly a model. She was also quite clearly a nighttime guest of Omri's.

I made coffees for both of us and offered to make her an omelet. She declined, but a fork appeared in her hand rather suspiciously as I sat down to eat my own. A pattern was emerging here, one that called for larger omelets.

Omri joined us as I was cleaning up, showering young Hélène with affection before she headed back to the bedroom.

"What happened to Amélie?" I asked quietly. "Hélène appears a little…detached."

"I know. But some nights, she wants a little comfort."

"Comfort, is it?"

"It comes in many shapes and sizes, *mon ami*," he said with a wink. "I will spend the day with her. And the timing is perfect because you need to begin your homework."

"Homework?" I asked.

"Yes. Your first assignment."

"Fire away," I said. "Since the president is gone, I can say that now," I added with a smile.

"Ah, speaking of that. You did not show me your photos of him last night!"

I went to the windowsill and grabbed the laptop I'd used for retouching the night before. Swiping and clicking, I pulled up three shots I was rather proud of. The first was similar to a portrait Omri had taken. It wasn't as beautiful as his, but it was reasonable.

"Very good," he said. He zoomed in and explained how the focus should have been adjusted and that it was slightly overexposed.

I swiped to the next one, the one of Omri and the president shaking hands. He loved it and said it told a nice behind-the-scenes story.

"Ok, show me your last one," he prompted.

I swiped to the image I'd taken with the president reading the note. The night before, I'd taken some time with the edit. The glint on the foil crest sparkled even more now, and the shadow on the president's profile was darker and somehow more mysterious.

"This is marvelous, John!" he said. "I love the drama. You know exactly who it is from the profile, and the flash of gold makes what he's reading look so important."

"It's probably just a dry cleaning bill."

"It does not matter. What you have done is create a mystery that shows how engaged he is. Well done!"

I was happy to hear his praise, if not a little embarrassed. "So what is my homework?" I asked, changing the subject.

"There will be assignments, some photos I want you to take. Portraits of some sort. And I would like them to be even better than the one you shot of the president, ok?" He continued, saying, "They need to tell a story, John."

"Ok," I said. The gravity in his voice had me feeling nervous.

"You are not asking why," he said.

I shrugged. "You're the teacher here, Omri."

"Yes, but it is ok to question me."

"Ok. Why?"

"I will not tell you now. Later."

"Jesus, Omri!"

He smiled. "You can use his name for emphasis if you'd like. But don't forget, I'm a Jew, so it really has no effect. Jesus was just another guy in the desert to me!"

"You know what I mean."

"Yes, but it is so enjoyable to make fun of you!"

"Ok, wise guy. What's my first assignment?"

A door closed, echoing down the hall.

"Your first one will be easy."

Behind me, there were footsteps. But I needed him to finish before we were interrupted, so I waved my hand for him to continue.

"I want a picture that tells a story. That tells something about your subject people don't know."

The footsteps came closer, and suddenly, two thin arms wrapped around me. A set of lips pecked my cheek.

"*Salut chéri!*"

It was Camille. I fixed Omri with a withering stare.

"Oh, John," she said. "It will be fun!"

They both laughed at my expense once again.

"What do you think? Shall we go into the studio? Or take pictures right here?" she asked.

I thought for a moment. How do you come up with a picture of someone who makes a living being photographed? How do you tell a story about someone who's had reporters all over the world cover her every move? How do you take a photo that impresses a photographer of Omri's caliber? I was way out of my depth. Omri teaching me to work the dials was one thing, but this was something else entirely.

Slowly, though, an idea formed. I picked up my phone and did a quick search. "We should go here," I said, turning the phone so only Camille could see.

She let out a little squeak of delight.

"Where?" Omri asked, trying to look at the phone.

I held it to my chest. "Sorry, but that's part of the 'story.'"

He made a shooing motion with his hands. "Off you go with your little secret, then. Be back for dinner. I will make something for us."

"Taxi?" I asked Camille. "Or is your car here?"

"I sent the car away," she said. "But this is very close, and it is a nice day, so we will walk."

"You're not worried about the paparazzi?"

"*Non*. People knew about the *Vogue* shoot. Today will be ok. But let's go to the wardrobe to see if there is a hat just in case."

She took me through the apartment to a room I hadn't seen before. Inside was row after row of rolling racks and shelves, all filled with a wide assortment of clothing.

"Wow, I had no idea this was here," I said.

"Well, Omri is a fashion photographer."

She weaved through the rows, and I saw that it was organized well. Monique's work, I suspected.

"Ah, how is this?" She pulled on a straw hat with a wide brim.

"Add some sunglasses, maybe?"

She found a large pair and put them on.

"Perfect!" I said.

"What would you like me to wear for your picture?"

I really had no idea other than I wanted her to look like a normal person, not a supermodel. "Your jeans are fine," I said. "But this top is a little too fancy. Let's find a T-shirt."

She led the way through the racks, eventually pulling one out. "This one?"

"Yes, that should be good. I really have no idea how you choose."

"This is good. The green will go with my eyes. Hold these," she said, handing me the hat and glasses. She began to take off her top.

"Camille, stop!" I said.

"Ugh!" she said. But she retreated behind a rack of clothing, honoring my request. "In fashion, we do not worry about dressing in front of others. You have no idea what happens behind a runway, do you?"

"That's where the passengers get on the plane, right?"

She reappeared, looking as normal as someone like her could.

I gave her a thumbs up.

"Now you," she said.

"I'm not getting my picture taken."

"I know. But this is fun, yes?"

She pushed me along into a section with men's clothing. Rummaging around, she eventually pulled out a pair of cream-colored jeans and a navy T-shirt, both probably exorbitantly expensive and entirely wasted on me. But she handed them over and made a show of turning around and covering her eyes. Still, I went behind a rack to change.

When I reappeared, she assessed me. "*Ah, bon!* You look excellent in these clothes. More muscle than the usual skinny male models. Maybe you will replace one of them for Omri one day?" she said with a smile.

I rolled my eyes. "That'll be the day."

Reaching out, she ruffled and fluffed the shirt a bit. "Now, better. We are ready."

We walked through the Marais and down to the Seine. Camille insisted she walk with her arm in mine and would not be convinced otherwise. She kept a running commentary of local culture as we went and had me practice a few phrases in French. Eventually, we arrived at Ile de la Cité. With Sainte Chapelle and the charred remains of Notre Dame drawing so many tourists, I was surprised to see the Marché aux Fleurs was relatively empty. We wandered through and around the glass-ceilinged halls of the flower market, looking for a good location. A long row of roses in a rainbow of colors reminded me of Omri's lesson on using leading lines to draw the eye. Camille removed her hat and glasses, and after shaking out her hair, took a pose with her body facing away and her head turned towards me.

With the camera set correctly, I took a few pictures. They were ok. But looking through the viewfinder, all I saw was a model in a flower market. Did it tell a story? Not really. Right now, the only story it told was that a weary widower was well out of his comfort zone.

"Do you want a smile? Or serious?"

"I don't know. This is all new to me."

"I will make a face like I am choosing," she said.

She pursed her lips and regarded some of the flowers. The proprietor of this particular stand, an older woman, stepped away from an arrangement she was making to get out of our shot.

I didn't press the shutter. It was all rather conceived. I lowered the camera and let it hang from the strap.

"Camille, this is silly. We are holding the florist up. And I don't have a clue what I am doing."

She came over to face me, and putting her hands on my shoulders, said, "Omri says you have a good sense of people. You have a sense of me. It is why you chose this place. Go one step further, John, and the idea will come to you."

One step.

The old woman had seen we were done and went back to the potter's bench to finish.

"Camille," I said. "Could you mess up your hair some? It looks quite model-y, if that's a word."

She ran her hands through her brown hair vigorously. Shaking her head a bit, she said, "Like this?"

"No. That's too…sexy."

She laughed. "Oh, you think I am sexy!"

I frowned and said, "We've been through this, Camille."

This only made her laugh more. "Yes, John, I know! But it is very fun when you are uncomfortable!"

"How do you do your hair on a Sunday morning when you're staying at home?"

She pulled her hair back and twirled it around, adding a band she took from her pocket. She spun to show the result. Errant strands of hair shot out from a loose bun she'd tied in the back.

"That's good. Now let's go talk to the shop owner. I might need your help."

With Camille translating and applying a little of her charm, we enlisted the elderly shopkeeper's help. Camille, now wearing the woman's dirty apron, stood at the bench finishing the flower arrangement that had been started. I found a good spot and took a couple of photos. At one point, the shop owner came over and changed something Camille had done. As she instructed Camille on how to do it correctly, I snapped a few more pictures.

I felt a tap on my shoulder and turned around.

A young girl of ten or eleven asked, "*Est-ce Camille Amari?*"

"*Oui!*" I replied.

"*Puis-je lui dire bonjour?*"

I didn't know what that meant, but it sounded like she wanted to say hello.

As she took a step toward Camille, I tapped her shoulder. She stopped, and I handed her some roses from a bucket next to me. She took them and walked over.

Camille bent down and gave the girl a lovely smile. They chatted for a moment, and Camille pulled a wooden stool over, placing it next to her. The girl climbed up, and through the lens, I watched as they added the flowers to the arrangement. When they'd finished, Camille looked across the bench and exchanged a few words with the shopkeeper. Together, she and the girl tied a bow around the arrangement and wrapped it in paper. The girl stepped off the stool, and Camille handed her the bouquet. The little girl turned around to her mother, a huge smile on her face. As if an afterthought, she quickly spun back to Camille, and they hugged.

The mother beamed.

The girl took Camille's hand and led her over for an introduction. I thanked the shopkeeper and paid for the flowers. When I was done, Camille had returned.

"She is adorable!" said Camille.

"And you were adorable with her," I replied honestly.

Camille returned the apron and fetched her hat and glasses.

Holding out the crook of my arm, I said, "Let's enjoy the day."

"*On y va!*" she said. *Let's go!*

We explored the island a bit longer before Camille said she would like a bite to eat. She suggested Omri's favorite place. As we approached, she explained it was run by a famous Israeli chef who had several successful restaurants in Tel Aviv.

"What do they serve?" I asked.

"Everything in a pita," she replied.

We took our place in a short line. When our turn came, the woman at the register didn't acknowledge us straightway.

"*Sli-ha,*" Camille said.

When the woman looked up, Camille gave her a smile and said, "*Shalom.*"

She ordered for us in French and ended saying, "*Toda raba.*"

The few tables inside were full, but two stools at the counter had just opened up. Laid before us was an arrangement of white rectangular dishes, each filled with beautifully colored produce. Four cooks worked feverishly chopping vegetables, spooning hummus, and filling pitas with a wide variety of ingredients. Their pace was impressive, and before long, our meals were passed over the counter. It was delicious, and I enjoyed the wonderful flavors and pita bread that was as thick and soft as a pillow.

Through messy bites, I wondered about Camille's background. Her hair was brown with amber highlights, but the combination of green eyes and light olive skin was curious, as was the way she spoke with the cashier.

"You used Hebrew earlier, didn't you?" I asked.

"Yes. From so much time with Omri."

"Ah, I was wondering if you were from Israel as well."

"*Non, non.* Quite the opposite. I was born in Paris. My mother was Arab. My father was French, but they were never married, and I never knew him."

I tried to remember if she'd referred to her mother in the past tense before and thought she might have. I resumed eating, letting silence ask the question. We finished our meal quietly, and outside, I crooked an arm for her.

"Where to?" I asked.

She put her arm in mine and said, "I would like to go to one of my mother's favorite places, John. It is a museum for the sculptor Rodin. It is a long walk, but Paris is a city made for walking."

Camille led us past the Louvre, through the Tuileries garden, and across the Seine. We spoke not a word the entire time. Our closeness and the warmth of the sun said enough.

Inside the Rodin Museum, we followed the prescribed route for a while. Rodin's work was incredible, the dynamic poses and textures captivating. Eventually, some of the visitors began to recognize Camille and ask for photos, so we moved outside to the sculpture garden. Weaving through the footpaths, we found a quiet corner and sat down on a bench in the shade.

"It is very interesting how you say so much, even when you are not talking," she said.

"The same could be said for you," I replied.

"Perhaps. But there is no one who listens like you when I do not speak."

I didn't respond, wanting her to take her time.

Eventually, she said, "It was an overdose. Heroine. I had just turned sixteen."

"I am sorry, Camille."

"Only a few weeks before, Omri had discovered me. He does not like to say he discovered me, but it is true. My mother was so happy when he called to ask if I could model for one of his clients. She liked our Omri, even if she only knew him from that one telephone call. After she died, I lived in Omri's apartment, working and finishing school. He is one of the most loving people I know."

"I have seen how he is different with you. He flirts with all of the other girls. But not you. I am glad to understand why."

"We are both lucky to know Omri, I think," she said.

***

Proving just that point, we found Omri back at the apartment that evening surrounded by a mass of vegetables, chopping away with a huge smile on his face.

"Hello! How was your day?"

"*Fabuleux*, Omri!" Camille replied as she went behind the counter and gave him a hug. She stole a carrot off the bench and said, "But we did a lot of walking, and I am going for a little rest."

As she walked out, Omri asked what we had gotten up to. I gave him the broad strokes, not mentioning our photos at the flower market. He was delighted we'd stopped at Miznon for lunch.

"She told me about her mother," I said.

Setting down the knife, he said, "Yes, it was terrible. It's why she isn't one of the party girls in this world. Sure, they go to Cannes, Ibiza, Dubai, and all. But Camille, she is the one who dances and laughs, and leaves when the drugs come out."

"Sixteen years old. She needed someone, and you were there."

"Then, yes. And now. Whenever she needs me," he said. "Ah, and how were your pictures?"

"Let's see," I said.

"Grab the laptop over there," he said, now back to chopping. "Find your best and show us at dinner."

I picked up the laptop and loaded the images. Scrolling through, I flagged some of the better ones and began cropping and retouching.

"She also told me something about you the other night," I said.

"That I am handsome and a wonderful chef?"

I smirked and said, "Not that."

He regarded me for a moment. "Yes, I imagined she would," he said gently. "You, me, Camille, we all have this in common. Losing someone we love. Losing the most important person in our lives."

"But you're so full of life. How do you do it? How do you get there?"

"Time helps. But it is love others give and you give to them that helps the most."

"I am not sure I can give love to anyone now, Omri. And I don't think I would be very good at seeing it come my way if it ever did."

He set his knife down again and said, "I will respond to this statement of yours two ways, John. First, loving and being loved requires a door in your heart to be open. This is why you are here. Here, we will open that door.

"The second thing I want to tell you is that you are wrong about not being able to give love yet. Monique turned to you for help with the president. You, not me. Gabriel was hurting, and you didn't hesitate. You stepped in to protect him without a second thought. And for me to see Camille now, it warms my heart. I have not seen her so trusting of someone in years. This trust you have earned from them in only a few days comes because they feel you're open to them. You can give love, John. We can feel it. You just haven't realized it yet."

Heat rushed to my face as he spoke. Embarrassment mostly, though I didn't need to feel this way. I shouldn't with these wonderful people who had been so kind. I also was taken aback by his expressive analysis. This paratrooper-turned-photographer was able to cut right through everything on the surface and see straight to the core.

He picked his knife back up and, knowing I was at a loss for what to say, kindly changed the subject. Waggling the tip of the blade at me with a smile, he said, "Now get your photograph ready. I have work to do!"

I smiled with thanks and turned back to the computer, my eyes a little swollen and my heart a little fuller. Once I'd finished, I set one end of the long dining table for the four of us and went to wake Camille.

The apartment had six bedrooms other than Omri's. I looked in two of them for Camille and did not see her. Before walking to a third, I smiled, turning back toward my own room. Opening the door, I saw her laying on top of the bed, curled into a little ball right in the center. I sat down gently beside her, and she stirred. Behind a few stray locks of hair, her eyelids fluttered, eventually revealing her emerald green eyes. She made no move other than a tiny smile.

Softly, I said, "When you lived with Omri, this was your room, wasn't it?"

She nodded her head, and her smile widened.

He was a mischievous one, our Omri.

***

Dinner was delightful, a mix of French and Israeli dishes that were both beautiful and delicious. I sat next to Hélène, who was more cautious in the flowing conversation and seemed rather shy. The large Israeli was tender with her, making me wonder if she was another lost soul like I was and Camille had been. I made sure to keep her engaged, to let her know we were all there together as one, just as I'd been treated.

At the end of the meal, Omri said, "John, I believe you have some homework to share."

I got up from the table and wheeled the monitor over, rotating it to stand vertically. I connected the laptop, and an empty frame appeared.

Nervously, I asked, "Can I share the runners up first?"

"No, John. Just one. Your best. Tomorrow, perhaps, we can see the others."

I tapped a key, and the photo filled the screen. It was of Camille finishing the flower arrangement with the little girl. Both their hands held flowers, and Camille's expression was priceless. The tip of her tongue was poking out the slightest bit, and you could tell that she was entirely focused on making the arrangement beautiful. The girl was up on her toes, her head crooked to the side and her eyes on the flower Camille was placing, assessing whether or not she was making the right choice. They were framed on the bottom by the rough texture of the potter's table and the dirty apron, and on the top by soft, blown-out clouds of colorful roses in the background.

I was actually rather proud of the picture, if not a little surprised it came from my rookie hand. But unlike the presentation of photos after the fashion shoot, there was no applause. I looked up from the laptop, wondering if I'd somehow failed the first test.

Camille's head was nestled in Omri's chest, his arms around her shoulders. He tenderly kissed the top of her head. She collected her breath and turned to me with tears in her eyes and a beautiful smile.

Hélène reached over and squeezed my hand.

Camille got up from her chair and came around the table. She pushed the computer out of the way and sat down on my lap. "You saw us there, John. My mother and I," she said. She wrapped her arms around my neck and gently sobbed. In the whispers between, as if only to herself, the tiniest voice said, "*Ma mère. Ma mère et moi.*"

I looked across the table at Omri. His brown eyes were as soft and gentle as I'd ever seen them.

He smiled and said, "That photograph, John, that is you seeing something no one else could. That is your heart opening. That is giving love."

5

In the days that followed, Omri's schedule became hectic. It was all hands on deck as a few fashion houses simultaneously needed photographs for their upcoming collections. Day and night, the apartment was a hive of activity. Models, male and female, came and went sometimes quietly, sometimes in a torrent of drama. Clients and art directors were in and out, and they needed to be carefully handled and well-fed. Caterers operated the kitchen in seemingly endless shifts. The number of deliveries was staggering. Clothes, lights, food, props, and more came and went all hours of the day. New contractors supported Omri and Gabriel, working around the clock on set changes and a staggering amount of retouching.

I spent time with Monique, and together, we solved the organizational challenges of so many people and so much *matériel*. We complemented each other perfectly, easily coming up with procedures and checklists to ensure everything and everyone could move as efficiently as possible.

Amélie was in a shoot one day, and Chloe and Hélène worked a few days. Camille had business meetings in London and Florence, and while we didn't see her, all of us exchanged jokes and gripes with her via text as time permitted. Monique introduced a few of the other regular models and photographers in their circle, and it was nice to get to know some new faces.

Despite it being so busy, the early mornings were always quiet in the kitchen. My routine of coffee and breakfast with whichever model had spent the night continued. Omri had indeed opened the door to his heart. And the one to his bedroom certainly had well-oiled hinges.

Once the big push was over and the last of the files went out to the agencies, it took three days for Monique and I to bring things back to normal. We let Gabriel and Omri sleep, shooing away any interlopers. And after the last crate had been put away or sent out on the back of a truck, Monique returned to her home for a well-deserved rest and I hunkered down.

We settled into a nice routine with a healthy balance of light and busy days. On weekends, I explored the city, sometimes alone and sometimes with Omri or Camille. On several occasions, the three of us ventured out to lovely little villages in the French countryside. The bond that connected us grew, bringing comfort and happiness. It reflected our vulnerability, and through that, our mutual trust with one another grew strong.

Until it was tested.

It was months later that Omri came back to my homework. My second assignment came up casually as we walked along the bank of the Seine one afternoon. He wanted a portrait of a widow.

I skipped dinner that night, retreating to the safety of my room, avoiding any further discussion on the matter. Despite trying to block it out, I became angry, upset that Omri was reopening a wound. I'd made progress in my grief, with more happy moments than not lately. Omri asking me to do this felt vindictive, as if he'd betrayed my trust.

For hours I stewed, my heart darkening.

I'd stayed too long, become too comfortable.

Maybe it was time to leave.

It was an easy kill button to press, right there in front of me. So easy. So close. I opened drawers in the dresser, throwing clothes at the backpack in the corner. At one point, I pulled out a nice shirt that had come from the wardrobe room. I remember Gabriel had chosen it, saying it was the perfect style for me. I jammed it back in and slammed the drawer closed.

The door opened, and Camille stepped quietly through the threshold. Slowly, she closed the door behind her. I broke down, falling to the bed in tears. She sat next to me, uttering not a single word. Through the night, she stayed by my side, dozing in and out as I did, soothing me when I stirred, still saying nothing.

In the dismal hours before dawn, I'd settled enough to listen, if not yet speak.

"Omri loves you as I do, *mon chéri*. He did not suggest this to be cruel."

"Then why, Camille? Why?"

"I don't know, John. But do you trust Omri?"

"I did. Now, I am not so sure."

"Then you do not have to take this picture, John. If he has lost your love, then do not take the picture. He loves you so much, John, that he will understand."

The word love was thrown around often during the months I'd been here. In the beginning, I'd thought it fell too quickly off the tongues of the friends I'd made. I'd thought it was flirtatious and flippant. My personal stereotype of the French, along with my broken heart and tendency to over-analyze, had misguided me. As time passed and I grew closer with the people in this new world, I understood they used the word to mean something entirely different. In truth, the word showed the most profound and genuine care one could give. And with that understanding, I knew that I loved both Camille and Omri. I'd told them as much, but it had always been in lighthearted ways. The pain was from making myself vulnerable, the essential ingredient in love.

"I do love him, Camille," I said. "I love both of you."

"We know you do, John. We share this, the three of us."

"And I do trust him," I said. "But I'm scared."

She held me tighter. "We know you are scared, my darling. But we are right here with you." And then she squeezed with everything she had. Every ounce of her heart.

The door to the bedroom suddenly flew open. It was Omri, an alarmed look on his face. "It's Hélène. Come, I need your help."

We jumped out of bed, and the three of us ran to Omri's bedroom. Hélène lay still on the bed. Alarmingly still.

Omri went to her side, and gently squeezing her hand, he called her name. "She was stirring. I thought it was a nightmare, but she didn't wake up. She's been breathing, and her pulse is slow but ok. I don't know what it is," he said.

I placed a cheek by her mouth and checked her pulse. She was just as Omri described. But the movement of her chest was gradually slowing, her breath on the side of my face weakening. "Call an ambulance," I said.

Omri had seen her breathing change too, and was already dialing.

Before Lauren and I had married, I'd insisted we take some first aid and emergency medicine classes. I was so obsessed with planning ahead that I wanted us to be ready in case anything happened to the other. As it turned out, what happened to Lauren was well beyond what any seminar could teach. But the lessons had stayed with me.

"Give me some light," I said.

Camille turned on a light.

Hélène's lips were blue. And then her breathing stopped.

I put a hand under her neck, and with the other tilted her chin up. Bending down, I pinched her nose and gave two quick breaths.

"Camille, any needles or pills around?" As soon as I spoke, I gave Hélène another breath. With respiratory failure, this had to be done every five seconds.

Camille looked around the bed. Nothing. She found Hélène's purse and quickly dumped everything onto the floor.

I continued breathing.

"No drugs," she said.

Omri had emergency services on the phone and was giving the address.

"Wait. There is a tin," Camille said.

I glanced over to see her opening what looked like a pack of mints.

Her hands fumbled.

I gave another breath.

"Pills," she said.

"Tell them to bring Naloxone, Omri."

I continued breathing for her, checking her pulse as well. It had slowed and weakened but was still there. It occurred to me Camille had been silent.

"Camille, get over here."

I gave another breath.

Camille hadn't moved.

"Now!" I said before giving another breath.

Camille came to me. "Get on the other side of the bed. Grab her hand." I gave another breath. "Hold her hand. Talk. She needs to know a friend is with her."

What Hélène actually needed was oxygen in her blood supply. But I wanted Camille distracted.

Omri and three paramedics entered the room. The paramedics covered her mouth with a manual respirator, allowing me to step away. They checked her vitals, and I handed a female paramedic the tin of pills. She looked at them, inspecting their size and markings. She spoke to another paramedic who injected a dose of Naloxone. I went to the opposite side of the bed where Camille stood, staring at Hélène, and clearly in shock. This was a horror story from her childhood haunting her again. Without speaking, I used my eyes to instruct Omri to stay with Hélène and the paramedics. He nodded, and I took Camille to the room next door, Omri's office.

The second we entered, I knew it was a bad choice. Above the couch, printed and framed at nearly a meter tall was the photograph of the little girl and Camille in the flower market. I remembered being so proud he'd hung it in his own office. Not tonight. I steered her around so that we sat below it, keeping it out of her line of sight.

"Camille, I want you to look at me, ok?"

She did, shaking now and breathing quickly. I slowly rubbed her arms. Speaking softly, I asked her to breathe with me. Starting with a slow, deep inhale and then a long, slow exhale. After the third time, she was able to match my cadence. After three more, the muscles in her arms relaxed and the shaking subsided.

"There you go, Camille. That's it. I know that was hard to see."

"Will she be ok?"

"I think so. They were very thorough and gave her the right drug."

"I don't want her to die, John."

"I know, Camille. I don't either."

I held her until the paramedics' stretcher clicked and creaked. They'd moved Hélène off the bed.

"I am just going to the door to talk to Omri, ok? I will be right there."

She nodded, keeping her eye on me as I moved.

"How is she?" I asked.

The female paramedic responded. "She is reacting to stimulus now and stabilizing. Her oxygen level is low but rising, same with her blood pressure, low but ok. You did the right thing to respirate her. But we are going to have some questions."

"Thank you. And I understand."

To Omri, I said, "Someone needs to stay with Camille."

He shook his head. "You stay. I will go," he said.

The paramedics began to wheel her out. I sensed Camille step behind me and look around my arm. As they left the room, the female paramedic stopped in front of me.

"Is everyone else ok?" she asked. With drugs, it wasn't always just one person.

"Yes," I replied. Moving slightly so that the paramedic could see Camille, I said, "Shock. She saw this as a child."

The paramedic's expression softened as she looked at Camille. "Your friend is going to be fine, ok?"

I could feel Camille relax.

"Text us updates," I said to Omri.

He nodded, then said, "I will. Take care of her, ok?"

"I will. And Omri?" I didn't know what to say, so I just gave him a hug. He returned the embrace warmly, understanding. I pushed him toward the door, and he left.

The adrenaline had us wired. When it dissipated, combined with the fact that we'd been up most of the night, we would crash hard and fast. Fluids were needed to help the transition. I brought us to the kitchen and put on the kettle for tea.

"You saved her, John."

"She'd stopped breathing. Just happened to be while I was right next to her. Omri has plenty of trauma training. He'd have done it if he'd been closest."

"But it was you. You helped her breathe, and you knew the drug to fix it."

"The paramedics carry it now. They'd have known to use it."

I knew she was thinking about her mother, wondering if doctors had the same medicine when she'd overdosed.

Passing her a cup of tea, I waited.

She sipped silently.

I tried to distract her, and said, "You heard the paramedics. She will be ok. But she'll need treatment and support to stay clean."

Camille continued to sip her tea.

I did as well, still trying to calm myself down a bit.

"This drug, it is new?"

"I don't know, Camille."

She sipped her tea again. "It is good they have this drug, John. I don't want any girl to lose her mother again."

There was nothing to say. I saw her eyelids begin to lower. I guided her down the hall to our room. Our roles reversed, and I stayed by her side there until late the next day.

Eventually, Omri messaged to say Hélène would make a full recovery. We visited her in the hospital, exchanging shifts with Omri. We learned her dependency had started small with an opiate prescribed after a procedure. Then addiction had set its hideous claws, and she'd eventually moved on to morphine. The need continued to escalate, and it was a combination of benzodiazepines and fentanyl she'd thought was morphine that triggered the overdose. Once she was stable enough to move, she checked into a recovery clinic in Northern France Omri had arranged. We knew her path would be long, slow, and challenging and held faith she would return confident and strong.

In the days that followed, the mood in the apartment was somber. The pace of work provided a needed distraction. We carried on, receiving occasional updates. Eventually, we heard that Hélène's parents would bring her back to the family apple orchard in Normandy after treatment, and she would step away from modeling. They said she was happy with the decision and knew the lifestyle change was what she needed. The collective sigh of relief in the studio was likely felt for miles.

6

"Let me help you with that, Madame Mercier," I said taking the grocery bag from an elderly woman in the courtyard of Omri's building. I'd been heading out, but seeing our neighbor with a rather heavy bag, decided to lend a hand. There were no elevators in the old building.

Mrs. Mercier lived alone in an apartment below Omri's. I'd occasionally see her coming and going, always dressed nicely with a small purse on one wrist. At first, we just said hello. I'd eventually introduced myself, and from then on, we'd exchanged pleasantries outside or in the stairwell.

Reversing course, I followed Mrs. Mercier back into the building and up the wide staircase. She unlocked the door, and I followed her into the kitchen. It was as you'd expect an elderly woman's home to be—slightly over-filled, a little dated, and tidy.

I set the bag on the counter, and she thanked me. Taking my leave, I turned back to the door.

"Monsieur Winter?" she said.

"Yes, madame?"

"Will you join me for a cup of tea?"

I didn't have anything on at the moment, and it wasn't lost on me that I really didn't have anything on for the foreseeable future. "I would enjoy that," I replied.

She put the kettle on, then fetched some cups and plates along with a small package of biscuits. We sat in the kitchen at a small table for two, and as we waited for the water to boil, I said, "Tell me about yourself, madame."

"I am an old woman, Monsieur Winter."

"I still wish you would call me John."

Ignoring the original question, she asked, "How is Monsieur Uziel?"

"He is fine. Happily working upstairs."

"The business with the ambulance and the young woman was unfortunate."

I replied carefully. I didn't know what Omri had told her and had come to learn that opiate addictions were a taboo subject in France. The president was establishing programs to shine light on the problem and how to stop it, but it would be a long process. "Yes, it was very sad. But she is with her parents in Normandy now. We've heard from her, and she is healthy," I said.

Mrs. Mercier nodded. The kettle whistled, and she made us each a cup of tea. "I am from Normandy, you know."

"I didn't know that," I replied.

"My father made calvados. It is an apple brandy."

"What brought you to Paris?"

"My husband. He was a businessman here."

"Where did you meet?"

"We met in boarding school. There was a social event with a school across the valley, and I was taken with him the moment he asked me to dance. After school, we married. In those years after the war, there was much rebuilding and he was given a job here in Paris."

As I had never seen a Monsieur Mercier, I knew how this story ended. And I knew all too well not to ask. I'd noticed some pictures in the foyer as we entered, photographs that included adults and children.

"Tell me about your children," I said.

And so she did. There were three scattered across France, each with children of their own. She told me about their lives, their successes, and their failures as we drank our cups of tea.

The biscuits went untouched.

"And you?" she asked. "What has brought you to Paris?"

"I lost my wife several months ago," I said.

Her wrinkled hand reached out and covered mine. It was warm with a shared understanding.

"She left a letter, a letter telling me to go see the world. She wanted me to move on, I think. I will never know why."

"If you had died first, would you want her to spend the rest of her life sad?" she asked.

"I wouldn't have wanted that," I replied.

"This is why," she said.

I'd felt this of course. It didn't always help. But sometimes it did, and perhaps a little more as each day went by. "How did you move on?" I asked.

She thought for a moment, then replied, "Distractions, mostly. I had children to feed, to send off to school each day. As they grew older, I realized that they helped me and I helped them. But there is no choice. You have to take each day and make the best of it."

"That is what I am trying to do. Take it one day at a time. Omri has been a wonderful help."

"Monsieur Uziel is very kind."

I looked down at the table. Seeing the untouched biscuits, I asked, "Did Monsieur Mercier take biscuits with his tea?"

"He did. He liked these molasses biscuits very much."

"Madame Mercier, would you mind if I took a photograph of you?" I asked.

"A photograph? Why would you want this?"

I didn't want to answer precisely why but understood why Omri had given me the assignment now. "Because, madame, there are days that I feel very alone. And talking with you has made me realize that I cannot feel sorry for myself. That I am *not* alone."

"Very well. If it will help, you may take this photograph. I will prepare."

"Please don't. I would like to remember this moment just as it is. I will be right back!"

I dashed back to the apartment and grabbed my camera, locking on a short lens as I rushed back to see Madame Mercier, precisely as I'd left her. I removed my teacup but left the empty plate where it was. Sitting just back from where I'd sat before, I took a single photo.

"This is what you want?" she asked.

"It is, thanks. You are lovely to allow me this picture."

"Of course."

As I helped her set the dishes in the sink, I said, "Madame Mercier, would you like to join Omri and I for dinner tonight?"

She let out a little laugh. "I am afraid I am fifty years past the women I see having dinner with Monsieur Uziel."

I laughed as well. "That is true, but also why it will be good for him!"

***

She joined us that evening, and it was wonderful to hear stories about years past in Paris. At one point, we noticed her sound just a bit cheeky. We nudged her on and found she had a wonderfully wicked sense of humor. Omri and I were still in stitches as we walked her back to her apartment at the end of the night.

Later, in Omri's kitchen as we cleaned up, I showed him the photo I'd taken. He critiqued it as a photographer, explaining what I'd done well and what needed work.

"This assignment of yours wasn't about light and composition, Omri," I said when he'd finished.

"It was not," he said. "What do you think it was about?"

"Me seeing how another widow lived with loss."

"That is what I wanted. And now you have seen how I have and how Mrs. Mercier has."

"So what's next?" I asked.

"I think, John, that you are done."

"Done?" I asked. "How is that?"

"This photo, this was for you to talk to a widow, yes. But really, I wanted you to engage. Engage with life. Taking a portrait, a good one, means engaging. It means listening and hearing that person's story. I wanted to give you a camera because, for me, it is a tool that lets me get close, lets me ask questions." He stopped scrubbing the pot in his hands and asked, "But do you know what I saw?"

"What?"

"I saw that you don't need a camera. You are good at talking to people, John. I see it when you first meet someone. You always say, 'tell me about yourself.' You do not ask what they do or where they are from. You give them a natural invitation to open up."

I hadn't even noticed that about myself.

He continued. "If you struggled, I would have made up some more homework. But you do not need it."

"Well, that's a relief," I said, trying to lighten the moment and deflect a little bit.

"But please, do something for me," he said. "When your journey continues, talk to people right away. Don't go to see the sights as you did here. Engage like you did with each of us. If you need the camera, use it. Use it to find a story for yourself or tell a story to someone else."

"Is it time for me to go, Omri?" I asked quietly.

"I am not asking you to go, John. There is nothing I would like more than for you to stay here forever, and I mean that sincerely. But I want you to know that you are ready."

I'd known this moment would come. Lately, I'd felt the time was coming sooner rather than later, but every time the feeling rose, I had distracted myself with something else, hoping to make it go away. Now, it was exposed to the light.

"I suppose you're right," I said.

"I have something for you," he said, drying his hands and retrieving an envelope from a nearby table. "You've probably run out of time on your tourist visa. Inside is a French freelancer visa. It will allow you to stay in the Schengen Area for two years longer."

"Thank you, Omri. I hadn't thought about that at all and am so glad that you did!"

"It wasn't me. Thank Monique. She was the one that stole your passport and did all of the paperwork. She has offered to help you wherever you go with this."

"I will thank her."

"Remember, John, there is no rush. Take the time you need."

***

I carried on the next week as before, setting up and breaking down for the scheduled shoots. I didn't want to say goodbye, nor really know how. So I hoped, unfairly so, that Omri would tell everyone my time had come to an end.

The day before I was to depart, Camille came to the apartment. She was excited and exceptionally animated. Her cosmetics line had launched to great success and, most recently, a global retailer had inquired about putting her name on a new line. The 'super' in supermodel, I'd learned, was earned by turning success on the runway into business, and Camille was at the top of her game in both departments. Over lunch, she shared details of the discussions she'd had lately in long-table boardrooms in New York, London, and Milan. And while she had us laughing and animated most of the time, her stories also showed her incredible focus as a businesswoman.

Omri offered coffee after we'd finished. Camille said she'd like to have me to herself and excused us to go off for a walk on our own.

With her large hat and glasses disguise in place, we set off through the small door set in the courtyard's gate once again. I held my arm out for her, and she led us through the Marais to the Seine. Like before, like always with Camille, words weren't needed. We crossed a bridge onto Île Saint-Louis, and I could see we were headed for the small park at the very end of the island. We found a spot beneath a tree with some shade and no one around. Hopping up on one of the small retaining walls, we lay down on a slope of warm, dry grass. Above us, the leaves in the tree fluttered. It was awhile before she finally spoke.

"Where will you go?" she asked.

"Rome," I said.

"When?"

"Tomorrow."

The flutter of leaves was joined by the sound of water running along the ancient stone wall beneath us. Together, they blocked out the sounds of the city, leaving us alone with our thoughts.

"We will see each other again, yes?"

"I am sure we will, Camille."

"I will miss you, you know."

"I'll miss you too."

"There is no one who understands me the way you do," she said. "And I understand you too, John. I understand why Lauren loved you so much."

"When I moved into the apartment, Omri said, 'we will open your heart.'"

"Omri can be very dramatic."

I looked over at her and smiled. "That is true."

"But did he open your heart, John?"

"He pushed hard, our Omri, and yes, he did." I turned to her before continuing. "But when he pushed, it hurt. And you were the one to tell me it was ok. You were there when I tried to close it again."

"I will always keep your heart safe, John."

I rolled back, staring at the tree once again. "I have to do this, Camille. I have to keep going."

"I know you do, John. It is what Lauren wanted, and you should honor her. I did not bring you here to change your mind. I love you too much to do that."

"You brought me here to say goodbye," I said. "But I don't know how to do that with you, Camille."

"We will walk through the city and laugh and tell stories. You will take me to dinner, where we will laugh some more and cry. And then you will walk me home. On my doorstep, you will not say goodbye. You will tell me you love me and say *au revoir* so that I know I will see you again."

"And there you are, protecting my heart once again," I said.

She squeezed my hand and said simply, "Always."

***

Sitting at the gate at Roissy-Charles de Gaulle the next morning was not easy. I'd been spoiled in Paris, living in luxury with such adoring friends. Moving forward meant knowing I would be uncomfortable. Knowing there would be lonely times. But I had to go, and the anxiety would just have to be ignored.

I decided Ashton had been right, that I didn't need much and would travel light. All I had was the small backpack filled with a few changes of clothes and Omri's camera.

With an hour to wait, I pulled out my phone and thumbed through to see the faces I was leaving behind. Amélie had posted a picture of a cat yawning on my chest as I slept on Omri's couch, with a kind caption wishing me well.

Omri had done the same, but with a photo that showed me in the courtyard and three of the girls cutting my hair. I remembered that day, sitting there wrapped in a tablecloth while Camille and her friends butchered my hair. They'd had to bring a stylist over to repair the damage.

Camille had posted a photo as well. It was from one of our weekend trips to the countryside with Omri. We'd stopped for ice cream, and during a rather animated part of the conversation, Camille had knocked into me, sending ice cream down my shirt.

The photo Omri had taken was one of my favorites, with Camille trying to clean me up and both of us laughing hysterically. Her caption read, *Take care of my John, world!* followed by a series of hearts in every color.

There were thousands of comments. Friends and strangers wishing me well, asking for updates as I ventured on. Even the French president, with whom I'd exchanged a few messages since our shoot, wished a *bon voyage*. It was a strange world I'd fallen into in Paris, but I'd loved every minute. Even the hard times.

A speaker above me pinged, and it was time to go. It was time to see what was around the next corner.

7

Omri had helped me select a place in the Colonna neighborhood of Rome, insisting it was better to take an apartment there than book a hotel, especially a brown chain hotel. I'd reserved a studio for a week, thinking that would be enough. Outside of Fiumicino Airport, I followed the apartment owner's tip, ignoring the men shouting "Taxi, taxi!" and instead going to the official Taxi sign.

I was more than an hour early for our meeting and went to find a café. Matching my vision of what Rome would be like, I naturally found one minutes later.

I knew all but two words of Italian and greeted the bearded man behind the counter by saying, "*Buongiorno.*"

He returned my greeting, saying, "*Buongiorno, signore.*"

"Would English be ok?" I asked.

He shook his head and said, "*Non parlo inglese.*"

I resorted to hand signals, pointing to a sandwich that looked rather good. There was a hot press behind him, so I said, "Panini?"

"*Pannin-o,*" he corrected rather tersely.

I nodded, and he used some tongs to pick up a sandwich entirely different from the one I'd selected. He raised his eyebrows, asking if there was anything else.

"Cappuccino?" I responded.

He gave me a disapproving look, and I remembered the unwritten rule about not having milk in coffee after noon. Whoops. He pointed to the amount due on the register, and I paid and took a seat.

When the apartment owner finally arrived, he was half an hour late. A few months ago, this would have infuriated me. I had always been quite careful with my schedule, making an effort to be on time and expecting the same of others. But right now, leaning against a wall watching the locals stroll by, I wasn't bothered in the slightest. Perhaps that was progress.

A sharply-dressed man about my age approached. He walked hurriedly, tapping away at something on his phone. I'd seen on the booking site that he was a British expat.

"Nigel?" I asked.

"You must be John," he said, putting the phone in his pocket. "I am terribly sorry to be late. It's been just a dreadful day."

"That's ok, Nigel. It's nice to meet you."

"Thank you," he said, shaking my hand. "I have a few rentals now, and balancing my actual job with them is getting rather difficult."

"I can imagine."

"Yes, well, there's a rental agency hot on my tail that wants them, but the cut they're after is outrageous." He opened the door to the building, and we entered. "There's a lift," he said, pointing at a small elevator door. "But it's so tiny that I prefer the stairs."

"After you," I said.

We walked up to the third floor where he used a key to let us in. The studio was sparse but clean and entirely new. It was exactly like the photographs and would be perfect.

"Wonderful, Nigel, thanks."

"Well, John, if you have any questions, you have my number. And that's my apartment just next door."

"Do you own the building?"

"No, no," he said. Smiling, he added, "It's hard enough with the bureaucracy here to just own some apartments. Can't imagine the fuss they'd put up if I could afford a building."

I smiled, and he showed me where to find extra towels and how to operate the overly-complicated washer-dryer.

When he was done, he studied me for a minute. "You look quite familiar, John. But I am not sure why."

"One of those faces, I guess."

"One other thing. I have a list of places in the neighborhood for you. Favorite restaurants and the like. But I'm afraid I've left it at the office."

"Don't worry," I replied.

"It's just around the corner. How about I leave a copy with my assistant. You can pick it up if you like. And if you don't make it, I'll just slip it under the door tonight."

"That sounds great, Nigel, thank you."

He handed me a key and his business card, and we said goodbye.

The rest of the afternoon was dedicated to getting to know the neighborhood. I wandered the streets without a map or agenda, wanting to sense the pace and way of life. It felt denser than Paris, the diagonally-cobbled streets narrower and more filled with people. Tourists stood out more here, their backpacks and cameras allowing them to be easily separated from the locals carrying shiny leather briefcases and handbags. And where tourists always looked up at the magnificent buildings with their painted shutters and flower boxes, the residents moved with purpose, staring straight ahead or slightly down.

Magnificent churches were nestled amongst restaurants, apartments, and businesses. Small squares opened up unexpectedly around corners, filled with people eating ice cream, taking pictures, and enjoying life. I came across the Pantheon and was stunned by its vast open interior. At one point, I found myself in another public square and was surprised to see I'd arrived at the Trevi Fountain. I joined the mass of tourists and sat down on the steps.

A couple took turns throwing coins into the fountain, right hand over the left shoulder. Something Lauren and I would never be able to do together.

The thought saddened me.

I'd learned in Paris that distractions helped more than anything, so I pulled out Nigel's business card. Remembering I'd passed the street his office was on earlier, I set off to find it and collect his list of favorite neighborhood spots.

The office building was a classic example of Roman architecture on the outside, but inside was completely modern with glass walls and steel accents. I asked to speak with Nigel's assistant at the reception desk and took a seat in the waiting area.

After some time, a well-dressed middle-aged woman greeted me. "Mr. Winter, it is good to meet you. I am Milena Bianci, Nigel's assistant."

"Nice to meet you, Signora Bianci. Please call me John. I'm one of Nigel's tenants," I said, shaking her hand.

"Very well, John. Please call me Milena."

"Your English is wonderful, Milena. I am afraid I don't speak Italian."

"Thank you. The result of too many years at university. Come, we will go to my office."

She led me down a long hallway, her tall heels clicking on the polished concrete. She held herself with some authority, and as she opened a door for me, the impression was that she was more of a corporate leader than an assistant. The glass-walled room was small but perfectly organized. Only a few folders sat on the white desk, each at perfect right angles and equally spaced. There were no knick-knacks or silly items one might usually find in an office other than a single photo that appeared to be her with two grown children. A closed glass door connected her to another larger office. By contrast, it was a complete mess. Stacks of papers littered the desk, and a small conference table had taken the overflow. A cricket bat rested in one corner, making it Nigel's office.

She gestured for me to take her one visitor's chair and sat down across the desk from me.

I smiled, and tilting my head toward the connecting office, said, "Quite the contrast."

She remained professional for a second before showing just the hint of a smirk. "How may I help you, John?"

"I checked into one of Nigel's apartments today. He said that he would leave a list of local recommendations with you."

"I am sorry, he did not," she replied. "But I have seen this list before. Let me have a look in his office." She came around the desk and pushed open the connecting door. She began at the small conference table, carefully searching.

I went to the doorway and asked, "What is it you do here?"

"Commercial real estate. Mostly offices and retail buildings. Nigel is one of our brokers." She had looked through everything on the conference table and moved on to search his desk.

"It's a pity he's not as well organized as you are."

"Ah, here it is!" she said. "Let's sit down and take a look."

Milena led me back to her smaller office, and we retook our seats. She grabbed a pair of reading glasses that had been folded neatly beneath her laptop stand and put them on. Setting the paper down, she pointed to a list of three addresses at the top and said, "Which of these are you renting?"

I looked at the street names and pointed to mine.

She nodded and scanned the list. Picking up the one pen on her desk, she drew a line through a restaurant name, saying it had been closed. "This list is good," she said. "I will just add one more restaurant that is quite nice. You are alone?"

"I am."

"That will be fine here. They have a bar around the kitchen, which is a nice place to sit when you are alone."

As she wrote the name and address, I noticed a detailed spreadsheet on her monitor. "Do you do Nigel's financial analysis?"

There was a little suspicion in her eyes when she looked up. "I assist him with his models, yes." The contrast in offices and the way she held herself was odd.

I didn't respond, wondering what I was missing.

"How do you know what this is?" she asked.

"I am an accountant," I said. "Well, I was, at least."

She relaxed a bit. Removing her reading glasses, she said, "Nigel sometimes struggles with these, so I will often help. I have a masters in finance."

I realized I'd made a mistake. Her conservative and well-fitting suit, combined with an advanced degree, meant she must be Nigel's business partner, not his secretary. "Oh my," I said. "I had a different impression of what an assistant was. Sorry, I am completely unfamiliar with businesses in Europe."

"No, John, assistant means the same here," she said, a hint of embarrassment in her tone. "I stopped my career to raise my children. Recently, I have needed to come back to work, but after being away for many years, this was the job I could find."

The picture did not show a husband and she didn't wear a ring. "Nigel is lucky to have you," I said.

"Thank you." She studied me curiously after answering.

Feeling uncomfortable, I began to get up to say goodbye.

"John, have you been living in Paris?" she asked.

I couldn't remember if I'd mistakenly used a French phrase or not but answered, "Yes."

"And might you be friends with Camille Amari?"

I let out a laugh. "Camille and I *are* friends."

She leaned back in her chair and said, "She has posted a lot of pictures of you."

"Well, we spent a lot of time together."

"Are you dating?"

I smiled. "Just good friends."

She gave me a knowing look. Only she didn't know. "What is she like?"

"She is a wonderful person. Fun, independent, and smart. I also know her to be especially giving, not unlike yourself helping cover for Nigel."

She smiled her thanks for the compliment.

I stood, taking the sheet of paper with me, and said, "Thank you so much, Milena. I appreciate your advice on the restaurant."

***

I spent three days walking all over Rome. Going against Omri's advice, I did visit many of the sights. But I found that it was different this time, and the loneliness wasn't as oppressive as it had been my first days in Paris.

Walking alone in a city for days on end meant there was plenty of time to think about things. I realized that the first difference was not staying or eating in a hotel. They're insular by nature, with guests there only for a few days at a time, each set in their own individual sterile cocoon. Staying in an apartment somehow made me feel a bit closer to the city. Just going to the corner shops for milk and toothpaste provided the opportunity to feel part of the community.

I also noticed that just as Omri said, the camera was a powerful tool to carry. It gave a reason for being somewhere. It provided an excuse to ask questions. And in an awkward situation, it was rather nice to hide behind. Mostly, though, it provided courage. It helped me walk into a bakery at dawn to see the baker make dough, enter an archeological site to see restorers tediously clean a mosaic, and even join in with some of the dodgy characters selling fake purses. Language was a problem here more than Paris, but showing kindness and interest, even with only hand signals, seemed to be enough.

I would occasionally post photographs, and it was always nice to see comments from Omri and the friends I'd made. Even Nigel's assistant, Milena, sent a note after seeing a picture of the chef from the restaurant she'd recommended.

Coming home after dinner one night, I ran into Nigel in the hall. Ever since he'd learned I was friends with Camille, he treated me a little differently. More like a special guest than a regular renter. It was a bit odd, but I couldn't complain.

"John, so glad to catch you!" he said.

"Nice to see you too, Nigel. What can I do for you?"

"I have to run to Florence tomorrow, and a new guest is checking in to one of the apartments."

"I'm not terribly fond of cleaning toilets, Nigel."

"No, no. We have cleaners that take care of that. But the handoff of keys and so forth, it would be lovely if you could help. I would be happy to discount your rate if you stay on longer."

"What exactly do you need?"

"If you get the keys from the last tenant at eleven and hand them off to the new guests at two, that would be wonderful. I know it's a lot to ask, but I am really in a bind."

Having a purpose had proven quite good for me, but with Nigel being so disorganized, the risk of this turning into a disaster was pretty high. "Sure, Nigel, I can help. But just in case, it would be helpful to have contact information for the cleaners and both guests."

"Brilliant! I can't thank you enough for this, John. The numbers are at the office. Can you pick them up from Milena tomorrow?"

"Of course, Nigel. Have a good trip."

The next day, Milena and I had a good laugh trying to find a contact number for the cleaners. We were eventually successful, and the handoff went without a hitch. At least until the next day, when Nigel called to say he needed to go straight from Florence to Milan for at least a couple of days.

"I really hate to ask, John, but would you mind doing another handover the day after tomorrow?"

"Sure," I said with a laugh. "I'm enjoying myself here, but I was thinking you could do with a little organizing."

"I know. I'm a bit of a mess right now. I was planning on getting things in order once work settles down."

"I can help with that, Nigel."

"What are you proposing?"

"How about I stay for another week or so. You can give me a break on my rate, and I could systemize things a bit and deal with any renters you have coming in."

"I could use the help," he admitted after a time.

"And I'm ready and willing."

"Well, then," he said, "let's do it. The studio is all yours for whatever time you need."

***

Holding a sticky note high in the air, Milena said, "That's thirty!"

I smiled and shook my head as she read the note and placed it with several others on the glass wall of Nigel's office. He appeared to be particularly fond of the sticky neon squares, and we'd been finding them everywhere.

While I knew it would be a challenge to find all of the contacts Nigel used for maintenance in the apartments, I wasn't prepared for the task we'd undertaken. Flipping through the stacks on his desk and table had become a bit of a mess. Given Milena's schedule was lighter with Nigel gone, we decided together we'd straighten him out for good. We plowed through almost everything in his office, categorizing according to work, rentals, and personal. Milena took the work papers, as they were surely confidential and I was already getting some sidelong glances from their colleagues. The rental items I took, and personal items were being carefully stacked on a small credenza.

Finally getting to the bottom of the last pile, I found an iPad. I held it up and remarked, "This is brand new. It still has the plastic wrapper!"

"That was a gift from a construction company. I don't know why he doesn't use it," Milena said.

"I think we should use it for the apartments."

We worked late into the night doing just that. The web site he used for bookings was wired to his calendar. The maintenance vendor contacts were indexed, each associated with their respective contracts. And after finding so many usernames and passwords on sticky notes, we made sure all of the accounts were linked correctly and updated his security. We even went so far as to go into the apartment profiles, updating the copy and other details. Then Milena took things a step further and analyzed his occupancy rates and pricing compared to similar rentals in the area. Seeing there was an opportunity to increase bookings and revenue, she went so far as to reset his prices on the booking site. By the time we turned off the lights, Nigel would have everything he needed on a single device, something oddly satisfying to both of us.

We celebrated over dinner, each enjoying both our accomplishment and one another's company. We talked at length about life in Italy and her two children, now grown up and living on their own. As our plates were cleared, she asked about my journey. I told her about Lauren's note, and she asked me a question I'd been too scared to ask myself.

"What do you think she wants you to find?"

I deferred, as I usually did when my mind wandered in this direction, and said, "I don't think she wanted me to find anything in particular. I think she wanted me to do something I'd be too reluctant to do without a push."

"You don't ask someone to do something without reason, John."

"We'd always wanted to travel, and I think she wanted me to fulfill that wish, even without her. Maybe by my going away, she could somehow experience it in heaven."

"I am sure she is watching over you, John. But I don't think this is her reason. I think she wants you to find peace."

"To find peace."

"Yes, John, I think that's it."

"I'm not sure I even know what it looks like, or where it might be."

"No one really does, but it's inside you somewhere, and it will come out when it's ready," she said.

***

Nigel was thrilled with our work and offered me to stay another week for free. I only accepted once he'd promised to give Milena responsibilities more in line with her capabilities. I sincerely hoped he would live up to his word.

I used the time to explore Rome and photograph more, but also to think about what Milena had said, that it was peace Lauren wanted me to find. When had I felt peaceful since leaving? Really, the only times I'd felt settled were when I had a purpose. Stacking bricks, setting up for Omri's shots, and even organizing Nigel.

Were these moments helping me find peace? Or were they distractions, a way to avoid facing my reality of a life without her?

Perhaps they were both, I thought as I boarded the train in Termini Station.

8

A pattern was emerging. With each city, I needed to see the feature landmarks, the places one must see. Their omnipresence in travel media made them a frequent topic when Lauren had brought up our trip. I was going against everything Ashton, Hailey, and Omri had said as I wound up the terraced streets of Amalfi and Positano, looked down over the port in Capri, and paddled into the Blue Grotto, but I decided that at least in this regard, they were wrong. Soaking in these sights was for Lauren, with the hope that in some way she could experience them through me.

After two weeks in southern Italy, I sat at a café outside the Napoli Centrale station, planning to head north and then make my way over to Venice. At the table next to mine, two young women laughed away, sharing stories in what sounded like German. Sipping my caffé, I regarded them as I often did backpackers, jealous of their ability to move freely and without care, always optimistic about what was to come. Two Italian boys approached, their broad smiles and energy immediately captivating the girls, and I heard them switch to English to bridge the language gap. Soon, chairs were pulled over, the charm dialed up, and the mating ritual of young travelers began.

I smiled to myself and pulled out my phone to double-check the departure time. Finishing my caffé, I stood up just as the young people did. They turned back toward the city, making their way to the sidewalk just as I put on my pack.

I'll never know what piqued my antennae. Perhaps it was the way the boys had positioned themselves, leading the girls right to the edge of the curb. More likely, it was the fact that they had suddenly gotten louder. One of them spread his arms wide, as if at the central part of a story. But the other boy didn't look at his friend. Instead, he glanced down the street behind me.

A scooter engine revved. Not the sound of puttering along or even leaving an intersection. It was the distinctive sound a scooter makes when it's taking off with some urgency, the rapid change in tone that instinctively lets you know it's time to get out of the way.

I turned as two men not ten feet away from me accelerated toward us. I'd taken two strides toward the girls just as the scooter slowed and the passenger on the back reached out. His hand brushed my side as he went to steal the bag off the shoulder of one of the girls. The driver accelerated again, but burdened by the weight of two men, my momentum proved faster and I was able to get a hand on her bag. The passenger had a solid grip as well and did not want to let go. I began to lose my footing as I was pulled forward. Just then, my feet struck a café chair, and I was airborne in an instant.

Stretched out horizontally, I crashed down onto the edge of the stone curb. Ribs cracked as both our grips released simultaneously. The last memory I had before rolling and knocking my head against the cobblestones was the girl's bag spilling across the road.

***

I woke in a dim, gray room to the most horrendous headache I'd ever felt. As I went to slowly prop myself up, pain shot like a knife through my side. I let out a groan, surrendering.

A gentle female voice said, "Shh, shh. Please be still," in heavily accented English. Hands slowly pushed me back.

I opened my eyes again to see it was a young nurse with deep brown eyes filled with sympathy. "Where am I?" I asked.

"You are in hospital, signore. My name is Gaia."

"What happened?"

"Signore, you have two broken ribs and a concussion. We have wrapped your ribs and cleaned some wounds. Your concussion is what you feel now."

"How long have I been here?"

"Since yesterday. Tell me, signore, is there someone I can call for you?" She pointed to my wedding ring and asked, "Your wife, perhaps?"

"No, Gaia. I am alone."

She hesitated a moment before saying, "I will get the doctor now."

I closed my eyes, hoping the pain would go away.

"Signore? Are you with us?" Gaia asked.

I mumbled, "Yes," and opened my eyes to see a bespectacled man with a short beard leaning over me. He showed me a penlight before turning it on and shining it into my eyes. It was clear from the stale smell of smoke on his coat that he'd just returned from a cigarette break. He checked a computer monitor by my shoulders and then spoke to the nurse.

"Signore, this is Doctor Romano. He does not speak English, so I will translate. He says that you will need to stay in hospital another day or two to monitor your progress."

They spoke together, and then again, Gaia translated. "He says that your ribs will heal, but it will take time. Resting will be good for them because there is nothing else that can be done."

After a final exchange with the doctor, she said, "He is going to check on you in a few hours, signore."

"*Grazie*," I said.

The doctor bowed his head and left the room.

"Rest, Signore Winter. I will be back soon," Gaia said before exiting.

***

It wasn't until that evening that the queasiness in my stomach subsided and my headache came down to a more manageable level. Gaia checked in on me regularly, and reluctantly told me she'd lengthened her shift to make sure I was ok and could communicate with the doctors on duty. She was rather upset that I didn't have someone to call. To placate her, I asked if my pack had made it to the hospital. She was happy to show me that the paramedics had, indeed, brought it in with me. I had her retrieve my phone so I could send a message to Omri.

Fell and had a bit of an accident in Naples. I am fine, and only sending this to you so the nurse will stop worrying. Hope you're well. Love, John.

My phone rang less than a minute later. After I explained to Omri that I was fine, he asked to speak with a nurse or doctor.

"It's for you," I said, passing Gaia the phone.

They spoke for a few minutes before she handed it back to me. Omri was insistent that he fly over, but I told him there was nothing he could do and I simply had to wait it out. After finally talking him out of it, I promised to call in the morning.

Hanging up the phone, I said to Gaia, "That goes for you too, Gaia. You must be exhausted, so please go home and get some rest. I am just going to sleep and will be fine until you're back tomorrow, ok?"

"If you are sure, signore," she said.

***

I woke up with morning light filtering through the dirty window, surprised that my head felt much better. Between the bed and the window, two chairs had been pushed together. In the center, a figure was nestled in a cocoon of hospital blankets.

With a smile, I said, "Good morning, Camille."

She stirred and opened her eyes. "John!" she said, jumping up and wrapping her arms around my neck.

The slight pressure on my side caused me to grunt, and she immediately let go.

"Oh, I am sorry!"

"It's ok," I said, gathering my breath as the pain in my ribs receded. "What are you doing here?"

"Omri called to tell me what happened. I was in Florence with Gucci, and they flew me down here right away. What happened?"

I told her the story, not a little embarrassed that I'd propelled myself across the cobblestone streets. She laughed at my version of events and wanted to hear everything else I'd experienced over the past month.

"How have you been?" I asked.

"I have been busy! But it has been more business than anything else this month."

"Cosmetics?"

She nodded yes. "And influencer contracts. But now, Gucci would like to collaborate with me on some accessories. That's why I was in Florence." She didn't appear as excited as I thought she might have been.

"Why aren't you happy about this?"

"I *am* happy about it. Opportunities like this are very rare. I am lucky to have this offer, plus one from another Kering brand. I know the industry and I know the market, but the finances for deals this large can be complicated. More than my two years in university can get me through."

"Do you have representation? Advisors? Deals like this, my guess is that it's a good idea to have a lawyer set up the right structure. They should be able to drive negotiations on your behalf too."

"Omri's lawyer is doing this, but the terms can be very complex."

"You might need a finance expert to work with the lawyer, then."

"I was hoping you—"

"I'll stop you right there, Camille. An accountant is different than someone in finance strategy. Plus, I don't know a thing about deals in the EU."

She sat back and let out a deep breath.

"But I have an idea," I said. "If you could pass me my phone, I'll make a call while you find us a coffee."

Camille shrugged as she handed me the phone before leaving.

"Are you serious, John?" came the voice on the other end of the line after I'd explained the assistance Camille needed.

"Absolutely, Milena."

"This is a dream job! I cannot believe it! Thank you so very much!"

"You still have to convince her. And deal with Nigel."

"Nigel will be fine. He's been very complimentary since you left, and he will understand."

Camille walked into the room, and I said, "Camille is here now. Let me talk to her, and we'll call you back."

I closed the line, and Camille said, "Who was that?"

"That might be your new finance advisor, Milena Bianci. I met her in Rome, and she's intelligent, capable, and extremely professional. She's being wasted right now assisting someone in real estate, a job she recently had to take. Here's her résumé," I said, passing my phone over. "There's a gap in there from time off to raise her children, but she has a masters in finance and plenty of experience in retail and consumer products."

Camille scrolled through and called out some of the highlights. After a few minutes, she handed the phone back to me. "This looks very good. Do you trust her, John?"

"I do."

"Then call her back."

I did, and Camille took the phone out into the hallway. Sometime later, she returned, still on the phone and saying, "Thank you, Milena. I look forward to seeing you at the airport tomorrow. I will text you the tail number." She went quiet as Milena spoke, then said, "I am with him now, Milena, so we will have to save that discussion! Ciao!" Turning to me, she said, "Milena sends her best wishes. She had no idea you were in hospital."

"Did I hear you say tomorrow?" I asked.

"I did. I made her an offer she couldn't refuse and asked her to join me in the negotiations the day after tomorrow."

"You are certainly decisive."

"You said you trust her, John," she replied. "This is all I need."

We spent time catching up, sharing stories, and laughing. Well, Camille was laughing. I was trying not to because even the tiniest chuckle caused my side to erupt in pain. But still, there were times I couldn't help it. As she sat on the foot of the bed with her legs crossed, finishing a story about a caterer's pressure cooker exploding in Omri's kitchen, the door opened.

"Good morning, Gaia," I said.

Looking down at her clipboard, she said, "Good morning, Signore Winter. How are you—" She froze and went silent, staring at Camille.

"Gaia, this is Camille—"

"Camille Amari," she said, still rooted in place and somewhat dumbfounded.

"It is nice to meet you, Gaia," Camille said, leaning across the bed and extending her hand.

"It is a pleasure to meet you, Signorina Amari."

"Please, call me Camille."

Gaia blushed slightly and said, "Signore Winter, I thought you said you were traveling alone."

"I am, but lucky enough to have a visit from a friend."

"How are you feeling?"

"My head feels back to normal, thank goodness. The ribs still hurt, as do the scrapes."

"That is good news. Let me check your dressings."

Camille hopped off the bed as Gaia went to work.

"Did you get some rest last night, Gaia?" I asked.

"Yes, signore. I am fine."

Camille let out a little laugh and said, "Has he been worried about you, Gaia?"

"He was very hurt yesterday but did not want me to stay later than my shift."

"This is our John, Gaia," Camille said. "Always wanting to make sure everyone is ok."

"I think it's you two that have been taking far more care of me lately," I said.

Gaia went into the corridor and returned with bandages and other supplies. She carefully changed the dressings on my arm, hips, and leg. When she was done, Camille followed her into the hallway. They were gone for some time, and I dozed off.

***

The next morning, I was checked up on by several doctors and nurses, something that had been the case the previous day despite my improving condition. Some were so transparent in their desire to meet Camille that they didn't even check my pulse on the monitor. Ah, Italy.

When Gaia arrived, she wore typical attire instead of her blue nursing uniform. She also pushed a wheelchair.

"Good morning, Signore Winter," she said.

Camille, who had been packing up for her return to Florence, said, "We have a surprise for you, John. The doctors said you can be released today."

"But they also said you need to rest and let your ribs heal," Gaia added.

"So what's the surprise?"

"Let's get you dressed and find out."

Once they had me dressed and settled in the wheelchair, which was apparently a requirement to exit the hospital, I was pushed down the hall. I gave my thanks to the staff and was assisted downstairs and into a long, black Mercedes. We drove for a few minutes, eventually merging on to the waterfront and passing the port. As we pulled under the portico of a luxury hotel overlooking the water, I turned to Camille and told her this was unnecessary.

"John, I have to go back up to Florence, and you need to rest. This is already done, so there will be no complaining, *d'accord*?"

I grumbled in protest as they helped me out of the car.

"If I cannot look after you, then it should be someone I know will take good care of you. Gaia is feeling too ill to go to work today, as she will be for the next few days. After that, she will come to visit you on her way to work and on the way home."

"Wow, Gaia, I sure hope I don't catch what you have," I said, rolling my eyes.

They both gave a little laugh and then hugged goodbye.

"I must go now, my love," Camille said.

"Thank you, Camille," I replied. "And I hope you and Milena knock 'em dead in Florence."

We exchanged a tender hug before Gaia helped me inside. The elderly tourists in England; Ashton and his friends; Omri, Camille, and now Gaia—all of these lovely people—always picking me up and putting me back on my feet.

Back on my feet so that I could carry on.

Carry on down a path with an end I still couldn't see.

9

As the summer days began to shorten, I made my way north to Venice, eventually carrying on into Switzerland. Whereas Italy's beauty came from its history and culture of family, food, and fashion, I found Switzerland beautiful for the striking contrast between the precision architecture, lush green hills, and jagged mountain peaks. I stayed a week in Zurich before moving on to smaller towns. From a little red guest house in Urnäsch, I set out to climb the mountain just to the south, Säntis.

The pain in my ribs had gone, and the abrasions down one side had healed to pink blotches. It was a beautiful day, so I set off for the weather station at the summit to take in the view and then enjoy a pleasant ride down on the tram before dinner.

The rolling hills at the base of the mountain were brilliant green, the grass thick and lush. The path, used by both hikers and livestock, carried me through sweeping curves, over hills, and through meadows. Occasionally, a cow appeared complete with the classic, heavy bell around her neck. I used the camera, which thankfully hadn't been damaged in Naples, to take a few photographs, doing my best to capture the glorious landscape. Eventually, green turned to gray as I transitioned to the limestone core of the mountain. As the trail turned steep, breathing became more difficult. Perhaps my ribs weren't exactly one hundred percent after all. I pushed on, occasionally stopping for water.

The view became more and more spectacular as I climbed. Thankfully, the trail wasn't technical. There were even a few nice flat areas, and I selected one to stop for a rest. I'd picked up some bread, cheese, and sausage that morning, which I pulled out to enjoy high above the small villages.

Lauren would have loved sitting there high in the Alps, the air fresh and clean, and the view almost limitless. I could imagine her vibrant smile lighting the meadows below. The thought made me smile, and the balance of my emotions when I thought of her were tilting further from the sadness that had paralyzed me not long ago.

At some point, a stiff, cool breeze reminded me that I'd sat too long. I packed everything back up and resumed the ascent. The trail, which had been so clear before, was less evident on the rocky surface. I had to backtrack a few times, finding hints of the path upward until eventually losing it entirely. But the modern, hard angles and tall spire of the weather station were in sight, so it was just a matter of carefully selecting the right approach. The mountain shadows grew long, and my progress slowed. The climb became more treacherous as the winds began to pick up. I'd undertaken a challenge I wasn't entirely ready for and might be fighting darkness before long.

With some urgency, I continued, and eventually found myself immediately below the weather station. The tram came into view, and my heart fell as the massive motor clanked to a stop. A set of stairs came into view that looked to lead to a viewing deck. I made my way to them and climbed. The wind had picked up significantly and carried with it the chill of fall. I soon found myself in front of a long glass wall, the other side of which was an empty space, merely a lobby. The lone door leading inside was locked.

Pulling on a jacket from my pack, I searched for additional doors. Finding none, I knocked loudly on the metal frame. There was no response, and I began to worry. I banged the soft side of my fist on the glass, louder this time. I banged and banged, hoping someone was still inside. I cupped my hands and tried to see into the building when to my complete delight, a man came from the back of the open room. As he walked to the door, it was clear he was displeased. But after finding a key on his substantial keyring, he unlocked the door and let me in.

As soon as I stepped through the threshold, I was given a thorough dressing down in the guttural tones of the local Swiss German dialect.

"I am sorry, sir, really! Thank you for opening the door!"

His brow furrowed and he said, "*Ach, Englisch.* You want tram?"

"Yes!"

He held out his watch and, pointing to the time, said, "Closed."

"I just heard it stop. Can you call down to the bottom and see if they could make one more trip?"

"*Nein!*" he said. "Closed!"

My heart fell. There was no way I could hike back down in the dark. There was nowhere to go. "I am very sorry to ask, but can I stay inside until the tram starts in the morning?"

"Nein!" he said again, this time crossing his hands with palms out, waving me off.

Outside, the sun had just kissed the mountaintops in the distance. Descending would soon be impossible. "Please, sir. It is going to be very cold outside."

The stern man furrowed his eyebrows and began to push me toward the door. He was likely one of the meteorologists, grumpy about having to take the night shift on the mountain. But there was no way I was going to sleep on the deck outside with the temperature plummeting.

I held my ground but remained polite. "Please? I can stay right here in the lobby."

He eased up and thought for a moment. "*Heir*," he said, pointing to the floor. He turned and pointed to the stairwell door from which he'd come and said, "*Nein*."

I took this to mean I could sleep in the small reception area but not go inside the station. It wouldn't be pleasant, but it was better than facing the elements overnight.

"Ok?" he asked, his face still stern.

"Yes," I said. "Thank you so much." I reached forward to shake his hand.

He didn't look me in the eyes but gave my hand a curt shake before making a swift about-face. The sound of the bolt hitting home a few seconds later let me know I wouldn't be seeing him for the rest of the night.

A quick survey of the space showed it was a simple rectangular entryway with the grumpy man's door on one side and a locked set of double doors to the tram platform opposite. The long back wall was covered with an oversized photo print of the tram I'd missed. In the center was a tall counter where clerks would greet hikers and hand out maps and information. I stood behind it and looked through the windows spanning the wall around the entrance. The sun had fallen behind the mountains, framing them in a silhouette of light blue that gradually faded to the darkening sky above.

With my pack on the counter, I pulled out the remaining bread, cheese, and sausage along with a scant amount of water. It wasn't the dinner I'd hoped for, but it would have to do. At least the view couldn't be beaten.

After cleaning up, I finished a bottle of Evian a worker had left on a shelf by the brochure supply and dragged the rubber standing mat out to the center of the room. It wasn't long enough to be a bed, but it was close enough and would keep the metal floor from sapping precious degrees of body heat away.

I put on a few extra layers of clothes, created a small pillow with socks and underwear stuffed into a T-shirt, and stretched out for the night.

First my luggage, then Stonehenge, then Paris, and certainly Naples. Now this. Nothing, it seemed, was going how one might plan it. It was literally one mistake, or blessing, after the other. These ups and downs were becoming frequent enough that I was, in some strange way, accepting them. Progress, of a sort.

***

As autumn settled in, I made my way east into Austria, south to Trieste, and eventually down the Croatian coast into Montenegro. I found myself ignoring hotels, staying in rented rooms or apartments, as they gave me the chance to meet locals and feel the pulse of each new town. I would often stay for days at a time, shooting landscapes, architecture, and portraits.

I was lonely less often, and not entirely due to the people I met. No, I think what helped was simply getting comfortable with myself. Getting comfortable being alone and less afraid to engage a stranger in conversation. More often than not, those strangers wanted to talk and we departed as friends.

Ashton and Hailey were right to tell me that social media was a powerful tool for travelers. I found the people I met would often connect me with friends in the next town on my path. I'd be invited for dinner, taken on a tour, or simply given tips for the best things to do, see, and eat.

I'd come to adding more detailed captions to the photographs I posted, telling the back story, or something personal about my experience. The network of Camille's fans that had begun following my posts in Paris merged with the network I'd built since then, and together they continued to grow. While the messages I'd received from friends were always positive, it was surprising to see words of encouragement from complete strangers.

It was just one of those comments that popped up as I wondered if I should brave winter in Romania or push down to Greece. The note was from a Kiwi, likely a friend of Ashton's, that read, *If you're looking for some work and a place to ride out the winter in Europe, come to Val d'Isère. I can hook you up with an easy gig photographing tourists at the resort.*

I'd been funding the journey with Lauren's life insurance money. While there was still plenty left, replenishing a bit wasn't a bad idea. Expenses on the house had picked up, with Mrs. Garland having recently informed me that the furnace needed to be replaced. In that same conversation, she'd asked if perhaps her daughter could rent it for her family. I had been reluctant at the time, but if I was going to stay in Europe for the winter and then continue, it did make sense. They were a lovely family, and the house could use some happiness. The next day, I messaged her my blessing and booked a ticket to Geneva, and soon found myself standing at the base of Val d'Isère learning "Say cheese!" in the different language of each guest.

It's fair to say the pay wasn't great. It barely covered meals and rent for a small room I'd taken. But the experience was priceless, not only for my language skills but for the glimpse into the wild world of traveling workers. They were a fantastic, eclectic young mix of people from all corners of the Earth. They worked hard and played hard and were an absolute riot. They knew every insider trick imaginable, from which runs to hit first thing in the morning to who had the cheapest drinks or a chef who could be counted on for a free meal outside a kitchen's back door.

The work itself I actually found quite fun. Couples and families wanted group photos to remember their holiday, and the photographs were simple as could be. Sometimes, they'd hire me to take some action shots on the slopes. At first, I was hesitant as I wasn't the best skier, but the more I skied on off days and early mornings with the other workers, the better I became.

When the days grew longer and the crowds thinned as the season came to an end, the workers began to scatter off in every direction with promises to stay in touch and cross paths again. I turned in the camera and badge, returned my ski gear to the underground community pile for the next set of nomads, and set off for Spain.

In Bilbao, I enjoyed the old mixed with the new. The historic buildings, meandering estuary, and narrow streets somehow matched perfectly with the shimmering titanium of the Guggenheim and the playful colors of the flower-covered Puppy sculpture. San Sebastian followed, with days hiking the hills and strolling the beaches before walks along the promenade into the old town for pintxos and txakoli. Eventually, I made my way down to Barcelona, taking a studio apartment in El Raval.

Walking home past graffiti-covered shutters one night, it became clear how much travel had changed for me. Or perhaps it was how travel had changed me.

When I'd first set out, I'd been nervous about everything. Concerns of where I would stay and how I'd handle language barriers mixed with fears of being robbed and diseases in tap water. I'd been terrified of doing anything I hadn't already planned and scared to ask for help when something went wrong. I'd been driven by fears and limits that were utterly arbitrary.

Lately, I found things were different. The most obvious was on the surface. My pack had streamlined down to a few hearty clothes I could wear anywhere, and importantly, wash anywhere. I wasn't as extreme as toothbrush-only Jack Reacher, but came to understand that I didn't need much beyond the camera, a few changes of clothes, and a local SIM card.

I was no longer a nervous wreck in airports and had come to roll with delays and cancellations. Rentals, in particular, were canceled at the last minute plenty of times. Busses broke down, train operators went on strike, and my sense of direction sent me the wrong way on plenty of occasions. I'd had to adapt, to improvise, and in the process became more comfortable with change and the unpredictability of life.

Lauren was right to send me away, to send me out of my comfort zone. And while I hadn't ultimately come to terms with living without her, this journey was helping. I needed to keep going, to push beyond what had become the comforts of Europe, and set off for North Africa.

10

Taxis, as a rule, are generally the most expensive way to get from an airport or train station to the center of town. Mapping apps solved the problem, giving detailed enough instructions for most people to figure out point A to point B on public transportation. But exiting the giant architectural soccer ball at the Marrakech airport, it was apparent that things weren't going to be as clearly marked and scheduled as they were in Europe.

Discarding the idea of solving which of the few buses in the central parking area would take me into town, I caved in and headed to the front of the queues of desert tan taxis. As soon as I took my first steps on to the oddly raised platform, men approached offering rides. I took the first one and showed him the address for a riad I'd booked along with a map the small hotel had sent.

After studying it for a bit, he simply said, "*Oui, bon.*" That would have to be good enough.

The fifteen-minute drive into the city made it clear I was in a far different place than I'd ever been. The landscape was desolate, with rocky sand as flat as could be in every direction. We rolled through two stop signs and a red light with only a brief glance in either direction before being enveloped by the city. The motorcycles we had passed on the main road now easily slipped around us as our progress slowed in the sudden mass of pedestrians and delivery men that flowed back and forth across the street. Gentle toots of the horn cleared the path enough for us to make our way to a haphazard roundabout where the driver stopped and explained in a combination of hand gestures and French that cars couldn't enter the medina. Pointing towards a corner of the square where we'd stopped, he explained that I would need to walk the rest of the way. I strapped on my pack and set off into the narrow cobblestone streets using only the small map and a bit of hope. I wound this way and that, getting more and more lost every turn. Men began to approach me, offering to take me to the riad. They made me suspicious, if not a little frightened.

In Paris, at the end of a particularly challenging day, Omri had once asked, "If someone offered you a button to press to send you instantly back home, would you press it now?" At the time, I'd answered, "No." But that was Europe and this was Africa, a continent with an entirely different pulse.

My chest tightened, and I began to sweat. The pride in my ability to travel only days before had disappeared. I shamefully knew that if I could find that button now, I'd press it. I stopped and tried to get control of my breathing. Long, slow inhale. Long, slow exhale. Again. This was part of the experience. This is what Lauren sent me to find.

I didn't need to check-in for hours, really, so why was I rushing? Was it habit to need to check in straight away? Hadn't I gotten past that? More likely it was the desire for safety. Not safety in the sense that I needed protection. The men with their hands out offering to guide me weren't thieves. They were just hustling. They were just looking for a little money to make their lives better. Like everyone else. No, the safety I was after was the safety of place. A place to belong, if only temporarily. During all the time in Europe, I'd formed a sense of belonging there.

I stubbornly told myself that right now, I belonged here, in the center of this maze, no matter how hard it was going to be. I put my phone in my pocket and looked up, took a deep breath and stepped forward. One step after the other. That was all I needed to do.

The noise was incredible, a cacophony of voices that I let soak in. Darija, the Moroccan dialect of Arabic, and French, for the most part, but English and a few other languages from tourists blended into the echoes off the cobblestones. Knives of sunlight sliced through bamboo slats overhead to be muffled on the dirty walls or amplified by tin lampshades. The smells of dust, spices, breads, and more were so strong that they almost had a physical texture. And the colors. Reds, blues, greens, and golds popped out of the shops from every tapestry, pillow, and ceramic dish. It was like no place I'd ever seen.

I passed a vendor selling wicker baskets, narrow and tall, short and wide, but each a blend of dramatic color. They were stacked so perfectly, in such precise rows, that I immediately remembered Omri discussing patterns with me.

I took the camera out of my pack and shot a few photographs. The seller, an old man with a magnificent mustache, sat on a stool and paid no attention to me as he simply smoked a wrinkled, hand-rolled cigarette. He'd been selling these baskets for decades and could probably tell a photographing tourist from a buying tourist a mile away. Taking the pack off my shoulders, I squatted down next to him. The camera went back into the bag. I was curious how he knew I only wanted to photograph the baskets. So many of the shopkeepers aggressively approached every passerby, but not this man. He simply knew that I wasn't a buyer, and I wanted to see what he saw.

He ignored me for a few minutes, and I pretended to ignore him. People walked by us in the narrow passage. The local women in dresses with long sleeves and sometimes scarves might be interested. The local men likely wouldn't be. Plump Americans in their safari pants and hiking sneakers were the most likely buyers. A basket was easy to pack and wouldn't break like a plate or bowl.

A middle-aged couple, European by the looks of them, slowed as they passed from right to left, looking at the shopkeeper's offerings. They cut a full circle and approached now from the left. The shopkeeper eyed them, waiting. The woman stepped closer, looking carefully. The man stayed a step or two back. I counted. One, two…and on three, the shopkeeper set his cigarette on the ground and stood up. He passed her a basket she'd been looking at closely. She held her hands up in a declining gesture. He rubbed the rough surface and presented it again. She looked past his hands for a moment, then said thank you in French and backed away.

The shopkeeper returned to his stool and picked up his cigarette. With two puffs, it came back to life. I stayed where I was, not sure exactly why. He cast a sidelong glance, not sure exactly why himself.

Another couple approached, but they swung in directly. Again, I counted. On four this time, he set his cigarette down and approached. Again, he offered the woman to hold a small basket.

She took it, turned it in her hands, and looked inside. "How much?" she asked. American. I should have guessed that before, as their clothes were rather bright.

He held out his hands, showing five fingers on the left and a fist on the right. 50, or about five dollars I knew, having taken some cash from the ATM at the airport.

She said, "Oh, that is too much."

He ran his fingers across the colored stripes, showing the quality. Oddly, he didn't speak. Perhaps he only knew Darija and French.

"How about thirty?" she said.

He furrowed his brow and shook his head. His hands went out again, this time, four fingers and a fist. I remembered that bargaining was common in markets and was curious as to how this would turn out.

She turned to her husband, and they spoke quietly. She agreed to his price and handed over four 10 Dirham coins. They went into a satchel hanging on his neck. He took the basket back and placed it in a small plastic bag before returning it. He bowed his head, and the couple thanked him in English. He put his right hand on his heart and nodded slightly again.

He hadn't said a word, even goodbye. It struck me that he couldn't speak. He returned to his stool and resumed smoking.

I was curious about their bargaining. *"Vous seriez descendu jusqu'à combien?"* How low would you have gone?

He turned to me and then pointed back to the couple that had just left.

"Oui," I said. *Yes,* them.

He held out two fingers and a fist.

He'd have gone to 20 but sold it at 40. I smiled.

To my surprise, he smiled right back. He finished his cigarette and stomped it out with a leather sandal. Reaching behind him, he grabbed a leather pouch and lighter. Another dun-colored cigarette appeared and was lit. He turned to replace the bag, but then stopped, offering one to me.

"*Non, merci*," I said.

He shrugged, and then together, we watched.

After a few minutes, another European couple did the slow pass and swing back maneuver. Again, I counted. On two, I held my hand up, thumb and finger raised. The shopkeeper looked at me, no doubt thinking I was more than a little strange, but he carefully handed me the cigarette. I held it there and watched the negotiation. This couple paid the full price for a larger basket. He returned with a broad smile on his face and took the cigarette back.

I set my hands on the top of my backpack and said a phrase I'd used so many times with skiers: "*Je peux prendre une photo de vous?*" May I take a picture of you?

He thought about it for a moment and then gave me a single nod.

I took the camera back out of the bag and found a position that offered a beautiful image. I took a few pictures with him looking away and as he caught a potential customer. When he set his cigarette down and rose, I packed up.

Catching his eye while the new buyers browsed, I placed my right hand on my heart as I'd seen him do. He returned the gesture and gave me a soft smile. It lifted my spirits immediately.

Through the months I spent in Marrakech, I never found that little alley or the basket vendor again. Perhaps it was because the medina is such a deep labyrinth. But some part of me always wondered if Lauren had sent him to me for just that moment.

***

A traveler once told me that when he's living away from home for an extended period, he'll often gravitate to certain place, feeling that developing a pattern in a new city gives him a sense of home. I'd found a little tea shop in the medina that I would visit every afternoon and came to know the owner and his family there. It began casually with nods of recognition, and after a few days, grew to the exchange of names and pleasantries.

Kadir and his wife, Hamisa, owned the modest café. While they made the tea and coffee, their two teenage daughters, Nisreen and Saeeda, served. Their young son, Hassan, was too small to help more than wiping the tables but was wonderful entertainment. He'd taken to sitting with me each day and sharing his drawings or the variety of spinning tops he'd made from bits of discarded material in the medina. Sometimes we would exchange a few bits of fragmented French, but for the most part, we communicated through playing with whatever home-made toy he chose to bring along.

One afternoon, it was Kadir who served my tea. Hassan, as was his habit, sat in the chair opposite me. This time, he hadn't brought a toy.

"He would like you to teach English," Kadir said.

"Sure, Kadir. I can teach him a few words," I replied.

"This is very good, Mister John. Thank you."

I had no idea how to teach someone English and wasn't even sure where to start, but the people I'd met during my journey always took the time to help me with language. It was my turn to return the favor.

"Hello," I said.

"Hello," Hassan repeated.

Getting started was as simple as that. For several days, I'd spend afternoons with little Hassan at the tea shop. He was like a sponge, soaking in nouns and verbs, quickly understanding how to string them together.

On what was to be my last day in Marrakech, I came to the café with my pack, planning to catch a bus out to the coast. The younger daughter, Saeeda, glanced at it briefly when she delivered my tea. No sooner had she returned to the kitchen than Kadir came out to see me. He'd always been quite respectful to me, from the way he addressed me to how he stood and poured tea, but this time, he pulled out the chair opposite mine and sat down.

"You are leaving, Mr. John?" he asked.

"I am afraid so, Kadir. Heading out to Essaouira."

"I see," he said. "You have travel schedule like the other tourists."

I laughed and said, "No, no schedule. But my room in the riad is booked for someone else now, so it's time to move on."

He considered this a moment and then said, "Hassan has learned much from you."

"It's been fun for me to teach him."

"I would like him to learn more. With English, he can be successful."

"Your English is excellent, Kadir. You can teach him."

"You are better teacher."

Kadir's expression was slightly sad. I didn't know what to say.

"You like Marrakech?" he asked.

"I do."

He nodded and then rather abruptly stood up and returned to the counter. I sipped my tea for a while, waiting for little Hassan, knowing that he was usually finished with school around this time. There was a little commotion behind me, and I turned to see him running toward the shop with some of his friends. There was a brief exchange, and the friends left.

Hassan took his chair. "Hello, John," he said.

"Hello, Hassan."

He, too, noticed my pack resting beneath the table. "Why this?" he said, pointing.

"It is time for me to go, Hassan."

"Go?"

I made as if I was steering a car and said, "Essaouira."

His face fell.

Just then, Kadir returned and they exchanged a few words. Kadir turned to me after the exchange and said, "We welcome you to stay in our home and teach Hassan."

Back at the counter, the girls were pretending to make something but were actually watching me. Hassan was bouncing up and down on his toes. Hamisa stared with more suspicion than anything. It was often the way she regarded me.

"Kadir, I don't think you want a stranger living in your house," I said.

"We do, Mister John. It is good for me. It is good for Hassan."

"What about Hamisa and your daughters?"

"They say good," Kadir said.

I wasn't so sure and looked back to Hamisa.

She gave me the smallest of nods before turning away.

Embarrassingly, my first thought was about what the conditions of their house would be like. That I would be sleeping on a dirt floor in a small hut with five other people and no water or electricity. I was disappointed in myself for feeling this way, for allowing my whole life to be rather privileged, from Lauren's and my beautiful house to Omri's large apartment, and every pampered studio I'd rented along the way. But beneath those superficial concerns, I knew this was part of the experience Lauren wanted me to have.

Which is why I said, "Ok, Kadir. I will live with you. But let's try it for a week and see how it goes, ok?"

"Thank you, Mister John!"

I looked behind him to see the two girls smiling. When they saw me look, they glanced back down and busied themselves.

"Kadir," I said. "We are friends now, so will you call me John?"

"Yes, ok. John."

"And since I am not a proper teacher, I think the best way to learn will be through practice. We will talk about everyday things in English, like Hassan and I have done here. Is that ok?"

"Yes, that is good!"

"Ok, then, Kadir. Thank you for welcoming me to your home," I said, extending my hand.

He shook it and, without letting go, led me over to the counter. They had an exchange in Darija, and at one point, the children all looked at me and smiled. They continued talking for another minute, and then Hassan darted off. He returned with my bag, and the elder daughter Nisreen came around the counter and joined him. She gestured for me to head out into the alley.

Apparently, we were going now. Just like that, with only one brief conversation, the course of my journey changed once again.

We wove our way out of the medina and through the city that had grown around it. All the while, Hassan and I kept a running dialog, practicing the English words for things that we saw on the way.

Nisreen was quiet as we walked, but I caught her snicker when I said something funny to Hassan.

Without looking her way or using her name, I said, "You understand me, don't you?"

She turned toward me and said, "A little, yes."

"Do they teach English in school?"

"No. I see on YouTube. And from tourists."

I smiled and said, "That is great, Nisreen. Does Saeeda learn this way too?"

"Yes. But our speaking not good."

"You sound great, Nisreen," I said. And I meant it, not just because it meant this new job was going to be far more manageable.

Hassan and Nisreen led me through a small archway between two shops, onto a narrow cobblestone alley. The buildings on either side seemed made from a patchwork of stucco and concrete in various muted colors stained from the effects of grime and time. After a series of rights and lefts, they led me through a wooden doorway, up some stairs, and into their home.

The center was a small, dusty courtyard that had seen better days. Underfoot were chipped tiles, some sections hastily patched with thin concrete. A small kitchen space was off to one side with a tiled counter, single sink, and cooking tools set on a series of sagging wooden shelves. Several similar rooms opened to the courtyard, filled with a jumble of furniture. Nisreen led me to one indicating I should put down my pack. I was to share the room with Hassan. My bed, like his, was simply a platform made of the building's concrete and a single mattress resting on the top. They showed me the other living spaces, the walls an assortment of colors, chipped and soiled with age. On the rooftop, there was a primitive washing machine and frayed strings for drying clothes. A few mattresses were scattered about, and I was told if it was too hot, I would be welcome to sleep there.

It was as rough as I'd imagined, but I could see the pride they took in their home. This was part of the experience, and whereas my instincts were telling me different meant worse, I knew that different simply meant different and I shouldn't judge until I understood what life here was truly like. This was an opportunity to experience a society that an outsider would rarely get, precisely something Lauren wanted for me.

A week with Kadir's family quickly became over a month, and I settled into the pace of life, getting a glimpse of a culture full of history, turmoil, and contradictions. Like so many places in the old world, Morocco had been seized by many over the centuries, from Phoenicians and Romans to Berbers and Arabs and eventually the French before becoming independent in the 50s. All of this meant that like so many places, the country was a quilt of varying languages, cuisines, and values. It was interesting with regards to women, where their strength from Berber culture combined with a more tolerant form of Islam practiced here to allow many barriers to be overcome. As a result, women in Morocco made progress toward equality; they drove, held office, studied at university, and built businesses. Some women wore hijabs, and some did not. As a suburbanite from the middle of America, my understanding of what the scarf signified was based on incorrect guesses driven by, and also themselves driving, over-simplified, knee-jerk opinions. Whereas I worried it was a symbol of oppressive male ownership, I found that, at least in Kadir's family, it was a choice. It was a way to show modesty before Allah, a form of respect. Hamisa and Nisreen wore hijabs, but despite being of age, Saeeda did not. My ignorance of the matter during my first few days in Morocco, I reluctantly admit, caused me to be a bit cautious. But after living with Kadir's family, I realized how ridiculous that was. I also realized that women covering their heads out of respect for God was not unique to Muslims; it was done in Judaism and Christianity as well.

There was, in fact, now only one woman wearing a scarf that I remained wary of, as she did of me, and that was Hamisa. There was a distance between us, and fabric had nothing to do with it whatsoever. She wasn't mean or aggressive, but suspicious might be more accurate. While I would catch her smiling to the rest of the family, it was an expression I'd never received. For weeks, I wondered why, conjuring up all sorts of reasons, from an American customer that had skipped out on a bill to a more tragic event in her past. I also never heard her speak English during our many hours practicing over meals and walks back and forth to the tea shop. I sensed she understood, though. So it was after a meal one evening while drying dishes in the dim kitchen that I built up the courage to ask.

"Hamisa, have I done something wrong? Something to offend you?"

She didn't look up and simply set a large bowl down on the bench for me to dry.

I continued. "I appreciate you having me as a guest. And I hope that it is ok to help practice English with your children, but I am worried that I have made you mad somehow."

She had been scrubbing a dented old pot, which she now set down in the sink. Taking ahold of an apron she had over her long, layered dress, she dried her hands. Without making eye contact, she grabbed my hand and pointed to my wedding ring.

"What about my ring?" I asked.

"Nisreen!" she shouted.

A moment later, Nisreen joined us. Hamisa said something to her in Darija, and Nisreen translated. "Mother says this mean marriage. She says you do not have wife here. She says you have left her. She is suspicious."

I looked down at my ring. Through all of our English practice and discussions of culture, I hadn't told them about Lauren. It wasn't that I was avoiding the topic, but more that I didn't want to burden them with my troubles.

"Please tell her that I did not abandon or leave my wife." I let Nisreen translate before continuing. "My wife passed away two years ago. I keep the ring on to remind me of how much we loved one another."

Nisreen translated, but I could see that Hamisa had understood already.

She held her hands to her mouth briefly, saying, "*Ana aasif. Ana aasif,*" quietly before wrapping my hands in her own.

"She says she is—"

"Sorry," I said. "I understand. Please tell her it is ok. Please tell her I am here because my wife wanted me to go on a journey to meet wonderful people like you and your family."

As Nisreen translated, Hamisa's eyes warmed as I hadn't seen before. Her strong hands tightened their grip on my own and our relationship instantly healed.

***

One evening sometime later, Camille messaged to say she would be in Marrakech soon for a Balenciaga cruise show. We hadn't seen each other in well over a year, and I was looking forward to her visit. While I'd started to enjoy meeting new people at every stop, there was something different about an old friend coming to visit, something comforting.

After cleaning the dishes, I approached Hamisa and Kadir to ask if the family might want to attend the show with me. Kadir explained that he had no interest and Hassan would likely feel the same, but after a brief exchange with Hamisa, he conceded that their daughters would probably enjoy it.

From one of the darkened doorways came a sneeze. Someone, apparently, had been eavesdropping on our exchange.

"*Hamdullah*," I said with a smile. "You may as well come in now."

Nisreen entered the room with Saeeda not far behind.

"Balenciaga?" Nisreen said. "That is very expensive!"

I nodded. "I think it is. And my friend Camille will be working there, so you'll get to see some of the designs up close."

"Camille Amari?" Saeeda asked.

I nodded, a little surprised she knew the name.

"Can we go, Father?" Nisreen asked.

"Yes, John may escort you to this show."

"Thank you!" they said in unison.

"I will look after them carefully," I said to Kadir.

"*Inshallah.*"

***

The Bahia Palace was done up for the show as none of us had ever seen it before. While beautiful on its own, filled with stunning tile and stonework from Berber, Arab, and Moorish artisans, the magical impression it gave was magnified several times over by the lights and fabric brought in by the show's production team.

"It is like a dream!" Nisreen said as we walked through the main entrance, toward a security team screening guests.

I was met with a disapproving look by a man holding an iPad just past the metal detector. While it was likely due to my pedestrian clothing, a Westerner arriving with two young Moroccan women probably wasn't regarded by a local terribly well either. But his demeanor changed as he found our names on the list along with a note Camille had left. We were quickly handed off to another well-dressed young man who escorted us around a courtyard where guests mingled over cocktails and to the back where the stylists and models were doing final preparations.

With only an hour-and-a-half before the show was to start, the back rooms were absolute madness. Models, makeup artists, hairstylists, publicists, agents, photographers, and designers briskly wove through the ranks of rolling wardrobe racks and dressing stations. The sound of their voices, each more urgent than the next, echoed off the tiles, making it almost impossible to understand anything being said.

Ahead of us, a photographer knelt, taking a picture of a male model having his hair styled. As he turned the camera vertical and gestured with his left hand, I knew immediately who it was.

Stepping up behind him, I said, "Excuse me, but do you think you could get us on the cover of *Vogue*?"

He turned around at the sound of my voice with a huge smile. Dropping his camera down on its strap, he opened his arms and said, "John!"

I hugged him and turned to make introductions. "Gabriel, I'd like you to meet my two guests, Nisreen and Saeeda."

The two girls were stunned, their eyes wide and taking in the chaos around them, but they turned their attention to Gabriel and said hello.

"Crazy, isn't it?" he said to them.

"It is magical," Saeeda said. "Is that the right word, John?"

Gabriel and I laughed. "That's the perfect word, Saeeda," Gabriel said. He was gentle as could be, giving them all of his attention just as Omri would have.

"John has to change out of his dreadful travel clothes," he continued, addressing both of them. "So we've made a special arrangement for you to spend some time with one of the makeup artists. Would you like that?"

Their eyes went as big as saucers, and together they said, "Yes! Yes!"

To me, Gabriel added, "It was Camille's idea. Would it be ok with you?"

"Absolutely," I said knowing they would enjoy the special treatment backstage.

"Fabulous. I will take them to Sofia," he said, pointing to a woman in the middle of a row of makeup chairs opposite a wall of mirrors and lights. "Camille has a suit for you just past there."

Sofia introduced herself to the girls, and I explained to them I would be back shortly. Just as I turned around, Camille appeared.

"Oh, John!" she said, holding her arms out.

I hugged her, taking care not to touch her makeup but enjoying the warmth of another old friend.

"You must be Saeeda and Nisreen," she said turning to the girls. "Who is who?"

The girls clarified and then thanked Camille profusely. It was adorable to see them so shy yet so excited.

"Now if you will excuse us, ladies, I am going to take our John and get him into something more appropriate." With a wink, she added, "He doesn't have quite the style the three of us have."

I rolled my eyes, and the girls giggled as Camille grabbed my hand. As we walked away, I said, "Arranging for them to have their makeup done was very thoughtful of you, Camille. Thank you."

"They have given you a home, John. They're your family. And since we are family too, then we must all take care of each other."

She led me through the madness to a little nook she'd taken over as her own. On the frame of a temporary changing room hung a dark gray suit along with a shirt, tie, and shoes.

"Thank you for the change of clothes. I didn't want to embarrass you but carrying only a small pack limits my wardrobe a bit," I said as I went behind the curtain.

"This is not a problem, John. There were so many crates of clothes coming here that having them add something was easy."

My regular clothes went into a small bag and I tried on the suit. The wool was smooth and light as a feather, and by the time I had the tie and jacket on, I realized it felt as if it had been made for me.

"Camille, how did you get this suit to fit me so well?"

"I am in the fashion business, John! I have known your measurements since the day we first met!"

I laughed and came out.

"*Ah, tu es magnifique!*" she said, adjusting my tie.

A flash popped, and I turned to see Gabriel. "For old time's sake," he said. He pulled a nearby stool over and joined us.

"How is Omri?" I asked.

"He is good. Happy, as always. Very happy that he does not have to spend all night on his feet working a fashion show any longer," Gabriel said.

He and Camille went on to tell me how everyone else in Paris was doing before Camille needed to do her final wardrobe change. I excused myself and went to collect the girls.

As I approached, the stylist said with a twinkle in her eye, "These are the nicest, most polite models I have ever worked with."

"I will be sure to tell their parents you said so," I said, genuinely appreciative.

Nisreen wore a new cream scarf with gold embroidery, and both of their faces had been done up in a beautiful but suitably conservative way. They held out their feet to show they now wore fashionable new sandals.

"They must have fallen off the truck," Sofia said.

"You are wonderful, Sofia. Thank you."

The girls thanked her and exchanged gentle hugs.

I took the bag with their other shoes back and set them with my own clothes before escorting the girls to our seats. The lights were dim, but we could see a raised runway had been set up to stretch from one end of the open-air courtyard to the other, detouring in a small circle around the central fountain, which strangely wasn't flowing. As we made ourselves comfortable, the background music faded away and the lights dimmed, building suspense. Slowly, a spotlight illuminated the fountain and the water began to gently flow out of the top before spilling over the edges, into the catch basin. The show was starting, and the girls went to the edge of their seats, phones at the ready. Music began to play and soft lights moved around the seating area. As the music reached a peak, we were suddenly surrounded by falling water. The walls of the courtyard had been set up with their own fountain system, effectively framing the space in curtains of water. More spotlights and lasers illuminated the fantastic scene, and even the most skeptic would have been impressed. As the models came out and took their turns on the runway, I watched the girls, both thoroughly enjoying themselves and snapping pictures like mad.

At one point, Nisreen turned to me and said, "It is Camille!"

I looked up to see Camille walk her first look of the night.

"She is beautiful!" Saeeda said.

I knew Camille would enjoy the compliment.

At the end of the show, when the guests had withdrawn to another courtyard for the after party, the girls and I went backstage to say goodbye. If what we saw before was frantic chaos, what we walked into this time was happy madness. I'd seen it before in Paris but was pleased to experience the excitement of an entire crew relieved to have pulled off a successful show. There were smiles all around as stylists disassembled the looks they'd worked so hard on only hours before and models changed into far less extreme outfits. We found Camille having gems removed from her forehead and two hairstylists detangling and returning things to normal.

Her face lit up as she saw the girls. "Don't you look pretty!" she said.

They smiled shyly and thanked her once again.

"I don't need thanks, *d'accord*?" she said to them. Noticing the phones in their hands, she said, "Should we take some pictures?"

The girls lit up once again and proceeded to take even more photographs with Camille, the stylists, and a few others who popped over.

I gave them plenty of time before saying, "We should probably head home and let Camille get to the party. I am sure her night isn't over yet."

"I think I can avoid the party tonight," she said. Turning to the girls, she lowered her voice and brought them in as co-conspirators. "If you can help me out without being seen, I can walk you home."

"I have an idea!" Saeeda said, reaching into her sister's bag. She pulled out the dark scarf Nisreen had worn to the event, folded it into a triangle, and placed it over Camille's head.

"*Parfait!*" Camille said as she tucked the shorter end under her chin and brought the other across her neck and over her shoulder.

I raised my eyebrows in question, and she gave me wink in return, letting me know this had been her plan all along.

"Can you have tea with us?" Nisreen said, her eyes pleading.

"*Bien sûr, mes chéries. On y va!*"

***

Leaving the house later that night, Camille put her arm in the crook of mine as we'd always done, and I said, "You certainly knew how to make them feel special. Thank you."

"They are wonderful, John. And so are their parents and little son. It was so nice of them to have me in for tea."

"You were nice to walk them home."

"It let me have this time with you."

She wasn't steering us toward La Mamounia, the well-known luxury hotel where I'd heard Balenciaga had put staff up for the show, so I asked, "Where are we going?"

"I did not want to stay at the company hotel. Even walking through the lobby, I have to be 'on.' Staying on my own gives some privacy."

We walked in silence toward the medina. Smoke from the open grills that crowded Jemaa El-Fna square still lingered, the last traces of lamb, cumin, and garlic slowly dissipating into the late-night air.

"Are you avoiding something, Camille?"

"I am, I think. There will be a day soon when this work comes to an end."

"You're not even twenty-four yet."

"But soon."

I was surprised that she was thinking about this. Her confidence and comfort with who she was had always held steadfast. Seeing this slight doubt, I knew that people in her circles would tell her she was beautiful no matter what her age. But she wanted a friend now, a friend to listen, not reply with superficial pleasantries.

I redirected the conversation slightly. "How is your business going?"

"Good," she said. "We have three licensing deals now. Milena and an assistant handle them along with the influencer contracts. She's moved to Paris, you know."

I did. One of the advantages of technology was all of the group chats between us. We'd kept up quite regularly, but it was on a more superficial level. There's only so much that can come through a keyboard.

I nodded. "What's next?"

A small spark of energy came through her arm into mine. "We have some exciting ideas! More collaborations and some investment opportunities. I love the idea of investing, taking a small company to the top."

"Sounds like you're enjoying it."

"Yes! Milena and I make a good pair, and I like discussing ideas with her."

"Is there an age limit to being a businesswoman?" I asked facetiously. "I think your answer's right there." She didn't respond immediately, and I realized she'd already come to that conclusion. "But you've already figured that out."

She nodded. "Yes, this is what I want to do. I will keep modeling for as long as the designers and agencies want to work with me. The exposure is very good for the business. But I want to be successful in this, John, and I worry about not having finished the last year of my *licence professionnelle*, my university degree."

"You don't need a degree, Camille. You've worked in the industry for almost eight years and have more practical experience than most. A degree is just a piece of paper that shows you've learned the rulebook on how to do something. Just ask Richard Branson. He doesn't have a degree. Plus, isn't that what Milena brings to the table?"

"I understand this, but a degree gives you credibility in business meetings. Some of these people look at me as a model and nothing more."

In the white-collar world, this was sad but true. A man can walk into a room thinking he knows everything, never noticing he's too ignorant to recognize his misconceptions.

"Ignore them. Or, if you really want, finish your degree. Some of it I imagine you can do online to allow for your travel schedule."

I noticed the corner of her lips turn up ever so slightly.

"You're already doing that, aren't you?"

She regarded me with a smile.

"Always a step ahead," I said.

"Yes, but I wanted to understand what you thought. Listen before speaking. This I learned from you."

"Not fair to turn the tables on me."

"But it is very fun, John." We turned a corner, and she looked up. "Ah, here we are," she said.

We'd stopped at an ornate door along an otherwise typical terra-cotta wall. Camille pressed the doorbell, and we were greeted and escorted across a majestic courtyard filled with delicately-lit towering trees and dangling vines. The young man led us to a door and unlocked it to reveal a beautifully tiled staircase. Camille declined his offer of mint tea and cookies before leading the way up.

At the top of the stairs, it was clear that her room spanned the entire roof on one side of the riad. We passed through an ornate living room to an expansive courtyard complete with a small pool and fountain. On the opposite side was a magnificent standalone bedroom framed in tall double doors on three sides. We entered and opened up the room, letting in the soft yellow glow of streetlights and cool night air.

While Camille went into the changing room to put on something comfortable, I walked around the space. Shelves towered between each doorway, laden with books in French about the history of *Maroc*, local design, and foods. In one corner was a wooden chest topped with a delicately-carved copper tray that served as the bar. Surprised to see a bottle of Armagnac in the selection, I poured two glasses.

Camille returned wearing a draping tunic, and I handed her a glass after she settled down on the bed. I stretched out on a large sofa in such a way that we could face one another and raised my glass. She did the same.

After taking a sip, she returned to our conversation, "Thank you for listening."

"You're good at everything you put your mind to."

"Almost."

"I'll be reading about you in a business journal someday. 'Amari Ventures Takes Over the Fashion World.'"

She let out a little giggle. "I hope this will be true, but enough about me. Tell me how you are doing."

"It's been an adjustment the last year, living without you and Omri."

She smiled. "There is only one Omri."

I raised my glass to that. "There have been good people, like the family tonight, but there have also been some rough encounters. An old curmudgeon in the Alps, some sour guesthouse owners, and border officers. I was pickpocketed in Barcelona a while ago too."

"Oh, no!"

I shrugged. "Took my credit card and some cash. Right after I got the replacement card, someone tried again. Gave the guy a fright grabbing his wrist when he went for it."

"You're lucky he didn't hurt you."

"I realized that as soon as he ran off," I said with a smile.

"The John we met in Paris wouldn't have confronted a pickpocket," she said.

I looked down at the amber liquid in my glass. "Getting my feet under me a little bit, I guess."

She sipped silently before asking, "Are you happy?"

It was a question I sometimes asked myself. "There are times when I'm happy. Peaceful. A few more of those moments every day."

"I think that is what we do, put the good moments together as much as we can."

"You're right," I said smiling. "They're still patching some holes right now, but nights like this, seeing you and the girls happy, go a long way for me."

"And that makes *me* happy," she said.

"What else is making you happy these days?" I asked.

She looked up at the thin fabric suspended above the bed and said, "This, I think. A quiet, gentle talk away from the crowd." Her eyes moved down to mine. "Give this moment a fireplace and a breeze from the sea, and I would be in heaven."

As if on cue, a puff of wind rustled the trees in the courtyard and sent ripples through the curtains.

We both laughed at the timing.

"You'll have to settle for the desert breeze tonight," I said.

"Time with you is never settling, John."

I smiled and closed my eyes, only to wake up hours later with the muezzin's dawn call to prayer echoing across the city. I was still on the sofa in my suit pants and dress shirt, though Camille had covered me with a light blanket at some point in the night.

Over on the bed, she slept peacefully. Careful not to wake her, I rose and retrieved the bag with my clothes before tip-toeing to the bathroom. Worried that the shower might make too much noise, I decided a dip in the pool might be a better idea, if not a pleasant morning indulgence. I swam a few short laps and then floated peacefully, listening to the early morning sounds drifting up from the medina. Pots and pans clattered, a baby cried, and shutters rolled up as merchants set up shop. Above, the sun slowly lit a clear sky, bathing the city in warmth.

"Good morning," came Camille's voice from behind me.

I quickly turned over. Not wanting to spend the day in wet underwear, I'd elected to swim in my birthday suit. After making my way to the edge of the pool and carefully hiding everything but my head from view, I returned her greeting.

"It is a beautiful day, yes?" she asked, her face lit with a cheeky smile.

"It is indeed." I did my best to be nonchalant.

"You just want to be *free* on days like this, don't you?" she asked.

We both laughed.

"Now that you've had your fun, why don't you turn around?"

"But you will need a towel," she said, taking one from a lounger. She brought it to the edge of the pool and held it out, making a show of trying to peer down through the water.

"Close your eyes, please," I said.

Her eyes closed, but the smile remained.

I pulled myself up and quickly wrapped the towel around my waist.

"I peeked," she said.

"I know," I replied, spinning behind her and pushing her into the pool.

She fell with a shriek, emerging in laughter a second later.

Our morning remained playful and fun. Breakfast was brought up, and we shared lighthearted stories over coffee, *b'ssara* soup, and square *msemen* crepes with olive oil. By the time she had packed, leaving me with a few more things for the girls, our voices had grown quiet, neither wanting to say goodbye. Our drive to Heliconia, the private aviation side of Marrakech-Ménara, was made in near silence. On the ramp, beneath the jet's stairs, we hugged, neither doing a very good job at holding back some tears.

Her head nestled against my neck, she asked, "Where will you go next?"

"The coast, I think."

"And after that?"

"I've been practicing letting my path unfold on its own, imagining it'll bring me home when it's time."

Her arms tightened around me before she broke our embrace. Holding my shoulders, she said, "You will tell me when you are ready to come back, yes?"

"I will." I leaned forward and kissed her cheeks, first right, then left.

Her grip on my shoulders lingered before she finally let go.

11

It was in the windy city of Essaouira a couple of months later, just outside a cabinetmaker's shop in the ancient, walled medina, that I met a travel photographer named Robert. I'd seen him in the old port the day before, photographing some fishermen in their traditional blue boats, and was surprised to run across him again. I introduced myself, and we ended up having coffee together and sharing a few stories.

Home for him was New Zealand, though it sounded like he only lived a few months of the year there. The bulk of his time was spent driving across central Asia, and now Africa, in a beefed-up Land Cruiser, shooting for travel magazines. He had an easygoing way about him, and we got on well enough that over several days, we'd become good friends.

At a tiny café near the shore, he looked up at me over lunch and said, "I looked you up online yesterday. Those are some great photographs of your journey."

"Thank you," I replied.

"Is Omri Uziel the one who taught you?"

I smiled. Robert really had looked through the trail of captions I'd left as a way of chronicling the journey. "He was. Lived with him for a while. But to be honest, I think he taught me more about life than photography. Do you know Omri?"

"No, I've never met him, but he's pretty famous in photography circles. How did you meet him?"

"Fate more than anything. A mutual friend introduced us."

"Did you work in the studio with him?"

I nodded. "A lot of unpacking and repacking gear, that's for sure. Why do you ask?"

"Well, I have another assignment in Dakar, Senegal and was wondering if you'd like to come along and get some shots of the coast with me on the way."

"You're driving?"

He nodded. "Through Western Sahara and Mauritania. That's why I was asking. I figure it's going to be a bit rough and probably a good idea to travel with someone and share the driving."

"Define 'a bit rough.'"

"Western Sahara is a bit of a no man's land. To Moroccans, it's Morocco. To the Saharawi, it's the Saharawi Republic, something the Algerians support because they have their eyes on it too. But for most of the world, it's considered an unrecognized territory without a government. And that means the roads are going to be shit."

"How about Mauritania?"

"Might get a little real there. Landmines off the track at the border and the occasional outlaw. But it would be an adventure. I've been through some rough places in Africa, and I'm still here."

"How long do you expect it to take?"

"If we went full gas, I'd guess three or four days. But the sights along the way could be spectacular, so let's say a week, maybe a little more? It'll be hot and sandy, but I've got AC in the truck and we'll get a good breeze at night in the camper tent up top."

"Robert, I have to be honest. Mines might not be something I'm prepared for."

"There are mines in more places than you know, John. But I've heard they've been cleared for a K or two either side of the road. Plus, they're only a worry at the border."

"Let me think about it, ok?"

"No problem. I'm off early tomorrow, around seven. How about I come by this café then, and if you're here, great. If you're not, I understand."

"Let's do that, but I'll see you here in the morning either way."

I'd like to say I enjoyed the rest of the afternoon and evening in Essaouira, but that wasn't even close to the case. I sat on the wall overlooking the sea much of the time, thinking and researching the drive on my phone. The State Department had travel advisories for most of the route, filled with words like malaria, landmines, kidnapping, and terrorists. I was sure they needed to cover their bases and err on the conservative side. The traveler forums, though, were more positive. But who wrote in those? Probably the road-hardened globetrotters who'd spent years adventure seeking, not suburban accountants.

I committed to letting this journey make its own path for me, but landmines and terrorists? Honestly, Lauren, is this what you wanted?

I was at the café at seven the next morning, pack on my back, ready to go. Ten torturous minutes went by while waiting for Robert. I probably second-guessed my decision a few dozen times.

When Robert finally pulled up in the Land Cruiser, he shut down the engine and hopped out. "Not up for it, I see. Well, thanks for seeing me off anyway," he said.

I shook my head and said, "Nope. I'm in. Doing my best to say yes more than no these days."

"That's the spirit! But this is all you've got?" he asked, pointing to my pack. "A twenty-five-liter day pack?"

"Long story, but it's proven to be all I need so far."

"Impressive. Have a sleeping bag?"

I shook my head. "Sorry."

"No worries. I've got an extra from the last guy that drove with me."

"What happened to him?"

"Landmine."

My jaw dropped.

"Only messing with you, mate! Get your bag in here, and we'll get some provisions for lunch and head out."

An hour later, we were on the N1 heading south in Robert's Land Cruiser that had been modified enough to tackle anything. It stood on beefy tires with a snorkel running up one side, a winch on the front, and a spare with a jack and sand ladder on the back. In the cargo space was a large case with a slide-out stovetop, fridge, and water dispenser, all beneath several bags of gear. The truck was impressive and efficient, and judging by the dents and dings, it looked like it had served him well for years.

I settled in, enjoying the view as we drove south through the hills. The pace was relaxed, and we swapped roles only once that morning so that I could get a sense of how the truck handled. It was heavier than I would have guessed, and Robert explained that it was due to extra tanks for drinking water and fuel, along with an air compressor and additional battery. Once I got used to compensating for the weight in turns and when braking, I found it quite solid and stable.

We took our time, stopping first at Paradise Valley, which was literally an oasis with lush green bush surrounding beautifully clean pools. We had lunch and cooled off in the water before heading over the hills to a small surfing town on the coast. At Robert's insistence, we rented a couple of boards and spent the late afternoon in the sea. I was utterly hopeless at first, but after some instruction, was able to ride a few waves as the sun set behind us.

We carried on for a few days, still taking the trip at a leisurely pace. In Tarfaya, Robert wanted to get some shots of the Casa Mar, the ruins of an old castle in the ocean about fifty meters from shore. As this town was the first I'd seen in Morocco without a single tourist, I wanted to get a sense of what the place was like.

Donkeys pulled simple two-wheeled carts down the main street, passing small groups of men discussing this-or-that. The few women that could be seen were covered head to toe, indicating this was a much more traditional town than we'd encountered before. It was a sleepy place with many of the buildings appearing to be abandoned. At one point, I came across a biplane sculpture and was surprised to learn that the aviator and author of *Le Petit Prince*, Antoine de Saint-Exupéry, had been stationed here for a time. A cobbler stitched sandals outside a small shop, and I stopped to watch his work. I said hello, and we had a brief exchange in a mixture of the Moroccan Arabic I'd picked up and French. It didn't take long for him to realize I was more interested in his work than buying a pair of sandals, but he was still friendly enough to demonstrate the process of trimming and stitching. After a time, I asked if I could photograph his work and then captured a few portraits along the way.

That night, after grilled lamb and couscous at a local restaurant, we shared photos from the day. Robert had taken some beautiful images of the castle in the sea that afternoon, but the ones he'd taken at sunset were astonishing, and I told him as much.

He seemed quite pleased with my shots as well, and when I asked for suggestions on taking pictures of tradesmen like this, he was happy to give some advice.

Afterward, he asked, "How did you choose him?"

"To be honest, since this town is so small, there weren't a lot of choices."

"But there were plenty of people working, like the fishermen and shopkeepers."

I shrugged. "Don't know, really. Maybe something in his eyes was different. Something hinted that he'd open up a bit."

"It's a talent you have, John. Especially in this part of the world. Most of the people here don't want their picture taken."

"I understand that. No one wants to be like an animal at the zoo, so I just talk, ask a few questions."

"Keep doing it, mate. These are great."

The next day, we drove deep into Western Sahara before camping just north of the Mauritanian border. The road was paved decently enough, but narrow, with rough shoulders of beaten earth. For miles in every direction it was simply stony desert, which Robert explained was called *hammada*. During my shifts driving, I fought to stay alert following the black ribbon through the vast expanse and was thankful when we finally found a suitable spot to lay up for the night.

Under the early morning sun, we exited Morocco and proceeded into four kilometers of no man's land. It was an entirely ungoverned buffer between the two borders and unlike any place I'd ever seen. Rocky sand as far as the eye could see, with the only indentations made by other vehicles making the transit. Robert explained that we needed to stay on the worn path and make sure it matched up with the track he'd marked on the GPS. Not long ago, some Frenchmen had lost their lives setting off an anti-tank mine when they veered off the trail. The burned-out shells of vehicles we drove past showed that hadn't been an isolated case. Touts lined the first few hundred yards, selling cars, machinery, weapons, and anything else best sold in a stretch of land without laws. We were going slowly enough that some came up and banged on the windows, offering their services as guides. They were some rough characters, and I was thankful when Robert increased his speed slightly. Eventually, we were entirely on our own, our eyes both darting between the windscreen and the GPS. The word *desolate* came to mind, but even that couldn't describe the sense I had of being somewhere so completely barren of absolutely anything. When we finally arrived at the two square towers marking the Mauritanian border, it was with great relief.

A police officer checked our passports and entered our details into a logbook. No computers here. He then indicated we needed to pay €120 each for visas. I was skeptical, but then saw he had a receipt pad ready and the same amount was listed next to names in the book. While it was outrageously expensive, it did appear legitimate. We paid and were sent on to a second building to clear Robert's truck. He provided the vehicle's Carnet, but the customs officer waved it off, saying that only a €20 fee was due. By the look on his face and his empty desk, we knew it was going straight into his pocket. Robert tended to some required vehicle insurance as well, and before long, some policemen unclipped a chain and allowed us entry into Mauritania.

While the route to Senegal was to our left after the border, we decided to turn right and drive down a peninsula that jutted into the Atlantic. The bay it formed had a fascinating history, and like many places around the world, that fame was for all the wrong reasons. It was the world's largest ship graveyard. Trawlers and cargo vessels are expensive to decommission at the end of their lives. Ideally, they're broken apart at shipyards with the scrap recycled or disposed of safely, but for many years, there was one place where for considerably less money, usually in the form of discreetly wrapped bundles of cash, owners could simply abandon their ships in the bay off the coast of Nouadhibou. The result was over 300 ships rusting and decaying right into the sea. Despite international funds dedicated to clean up, the ships remained. It was an incredible sight. Massive hulks of ships, many rusting into eerie shapes, rested on the beach and in the sea. They were ghost ships, scattered like skeletons waiting for a full moon to be piloted off into the deep.

We spent some time around the ones on the shore, taking photographs. But as sand pelted the hulls and the wind eerily howled through gaping holes, we became more than a little spooked. Resuming our journey south seemed to be the best decision.

We clocked mile after mile of desert for a couple of days. The road was paved for the most part but deteriorating the farther south we went. Vast strips of tarmac were occasionally windswept with sand, forcing detours and a little digging. The Atlantic would sometimes come into view, and seeing the Sahara touch the sea was astonishing.

Eventually, we came across a long-abandoned quarry on the coast. Robert was at the wheel, the plan to make lunch overlooking the sea and recharge before a last push to the Senegalese border. On a large, open plateau, he was swinging the

Land Cruiser in a broad arc when we came to an abrupt stop accompanied by a horrible snapping sound.

"Oh, shit!" Robert shouted as we slammed into our seatbelts.

"You ok?" I asked.

He held his left hand to his chest and said, "Mostly. You?"

"I'm ok. What the hell was that?"

"Don't know, but I'm going to need your help getting out."

I looked over to see he was gritting his teeth, his right hand now cradling his left.

"Remember when I told you that the only thing most people know about driving off-road is to keep your thumb on the outside edge of the steering wheel?" he asked.

"Oh no," I said.

"Yeah. Reminded myself the hard way."

I got out of the passenger side and walked around the front of the truck. A large piece of steel buried in the earth had grabbed the front wheel, snapping it to the side and right off the joint that held it to the axle.

Opening the driver's door, I released Robert's seatbelt and carefully brought it over his left arm. I was relieved to see he showed no signs of injury other than his hand. "Let's have a look," I said.

The bump near the wrist, where his thumb attached to his hand, had shifted back slightly, bulging beneath the skin. Fortunately, it wasn't an open fracture, but it was clearly causing some pain.

"Stay right there. I am going to get the first aid kit," I said. From one of the drawers in the back, I found the large first aid kit and brought it to the driver's door.

"Front wheel is buggered, isn't it?" he asked.

I nodded. "Hit a buried piece of metal. Looks like something left over from the quarry."

"Shit!"

"Well, at least it wasn't a mine."

He started to laugh, but the motion moved his hand and quickly ended in a grimace.

"Your hand is going to start swelling soon and then it's going to hurt like hell, so let's deal with that first," I said.

He looked down and said, "I don't know how to set that properly. Seen it done once, but…"

"Best to be done by a doctor, especially if there's damage to the wrist. Let's get some ice on it."

I took out a cold pack and banged the center with the side of my hand before shaking it. Once it was cooled by the chemical reaction, I set it gently on his wrist and thumb. After two packs of Paracetamol and half a bottle of water, he was anxious to get out.

"I want to keep it elevated a bit, so sit tight for a minute," I said.

Robert's first aid kit was a good one and included an inflatable splint as well as an arm sling. The sling would likely be enough for the time being, and I gently set his arm in it and adjusted the strap around his neck.

He carefully got out of the driver's seat and joined me at the front. The damage was discouraging and would require more than what even the best bush mechanic could handle. The only way the truck was getting out was with a tow, and that was something that would be hard to come by out there. Our situation was grim. We were on an exposed plateau about a kilometer from the abandoned quarry and three from the road. The last people we'd seen were in a small village about fifty kilometers back, and we hadn't passed another car since then. No one knew we were here. A check of the phone showed there was no signal.

"I've got a sat phone for emergencies," Robert said.

"And the number for African triple-A?" I asked.

"Better," he said with a smile. He went to the back of the truck and with one hand, started opening one of the camera cases.

"Let me do that," I said.

He directed me to the right compartment and the satellite phone.

I swiveled and extended the antenna and handed it to him. "Who are you going to call?" I asked.

"Emergency service called Global Rescue. They do field rescues and evacuation. Had their coverage for years, and they'll have the resources to help us out."

Looking at a number taped to the phone, he began to dial. Even with a call, help wasn't going to come instantly. Robert was going to need to sit down once the adrenaline wore off.

I opened up the tent platform on the roof of the truck, flipping the base out to act as a shade from the harsh sun. After getting some water and setting up two camp chairs beneath, I ushered Robert into one just as he was connected with an operator. He went through a process to confirm his identity before explaining the accident and answering a series of questions about his injury.

"How long?" I asked when he disconnected.

"They're checking. Crossing the border for a field rescue will add complications, so we'll likely be brought back up to Nouakchott first. They want the hospital there to X-ray my hand before planning the next step."

"Nice service," I said. "How are we getting back there?"

"They offered a helicopter, but we decided this wasn't serious enough. Told them if they could send a tow truck, we'd be happy enough to ride with them. Plus, it would get my truck to a garage."

We waited for the rest of the afternoon in the shade of the tent deck, periodically icing Robert's hand as the sun inched lower on the horizon behind us. When help finally arrived, the sun had nearly set. It was, unfortunately, still light enough for me to see that our rescue vehicle was in only slightly better condition than the ships we'd seen earlier.

It was some form of a heavy-duty van with four doors and a semi-open platform in the back, supporting what could only be described as a home-made towing structure. A well-dressed passenger stepped out of the front door carrying a sizeable medical case. The driver followed but waited off to the side. In surprisingly good English, the well-dressed man introduced himself as Amadou. He explained that he was contracted by Global Rescue and the driver, Papis, was a mechanic.

Amadou set down his case next to Robert and said, "Let's take a look at you first." He took his time, checking Robert's vitals and assessing his overall condition before taking a look at his hand.

"Your thumb is broken, and maybe your wrist. This sling is good, but I want to immobilize it for the journey. The road can be rough."

"We figured that out ourselves," Robert said with a smile, tilting his head to the front of the truck.

Amadou smiled, "Yes, you did." He exchanged a few words with Papis, apparently dispatching him to assess the truck. "Papis will prepare to tow your truck now," he said.

I went with Papis to the front bumper where we both got down on our knees. I took hold of the piece of metal that had stopped us. It was completely solid, apparently only the top of something substantial wind and time had buried long ago that had only resurfaced as our wheel pushed just enough of the sand away. Papis pointed to the casing that joined the wheel and axle and said something in Arabic before shaking his head at me. He didn't speak English, but it was evident in his tone that this wouldn't be fixed on the spot.

He pointed to the roof of the vehicle and, using his hands, illustrated that I should close the tent platform up. After warning Amadou and Robert, I did so. Papis then swung his truck around and secured the front of the Land Cruiser to his tow apparatus. By the time the sun had set, we were all in the cabin of the improvised tow truck, slowly making our way north.

It turned out that Robert's wrist wasn't broken, but his thumb fracture was significant enough to require surgery. Global Rescue, not wanting him to have surgery in Mauritania, arranged to fly with him to Paris early the next day. He was reluctant to leave his gear, so we agreed that I would stay and see about repairing the truck and finishing our transit into Senegal. I saw him off at the airport the next morning, where after the hundredth thank you, he gave me a pile of cash and his bank card. I promised to see him in Dakar when he was well enough to return.

I found a hotel near the airport and, after scrubbing days of desert off, promptly fell asleep.

***

It took four days for the parts Papis needed to arrive and another day before the truck was ready. I set off on my own through the desert, and with the help of a fixer set up by Global

Rescue's advisors, made it across the river and into St. Louis, Senegal by that evening.

Each country, I'd learned over the past year, had its own feel. There was simply a sense that transcended race, language, government, and religion. And the feeling Senegal gave was vibrant optimism.

Crossing the Senegal River had brought me into the West Africa I'd imagined. Vendors shouting in the streets as they sold their goods, women wearing the most colorful outfits I'd ever seen, drums banging, and seafood cooking over an open flame by the side of the river. It was magical, and I quickly found a small hotel in the center of it all with a secure parking lot and decided I'd stay for a while before heading on to Dakar. The French I'd learned in Paris proved helpful as I set about what I now thought of as my routine: walking through the day, watching, asking questions when I found something interesting, and photographing.

By the time Robert met me in Dakar, three weeks had passed. And after two weeks sharing stories and photographing with him, it was time to leave. There were still more places I needed to go.

Finding that it was somewhat tricky to get from West Africa to East Africa, I returned to Europe. I spent two months in Portugal before making my way across to Valencia where I took a job as a deckhand helping a captain and crewmate get a boat across the Med to Cyprus. I continued to pick up odd jobs like this, doing everything from scrubbing hulls in Crete to cleaning construction sites in Tel Aviv. I worked for cash or lodging, or any combination of both that would allow me to stay below the radar of the authorities, yet still let me learn about the people of each little region around the Eastern Mediterranean.

It was an incredible experience, and I could feel myself changing as each month went by. Physically, I had never felt stronger. And mentally, the fear I'd once had crossing into each new culture had given way to curiosity.

I migrated slowly south from Ethiopia to the Kazungula crossing. There, on the edge of the Zambesi river where Namibia, Zambia, Zimbabwe, and Botswana all meet, I used a little *ahem* money to bypass the massive lines queueing up for the ferry crossing and got myself on a small boat taking two Americans to the Botswana side. If the guide who met them was surprised to see a third passenger, me, get off the dock with them, it was hidden by his frustration that a tire on his Land Cruiser had punctured just when he parked. By this time, I'd had more experience with broken vehicles than just Robert's in Mauritania, so I jumped right in to help. Four hands proved faster than two, and in almost no time, we had the tire changed.

The guide, Tebogo, asked if I needed a lift somewhere in thanks. I explained that I really had no idea and just wanted to pick up a little work and go on safari for a while. He laughed and had me join him for the ride back to his lodge. By that night, I had a job working as the assistant to his head mechanic, complete with a bed in the workers' bunk room and three meals a day. It was dirty, hot, and sweaty work, but for nearly a year, I learned more about animals, vehicles, and, sadly, tourists than I could have ever wanted. In the four years I'd been traveling, the time I spent covered in grease in Botswana was by far the most peaceful I'd enjoyed.

It was in the lodge's garage over a plate of chicken and rice that a message came through from Ashton and Hailey. They were getting married in New Zealand and invited me to join the celebration.

12

The wedding was held in New Zealand's far north, in a tiny place called Peria. The old church was so small that it barely held everyone, something that made the ceremony that much more special. And as Peria was really only a collection of modest homes and a primary school, the reception was held a few kilometers away at a hotel on Taipa Bay.

In the days before the ceremony, Ashton's family adopted me as their own and immediately put me to work. We dusted and vacuumed the church, set decorations in the hotel, and even dug a pit in the center of the hotel lawn in which dinner was to be cooked. My skepticism of a hole in the ground acting as an oven was erased the moment I took a bite of the pork that had cooked there for most of the day. It was incredible, moist and tender with a small hint of earthy magic. I said as much to one of Ashton's aunties seated next to me at dinner.

Omri, who had flown down for the ceremony, laughed as my plate was piled higher and higher. "It is lovely, isn't it?" he asked.

"The food? Or the ceremony?"

"Both! Everything!" he replied. "It's positively wonderful. We should all be so alive. Look, they are going to sing again!"

I turned to see one of the groomsmen finish his toast and a group of women stand and sing what I'd learned was called a *waiata*. Their beautiful voices filled the room, and while I couldn't understand a single word, it wrapped me in immeasurable comfort.

When the last of the toasts had been made, songs had been sung, and perhaps more significantly, last beer had been finished, I found myself on the crescent-shaped beach of Taipa Bay with Omri.

He had aged more than I wanted to see. He'd gained weight and lost a little color, perhaps not enough of either to worry about, but it was troublesome. "How are you doing, Omri?"

"I am great!"

"I'm asking about your health, Omri. You look a little tired."

He made a dismissive gesture and said, "I am fine. My doctor has me on some medication for my heart, but it is handling things just fine. He did make me put a treadmill in the apartment, and I've been walking a few kilometers on it each day."

I nodded. "That's good, Omri. Do exactly what he says, ok?"

"I will."

We came across a couple of old logs laid on the beach in a V shape. We sat down and, for a moment, listened to the tiny waves ripple in the shallows of the bay.

"You look good," he said. "Tan and fit. Stronger too."

I looked down at my calloused hands. "Nothing like exchanging a desk job for labor to turn things around."

"You used to be scared of your own shadow. Now look at you."

"It's thanks to you, Omri. You're the one who gave me this courage."

He nodded and changed the subject. "Everyone loves seeing the pictures you post."

"I learned from the best."

"I think they love seeing you carry on. Seeing you continue this journey."

"How are they?"

"Monique is as wonderful as ever, still the glue that holds the studio together. She misses you, though. Gabriel is working on his own now and doing very well. I sometimes rent space and equipment to him because it's nice to have him around."

"And Camille?"

"Still the face of the biggest brands but putting a lot of focus on the business."

"Amari Ventures. I see articles about it sometimes, and I am always glad to see it's doing well."

"Did you hear about Milena?"

I nodded. "I did. CEO now with Camille as chairman. How about that?"

"You should see her now. Milena has inspired a courage and business strength in her that is incredible. She even returned to university and finished her degree, not that she needed it with the success they've been having. I've heard from a few clients that when the two of them walk into a boardroom, they come out with exactly the deal they wanted every single time."

"I knew they'd be a good match."

He paused again.

Our conversation had been circling something, and I suspected he was getting close to the point now.

"She wanted me to tell you something too, John."

"What's that?"

"She has started to date someone," he said gently as if it was a sensitive subject for him, which was puzzling. Camille and I were friends, close ones I could confidently say, but we lived in different worlds and each had our own stations in life.

"We exchange messages pretty often to check on each other. Not sure why she hasn't told me. Someone famous, I imagine?" I said.

"One of the Formula One drivers."

I let out a chuckle. "Well, that's the life she lives. Bright lights and red carpets."

"Hmm," he said.

"Is she happy?" I asked.

"I think so," he replied.

It wasn't what I hoped to hear and my protective instincts kicked in. "Please tell me he treats her well, with the respect she deserves."

"It is very new, and I have not met him yet. But from what she has told me, yes. She said that she 'calls the shots.' An expression I am sure she took from you."

"Well, that's good. As long as she's in charge. From what I understand, those guys can be cocky."

"Not with Camille," he said.

"If you ever think he's not right for her, break out the old paratrooper and kick his ass, ok?"

I expected this to give him a laugh, but he simply nodded his head. After a moment, he changed the subject once again. "Where are you off to next?"

"South Island here for a bit, then Southeast Asia."

***

A bit turned out to be two months. While photographing a farmer and his border collie on a farm outside of Nelson, he'd asked if I wanted to stay and help him shear his sheep. His son had just left for university, or "uni" as it's called, and he was short-handed. It was tough physical work, but I enjoyed learning what life on a farm was like.

I hopscotched my way north via Jakarta, Singapore, and Penang, eventually arriving in Ho Chi Minh City. I knew the journey Lauren had sent me on would include Southeast Asia. I'd had some reservations about this part of the world, that it would be too different, too much of a challenge. But I couldn't have been more wrong. It was positively amazing, and a feeling in my heart swelled even further when I arrived in Ho Chi Minh City.

Standing on a corner in one of the impossibly dense areas as I was, I should have been petrified. Scooters and small motorbikes packed every inch of the street, flowing like lava through the intersection. Everyone was going somewhere—to work, to be with family, to eat. They looked only straight ahead, and even with the constant beeping of tiny little horns, they followed an organically courteous pattern. A large mass passed through the intersection, and the following group slowed slightly, allowing another group to cross. Everyone went with the flow of the group around them, no single person feeling they were more important and pushing ahead. It was order within complete disorder, and utterly fascinating.

In the middle of the street, a woman's bag fell off the footwell of her scooter. She calmly stopped and pushed herself back to retrieve it. The flow around her simply parted, converging back as they passed. No one gave a rude gesture, no one yelled. After picking it up, she set it down again between her feet and rejoined, calm as could be.

The studio I'd booked was a few blocks away, down what the map showed to be some narrow streets, but I would need to cross the main road before me to get there. And given it was four lanes wide and there were no traffic signals whatsoever, I had no idea how to do it. So I watched. The locals fell into two camps: those who would wait for a break in the flow closest to the sidewalk, and those who would simply step straight into the street, not even breaking stride. But what they had in common was their pace. They crossed slowly and steadily, not stopping or starting midway, allowing their progress to be predictable. They stared straight ahead, trusting that everyone on the motorbikes would make space for them.

Astonishingly, they did. The flow just adjusted pace and direction slightly and continued on, leaving the precise amount of space pedestrians would need for their next step. It was like a slow-motion school of fish, adjusting perfectly as one.

I let a scooter carrying an entire family of four pass, then stepped off the curb and strode forward as if I belonged. And as mopeds and motorbikes and pedal bikes flowed around me, I knew I was in love.

A young, mismatched couple stood in the small hallway outside an apartment next to the one I'd rented. As I was struggling to get the lockbox open to retrieve the key, the man said, "Let me give you a hand. That one's a little tricky." From his accent, it was clear he was Australian.

"Thanks," I replied.

He re-spun the combination and nudged it around a bit until the door opened. "There ya go, mate."

There were two keys inside, and I retrieved the one with my unit number. Locking the box, I said, "I'm John."

"Nice to meet you, John," he said. "I'm James, and this is Claire."

We all shook hands. James appeared to be the full backpacker. Long, curly hair tied in a ponytail, T-shirt cut to be severely sleeveless, wrinkled shorts, and sandals. Claire was more put together, with long, nicely-braided blonde hair, cuffed shorts, and a linen top.

"Been here long?" I said, walking to my door and unlocking it.

They followed. "About a week here in Saigon. Two months in Vietnam."

"Two months? Must be great."

"Best place we've ever been," he said.

I gestured they could join me in the studio and looked around as we entered. It was remarkably inexpensive, so I'd expected it to be pretty shabby, but it was better than I'd imagined and would serve me just fine. There was a decent looking bed, compact but relatively clean bathroom, and a small kitchenette. Just what I needed, if not a little more, and I said as much.

James nodded. "We needed this place too. Couple months on motorbikes and staying in hostels...we'd had just about enough of the community bathrooms."

"Don't forget the outhouses in some of those little villages," Claire said.

James let out a laugh. "Those were a little rough!"

"Just a little?" Claire asked. She gave me a funny look for a moment and then said, "I know you! You're John Winter, the traveler, the one whose friends with those models and photographers!"

I tossed my bag on the bed. "That's me."

"Oh, man," James said flipping through his phone. "Look at all your followers! You must get all sorts of free stuff!"

"Afraid not, James. Patagonia sent me a new Black Hole backpack when I broke a zipper on the first one. That's about it."

He appeared a little shocked. "But you can turn that into something!"

"Right now, I'd like to turn it into something to eat. I've heard the food here is great."

"We were just heading out. C'mon with us, then," Claire said.

As was my habit, I grabbed the camera and slung the strap around my neck and one shoulder on the way out. It was new, a Fujifilm Omri had been sent for testing. He knew I appreciated dials over menus and had brought it to New Zealand for me along with a 50mm equivalent lens. To keep things light, I'd long ago streamlined down to just a prime lens, zooming with my feet when necessary. I'd been experimenting with the new setup on the way to Vietnam and was loving it.

They took me through some of the smaller alleys, and every street was bustling with vendors. They carried shoulder poles, the two baskets packed with produce, this way and that. They pushed small carts or rode bikes filled with foods and flowers. The colors were beautiful, and the scents—a mixture of fresh-picked vegetables, spices, sweat, exhaust, and a hint of incense—were extraordinary. Street food kitchens filled the sidewalks, each a jumble of pots and plastic baskets, always with tiny plastic stools arranged nearby. Each vendor's entire business was miniature enough to be easily packable and portable.

Claire had a particular dish in mind and wove us expertly through the mixture of tourists and locals as she scouted. "Ah," she said as she stopped. "This is what I was craving: *bun thit nuong.*"

"Sounds good," I said.

"*Xin chào,*" she said. Hello. Then she held up three fingers with a smile.

The elderly woman nodded and said, "Three. Ok."

The woman sat on a small plastic stool in front of a table that wasn't much more than a piece of wood over two buckets. Arranged around her was everything she needed: a small grill, two woks on burners caked with years of soot, and stacks of plastic colanders filled with herbs and vegetables. She set to work without getting up from the stool, merely pivoting through a series of well-practiced movements.

We sat down on little red stools at one of her two tables, the center of which was filled with a variety of condiments. Some sauces were in bottles like you would see in a store, but some appeared to be home-made concoctions poured into an old water bottle with a hole punched in the cap. I remember seeing this for the first time in Africa and being horrified. Now I knew it just meant there was something special inside, a secret recipe that had likely been passed from mother to daughter for generations.

The shuffle of flip flops and a string of Vietnamese I couldn't understand announced that our dishes had arrived. Rice noodles, grilled pork, an assortment of herbs and lettuce, strings of carrots, and a crispy spring roll adorned each bowl. Claire and James added fish sauce and chilies, and I did the same. The flavors and textures blended so wonderfully together that I knew by the second bite I couldn't leave this country until I tried absolutely everything.

James and Claire told me about the foods they'd experienced along their trip, how each region had its own specialty and motorbiking north to south had opened their eyes to the variety this part of the world offered.

I asked them where they were from and was surprised to hear that James was from The Gold Coast and Claire was from Melbourne. While I hadn't been to Australia before, I knew that the distances between any two cities could be vast.

"How did you two meet?"

They shared a knowing look before Claire said, "We just met in Hanoi."

Surprised, I replied, "Really? You look like you've known each other for years."

James reached over and held Claire's hand. "A mutual friend organized the trip. We planned to do it as three, but he fell down some stairs our first day here and broke his collar bone. Craziest thing. But he wanted us to take the trip anyway."

"I said there was no chance in hell," Claire said.

James waggled his eyebrows. "But I talked her into it. Said if our friend liked us both enough to travel with him, we would probably get on perfectly."

"'Perfectly' was a stretch, that's for sure," Claire said with a cheeky smile. "James is all over the place, so I have lots of training to do."

"And Claire's a bit too planned and predictable, so I have lots of training to do too!"

We shared a laugh, and I said, "I know exactly what it's like, Claire, taming the crazy ones."

"Your wife. She was wild?" She'd obviously been following me long enough to know about Lauren.

"Wild isn't the right word. Perhaps free-spirited would be better."

"Yes!" James said. "And you need that, don't you?"

I shared a knowing glance with Claire and said, "We do."

She nodded and said, "But we don't have to admit it to them."

"We don't. But we have to admit to ourselves that we're better together than separate," I said.

James nodded. "I think that's why we've found we are the perfect match. Secretly, we know that we complement each other."

"I make the plans," Claire said.

Raising his hand in the air, James said, "And I make the fun!"

They both broke into laughter.

"So," I said, changing the subject, "tell me how getting a bike here works."

"It's actually pretty simple," Claire said. "There are places in Hanoi and here where anyone can rent a bike or buy one. We bought ours, which seems to be fairly common. It's all set up, so you buy them up north and sell them after your trip down here. Then someone else comes along and does the reverse. It's not expensive at all. We bought ours for about a thousand US total, and just sold them for almost $800. Two hundred dollars for two months, which wasn't bad."

"Not bad," I said. "Do you need a license?"

They looked at each other and laughed.

"I said no," James said. "And I still think if you get pulled over, a little *ahem* money will solve it. Works at customs whenever I've overstayed a visa, so it'll work with the cops, I'm sure. But Claire would never let me try it."

"Yeah, yeah, I'm a rule follower. So I made us take the test for a license here."

"Is it hard?" I asked.

James shrugged. "They give you an easy pass through the written part. Our place didn't have an English version of the test, so they ask some questions and pretty much assume you know what you're doing."

"So we really just had to take the practical test, riding the bike between painted lines in the car park. You'll do fine and get all the paperwork back a few days later." Claire said.

"How are the roads between here and Hanoi?"

"Shitty," Claire said. "And a little dangerous. I'd pass on driving at night."

"But riding through the countryside is amazing," James said. "We can show you the place we just sold our bikes. Want to go?"

I stood up and paid the woman for our meals with some Vietnamese Dong I'd picked up at an ATM earlier. "Lead the way!" I said.

There are certain expectations Americans have for car and motorcycle showrooms, such as bright lights, gleaming white floors, and dozens of shiny new models to choose from. While I'd been on the road long enough to get used to the vast differences in what defined home or a business, I didn't expect the 'showroom' to be a sidewalk display of six bikes in front of what appeared to be the proprietor's home.

Seeing us approach, a man got up from the table where he'd been eating with his wife and two small children. He wore a red, orange, and yellow striped shirt with the Ralph Lauren polo player on the chest, which I noticed faced the wrong direction. With a broad smile, he greeted James and Claire by name.

"Hey, Quan!" James said.

"We'd like to introduce you to John. He's interested in buying a bike to take north. John, this is Quan," Claire said.

We shook hands, and Quan said, "So you want to go on a long trip! We have good bikes, all serviced!"

"They look great, Quan," I said. They were all clean and well-polished. I looked behind him and saw several bikes in various states of repair in what I imagined was his open living room but also served as the workshop. "How do you choose?" I asked all three of them. I'd ridden a small dirt bike a few times as a child and didn't really know much about motorcycles beyond that.

"The first choice is manual, automatic, or semi-automatic," James said. "Manuals are better for the mountains, but automatics are easier."

"Mine was a semi-automatic," Claire said. "And I kept up with you in the mountains just fine."

James conceded she was right with a shrug and then pointed out the two they'd used. James' was a Honda Win that looked like an old, beat-up motorcycle out of the 80s. Claire's was slightly smaller and looked like a blend of scooter and motorbike.

Pointing to Claire's, I said, "This looks like the type most of the locals are riding."

"This Honda Blade. Very reliable!" Quan said.

"That's true," Claire said. "James had a lot more mechanical issues than I did."

"But I looked good on it!" he said.

Claire rolled her eyes and then said, "When we were at a garage—and you will have some breakdowns because everyone does—the semi-automatics were always fixed and back out on the road faster."

James agreed. "Mine was definitely cooler, though!"

"Which would you get if you were riding back to Hanoi?" I asked.

"Probably Claire's. Since it's literally everywhere, everyone knows how to fix it." Turning away slightly, he whispered to me, "And mine was a bit of a dog, to be honest."

"You take for ride! If you like, I will give you very good price on new helmet and lock!" Quan said, pointing to Claire's bike.

After a few pointers, I headed out with James on the back for a loop around the block.

While it would never win a race, it was stable, easy to maneuver, and fit right in with the surroundings. There was also something fun about having the wind in your face and the sounds and smells of the city all around. As we returned to Quan's, I couldn't help but smile at the feeling that little ride had given me. An hour and several hundred dollars later, the three of us piled 'family-style' onto my new bike and rode back to the apartment.

I spent several more days in Ho Chi Minh City with Claire and James. They helped me with the driving test and license paperwork and offered a great introduction to the local food and culture. They were the perfect example of people I'd met on the road time and time again—positive, encouraging, and helpful. One hot and muggy morning, we said tearful goodbyes because the cute couple was heading back to Australia while I hopped on the bike to begin my journey north.

In that first week on the road, I spent more time lost on country roads than I did on whatever route I had planned for the day, but by the end of the week, it didn't matter. I loved it there, and as long as I kept the morning sun on my right more days than not, I would eventually make my way to Hanoi. So I packed the phone with its map in my pack and let the country show me the way.

In the cities, I stayed in small, inexpensive guesthouses or hostels. I'd mostly avoided the hostel scene over the years, feeling that they were a little too young and the party scene wasn't my cup of tea. But I gave it a try and learned it wasn't just young people in hippie elephant pants on a gap year. There were couples and solo travelers of all ages, each with their own exciting stories, and there's no one more willing to share a story than a traveler in a hostel.

I endured the standard "Where have you been?" "How long have you been traveling?" and "Where next?" questions because hostels were also inexpensive, something becoming more and more important as Lauren's life insurance money was beginning to dwindle. If I was careful with spending, I could keep going another year. If I continued to pick up odd jobs as I had been doing, it could be extended to a year-and-a-half. Some days that felt like plenty. But some days it felt like not nearly enough.

Mrs. Garland had suggested in a recent message that her daughter would like to purchase the house and had proposed an offer that made for a fantastic return over our purchase price. As tempting as it was, I still thought of the house as my last physical connection to Lauren, and I didn't think I could let go. As I usually did when these thoughts came to mind, I mulled it over for a moment and put it on the shelf for another day. Strangely, the notion of the house as my home didn't come to mind like it had so many times before. The road and the people I'd met along the way had oddly started to become home to me. It was a concept so foreign that I couldn't recognize what it meant.

What I could recognize was the stunning scenery Vietnam offered around every turn. Beautifully lush, green rice paddies terraced across hills and valleys. Majestic mountains peppered the landscape, covered in dense layers of jungle, often with their white stone core jutting through. A coastline that could just as easily hide beautiful little coves as it could stretch out to a ribbon of white sand for miles.

The riding, especially for someone new to motorbiking, was tough at times. The roads were rough, with ragged shoulders and plenty of potholes. Traffic could be absolutely hair-raising, with trucks and buses doing what they liked, when they felt like it, and that included driving on whichever side of the road happened to be convenient. There were plenty of dicey moments, from learning the hard way that the back brake was a better friend than the front brake, to understanding that taking turns when merging was entirely a western concept. When you need to merge, you simply do it. Unless you are merging with trucks, in which case you let them do whatever they want. They're going to do it anyway. But every time I had to wipe away the dust from a little off or push my bike into a petrol station, I found that I wasn't discouraged. In fact, I found that every scrape, muffler burn, and skinned knuckle made me a part of this beautiful country, and it a part of me.

The people were amazing in their trueness to self. Some parts of the world loved the spending power of tourists yet despised the tourists themselves. Other places, often those off the beaten track, loved tourists not just for their money but for their curiosity and willingness to visit their remote homes. The people of Vietnam, though, simply went about their lives. As a traveler, I was not despised but neither was a red carpet rolled out. I was simply welcome; welcome to see, do, taste, and experience as much as I would like.

One aspect of this was quite interesting. Throughout Europe, Africa, and New Zealand, I'd developed an approach to taking street portraits that involved asking questions, always with genuine interest, about what someone was doing before requesting a photograph. Usually, the answer would be yes, but plenty of people would decline. Here, though, there was a wonderful openness to street portraits. Shooting one child would lead to a group, which would lead to them doing all sorts of crazy antics, and which twice now led them to dragging me into a school to meet the teacher and share a few words in English. It prompted an elderly woman selling hand-carved whistles to take me back to her house, where she put on her Sunday best for a portrait she could send to her grandchildren. It let a group of men repairing a road invite me to share their lunch and, later, try the suspiciously-brown homemade moonshine one had brought along.

One bright, beautiful morning in the hills midway between Nha Trang and Cambodia, I found myself riding on a small dirt track between endless miles of rice paddies. There wasn't a car on the road nor a worker in the field for miles. At one point, I came across a picturesque farmhouse on stilts, complete with a couple of dilapidated outbuildings. I slowed, wondering if I should take a picture or not. Ultimately, I decided to carry on and find a town where I could stay for the night or a few days, but about a kilometer farther down the track, a man carried two bags of rice on his shoulders. I pulled to the side of the path, popped the dusty bike onto its side stand, and as I found myself doing often here, walked out to say hello. I studied the maze of ridges to find the paths that would intersect with the one he was on. One doesn't just walk through a rice paddy because even drained, the silky soil can be soggy and deep.

"*Xin chao,*" I said once I'd reached him.

He eyed me suspiciously and nodded, edging around me on the narrow path and continuing on.

I followed, saying, "Please, let me take one."

He stopped and turned to me, still wondering what a stranger was doing in the middle of nowhere, offering to help. "Heavy," he said, looking at the bag on his left shoulder.

He was about my age and considerably smaller, but wiry and undoubtedly strong. His face was brown from the sun, with wrinkles as clearly defined as crisp paper folds. The fact that he knew the English word *heavy* was unusual, as most of the farmers I'd photographed only spoke Vietnamese.

I held my hands out to take one and said, "It's ok."

He turned his right shoulder to me, and I lifted the bag off. It was far heavier than I'd expected. Once he'd seen I had it steadied on my shoulder, he turned and continued walking.

Our destination turned out to be the farmhouse I'd passed. We walked behind it to one of the small sheds. Pulling a piece of sheet metal aside, the farmer lifted up a tarp and flipped the bag off his shoulder on top of a few more that were already there. I did the same.

He looked at me and said, "Thank you for help."

"No problem," I replied. Offering my hand, I said, "My name is John."

"I am Cuong."

I looked across at the sun falling toward the horizon. There would only be a couple more hours of light. "Do you have more to carry?"

He looked back from the direction we'd come and nodded. "Tractor not work. Six more bags."

"Well, let's get to it then," I said.

"More?"

"Why not?"

Several hundred meters past my motorcycle, we rejoined the path I'd ridden down, and I saw why he was carrying the rice by hand. A trailer sat at a precarious angle on the side of the track, its left rear wheel snapped at the axel.

"Bad road," Cuong said, pointing at a spot in the road that had caved away to expose jagged rocks. He'd obviously hit them at just the right angle to snap the wheel.

We each carried two bags back to the shed and came back. In fractured English, he explained that he'd been on his way to the market to sell the rice when the accident happened. Rice farmers, I learned, used it to feed the family but also to trade for meat and produce and sell for a modest income.

I picked up the last two bags while Cuong disconnected the wagon from the two-wheel tractor. It was an interesting contraption made only of the components you need to pull something heavy and absolutely nothing else—a small engine with a large, exposed belt drive connected to a crankcase above a single axle and two wheels. Behind the wheels was a set of handlebars jutting six or seven feet back. The idea appeared to be that the driver would sit on the front of any attached wagon or farm implement, engage the gears to move forward, and swing the handlebars side-to-side to steer. He started up the little engine, its unmuffled exhaust a staccato assault belying its small size. Taking hold of the handles, he released the hand clutch and turned the tractor toward home for our walk back.

After making sure the rice would remain dry, we replaced the corrugated panel. The sun was low enough now to cast a beautiful golden glow across the valley, and Cuong agreed to let me photograph him. Returning to the bike, I hopped on and slowly rode it back to the shed. Unstrapping my pack from the back, I pulled out the camera and one of the large bottles of water I'd purchased earlier in the day. It was hot from sitting out, but I unscrewed the cap and offered it to Cuong anyway. It was the only thing I had to share.

I took a few photographs, pleased with how the sun accentuated his ruggedness. Afterward, I showed him on the small screen. He smiled and steered me toward the house, asking if I could show his family. As I approached, I could see his wife in the shadow just inside the front opening. Two small children peered out from deeper in the house behind her.

In America, I always thought of a home just as we drew them as children, with an A-shape roof, a door in the center with windows on either side, and a tree or white picket fence framing the image of prosperity and safety. But on this journey, my vision of home had detached from what the physical structure needed to be. I'd seen homes of mud, sticks, and dung; rough concrete blocks; and every combination of scrap wood and metal. Cuong's home was a perfect example. It sat a few feet above the ground to protect it from flooding. The framework was sturdy, even though the logs used were crooked and riddled with wormholes. The roof and walls were thatch, held together with precisely placed bamboo slats. One panel was propped open, allowing light inside while also serving as an entrance. Neither it's shape nor materials defined it as a home. What did was the kind, shy smile of his wife as we approached and the swing of Cuong's arm as he indicated I should enter first.

Untying my boots and placing them at the bottom of a set of uneven stairs, I walked up and inside the house. Smooth and worn floorboards creaked with every step. Cuong introduced his wife, Chau, who gestured I should have a seat on a woven mat. Two pots bubbled away above burners hooked up to a small propane tank. A round block of wood held an old knife and some chopped chicken thighs, and some plastic colanders filled with herbs sat nearby. Chau went behind the roughly-defined kitchen space and fetched a dirty red thermos. Popping the top, she poured two glasses full of brown liquid and handed them to Cuong and me.

"*Nuoc Sam*. Please. Is tea." She noticed my hesitation and smiled, saying, "Is ok. Water cook first."

I smiled and took a sip. It tasted like the countryside, earthy and fragrant with fresh greens. The combination was oddly refreshing.

"You like?" Cuong asked.

"I do. Thank you."

"Nettles and roots of grass and corn husk. Also sugar plant. No ice, sorry."

"It is delicious just the way it is," I said.

"You show Chau photo?"

I turned the camera back on and showed her.

She covered her mouth. Smiling behind her hand, she said, "Good! Good picture!"

Cuong said something to her in Vietnamese, and a lengthy exchange followed. He was obviously explaining what had happened to the rice and trailer.

My eyes had adjusted to the darkened interior, and I could see that the space had been divided by quilts sheets that likely separated the sleeping area. I was in what must be the general living space, complete with some nylon sacks of rice as seats and a television atop a makeshift table. The TV meant the family had power, and I followed the television's cord to a hazardous arrangement of power strips and tangled wires. Small footsteps behind me let me know I was being watched, and I turned to see two little faces above some bags of rice. As soon as I looked, they giggled and hid once again. I remained looking, knowing they couldn't avoid another peek. Sure enough, their heads popped up again. I made a funny face, only to have them laugh louder before hiding once again.

"Our children," Chai said. "Hau and Hoa."

"They are adorable," I said. I looked outside to see the sun was setting now. I was anxious to find a town and a place to stay, as riding a motorbike in the dark here was quite frightening. "How far away is the next town? I would like to find a guest room or hotel."

"Ten kilometers. This way," Cuong said gesturing in the direction I'd been headed before stopping. Chau said something to him, and they had another brief exchange before he continued, "Chau say it is dark. You stay here."

"No, I don't—" I started.

"Is ok," Chau said. "You eat. You sleep here."

It was this sort of hospitality that defined home. The structure didn't matter; it was merely evidence of available resources. No, home was the gesture of inviting someone in, sharing a place safe from the elements with a stranger.

They shared a meal of *com ga*, a rice cooked in chicken broth, served with chicken, fresh herbs, and strings of carrot and papaya. Afterward, we washed dishes in a simple bucket of water, and Cuong turned a soccer match on the old television until I was given some blankets upon which to sleep.

The next morning, after a bowl of broth and rice, there was a shout from outside.

"School," Chau explained.

The children ran past me and thundered down the little ramp to put on their shoes. I looked up to the road to see a horse pulling a two-wheeled wagon covered with a red tarp. A young boy shouted at Chau's children and then caught sight of me. He quickly darted back under the tarp, and a second later, four heads popped out simultaneously to stare at me.

"Hello!" one of them said.

"Hello!" I said back. "How are you today?"

"Hello!" he said in reply.

I smiled and waved as the kids climbed in and the horse set off for the next stop.

Who says a school bus has to be long and yellow and filled with rigidly-upright seats? If it only needs to be a wagon pulled by a horse, then perhaps that's all it really needs to be.

After saying goodbye to Chau, I gave Cuong a ride into town where he assured me that one of the men at the machine shop would give him a ride after he picked up what he needed to fix the trailer. We shook hands, and I thanked him for his hospitality. It had been one of the most genuine experiences I'd had in

Southeast Asia and has been a memory I've treasured for years for its simplicity and sincerity.

As Cuong headed to the back of the shop to search for the parts, I discreetly handed a fair amount of Dong to one of the shopkeepers. I pointed to where Cuong had gone and received a nod in understanding. The shopkeeper then pressed a finger to my heart and smiled before shaking my hand.

***

Five months went by as I slowly made my way north. There was no rush, only flavors to savor, beautiful scenery to behold, and culture to experience. When I finally arrived in Hanoi, there was a sense of balance and comfort I had not felt in years. There was a calmness to the people there, and they'd been kind enough to share it. But the country had also shared a tiny bit of unkindness I felt as my intestines gave a little gurgle. I'd had my share of the trots on this trip, and I knew it was typically short-lived, but I also knew that I wasn't really up for another dodgy toilet and decided it was time to splurge on a nice stay.

The Metropole is a Hanoi institution that maintains the same incredible level of service it has delivered for over one hundred years. The desk staff, in well-tailored suits and beautiful dresses, didn't bat an eye at my sweat-stained clothes and sunburned skin. They treated me as they would an ambassador or businessperson, with grace and professionalism. I was shown to a room in the original wing of the hotel, which exuded French colonial charm. I asked the bellman to arrange a doctor for me and informed him that I would have some laundry ready shortly. Stripping off my sticky clothes, I went into the beautifully tiled bathroom and washed off thousands of kilometers of dirt and grime.

Thoroughly scrubbed and clad only in a thick robe, I dug every bit of clothing out of my bag. Setting aside a single, moderately clean outfit, I put the rest in a pile and rang the butler. When he arrived to pick everything up, I handed him the bundle. At the last minute, I even emptied my toilet kit and gave it to him along with the pack itself. He smiled and said he would have everything back to me before dinner.

I used the rest of the afternoon for 'life maintenance.' The local doctor checked me out, and after reviewing my yellow card together, got me up-to-date and supplied some just-in-case-things-turn-bad antibiotics. On the way back to the Metropole, I picked up some toiletry supplies, underwear, and shirts before having my hair buzzed down at a dodgy sidewalk barber. Finally, I spent time on a computer in the business center making sure my savings were getting the best return and all of the bills were paid.

I returned to my room to find a tidy pile of clean clothes and my pack looking good as new. I changed into a fresh outfit and sent what I'd been wearing to be cleaned. Finally, with everything sorted, I went downstairs to the fabulously old school bar in the back courtyard. Sitting beneath a slowly turning rattan fan on a sumptuous couch with an excellent tequila on the rocks, I considered what to do next.

While there had been some exceptions, my general path had been east, so it felt logical to make my way up to Hong Kong, Shanghai, and then to Japan. A few months perhaps, and then back to America. Back home.

The thought of returning brought a lump to my throat. Was it sadness? Apprehension? What would I find there? My manager had said my job would be available when I returned, but five years had passed since that promise. And the house. Could I go back to the sadness I'd felt there? Could I live there alone for the rest of my life?

After Lauren died, every little item in the house had reminded me of her and brought terrible sadness. When I saw the pilled headband she'd put on before washing her face at night, I cried, knowing she'd never use it again. When I folded a tea towel the way she liked them folded, I knew she would never see I'd done it correctly. Every little memory in those months after her death had been of sadness.

But the memories from my time on the road, from her gift to me, had been magical. The experiences had shored up the damage to my spirit. They'd solidified her memory in my heart more than any house or tea towel ever could.

I took a deep breath. Then another. And then I sent a message to Mrs. Garland that I would be honored for her daughter to have the house and anything else she would like. I was letting go, letting go and moving forward.

As I took a sip of a second tequila, my phone rang.

"Well, Camille, your timing is certainly good," I said when the line connected.

"Why is that?" she said.

"Because I am presently staring at my second tequila of the evening, wondering if I should be sad, happy, or terrified."

"Oh, John, what happened? Are you alright?" she said with alarm in her voice.

"No, no. Nothing bad happened," I said quickly.

"*Mon dieu.* You had me worried. Riding that dreadful motorbike is not safe."

"You will be happy to know that the bike will be sold soon."

"Finally, you are being sensible! So why are you sad?"

"Because the bike isn't the only thing about to go. I am selling the house."

The line went silent briefly. "How do you feel about this?"

"It's time, I think. It feels right."

"Then you should not be sad, John."

"I know. I'm processing it. Adjusting. Only happened a few minutes ago." I took another sip and then continued. "But you didn't call to listen to me figure myself out. How are things in Paris?"

"It is beautiful here today! I was just calling to hear your voice. Messages are never the same."

"How is Jorgen?" I asked. Photos of Camille and her boyfriend at some of the mid-season Formula 1 races had been appearing in my news feed a little more frequently.

"Good," she said hesitantly. "It is stressful for him, fighting in the middle of the pack for points."

"Where is he off to next?"

"Hungary."

"You like the races?"

"A little too noisy for me," she said. "Where are you going next?"

She'd always been quite reserved when speaking about Jorgen, so her moving the conversation back came as no surprise. "That's the part I'm a little frightened about," I said. "I'm really not sure."

"You can come back to Paris perhaps?"

I chuckled. "Be pretty lonely there for Omri and I if you're in Hungary. No, there's still more in store for me."

"John, you've done so much, come so far already. Maybe it is time."

"There's still something, Camille. Some experiences that I need to have. Don't know what they are yet, but they're out there."

"How long will you be gone?"

"As long as it takes, I guess."

The line went quiet for a bit before she spoke again. "Take good care of yourself, John. I will always be here for you."

"I know you will, Camille. *À la prochaine*."

***

A newfound calmness came over me those final days in Hanoi. I spent time with street vendors, photographing them and enjoying my last tastes of *bun cha, phở*, and *bahn mi*. The bike that had been my entry ticket to this beautiful country was serviced and sold, and soon after, the last electronic signatures finalized the sale of the house.

Things would be different now, living with nothing more than what fit in my small pack. For so long, my life had been about collecting things on a list, assembling everything required for a career, family, and retirement. A job was followed by a car, which was followed by a house and grown-up furniture, not to mention a second car. The next things would have been paying for children to go to college and, eventually, a nice retirement house in the hills. But life had thrown me a curveball, and a terrible one at that. Through this journey, I'd adjusted. I'd hammered that ball straight back at the pitcher's head.

It was time to go. It was time to challenge myself, and there was no place that scared me more than India did. It was a destination for 'real' travelers, the ones who craved intensity. I'd never felt ready for it until now.

13

In the middle of the mass of travelers in the heat and humidity outside Mumbai Airport, I realized I still wasn't ready for India. By that time, it was too late.

To be fair, I'd chickened out a little. Not knowing the neighborhoods in this city of twenty million, I'd asked the advice of the Metropole's manager on where to stay. He'd thought I wanted a place of the Metropole's caliber and suggested the Oberoi. I'd shamefully not dissuaded him.

Public transportation options at the airport were limited, but a quick check of a ride-hailing app showed the prices were remarkably low. After a few taps, I was on my way in a boxy little car that rattled like a tin lunchbox and would probably be equally safe in a collision. I tried not to worry about it and took in the view. In the distance, the muted outlines of tall buildings were smothered in smog. Clear as daylight, though, were the slums. Clusters of tiny, colorful homes were piled together in slivers of land between buildings, on hillsides, and right next to the road. A road that was quickly becoming absolute madness.

As cars backed up, lanes and lights were completely ignored and everyone quickly filled any available gap in an effort to make forward progress. We wove between cars with inches to spare, every driver looking straight ahead, confident in their knowledge of the precise minimum amount of space they'd need to split a gap.

After crossing a long causeway that appeared to be only halfway finished, we wound our way through more dense surface streets before arriving on a wide, arcing boulevard on the water's edge. The traffic thinned ever so slightly, and I was pleased to see young couples and groups of friends strolling along the seawall. Just when it appeared we could go no farther, the driver took a hard left and looped into the Oberoi's small driveway. I thanked him and got out of the car to be greeted by a smiling, uniformed Sikh who took my pack and ushered me through the hotel's metal detector—a byproduct of the 2008 terrorist attacks—and into a small entrance hall. I took an elevator up to the main lobby. Seeing the vast space open to a ceiling at least a dozen floors up, I convinced myself that a few days of luxury would be permissible.

The next morning, after an entirely extravagant breakfast, I left the hotel's air conditioned embrace and headed out to Marine Drive. The humidity and pollution were everything people warned it would be: sticky, oppressive, and pervasive. But looking down the gentle curve of the seawall and across Back Bay, with my shirt quickly sticking to my back, I couldn't care less. I was here; fears be damned.

I roamed the Colaba for a few days, visiting the Gateway, Churchgate station, and the famous Taj Hotel. The one sight and smell that stuck with me was a pre-dawn visit to the Sassoon Docks. The fishermen had arrived under darkness, tired from a night spent filling their holds with every variety of fish. It's there that they bring their catch ashore, to one covered pier in particular where crowds of workers and buyers wait. As soon as the first basket hits the dock, the frenzy begins.

Women in beautiful saris carried baskets of fish on their heads, weaving around men pushing sharp, narrow carts back and forth between the docks and trucks waiting on the street. The humid air was filled with the pungent odor of fish, something made almost unbearable by the fact that those fish only hours before lived in the coastal waters that are essentially Mumbai's septic system. As the selling reached its peak, there were so many people that I found myself in full-body contact with someone every second. Then, just as the heat of the sun warmed the dock, the frenzy came to an end. Only a few men remained, their brooms attempting to clear oily kaleidoscopes from the concrete. While they were partially successful, the smell remained, ready to be revitalized the next day.

Suitably indoctrinated, I eventually moved to a modest hotel in Bandra West. While it's known as the home of Bollywood, it was the vibrancy of the neighborhood that drew me. There was constant noise, flashing lights, and people going every which way on the narrow streets all hours of the day. It was precisely what I'd been afraid of, yet as I stood on the edge of the road getting nearly hit by a *tuk-tuk*, I found it beautifully exciting.

Celebrating the little victory of crossing the street without dying, I found myself alongside a few teenagers. They were speaking to each other in English, but with different accents. I said hello and learned they were from a small traveling high school and spent each term in a different country. I didn't know something like this existed and asked them what a typical day was like.

"There's no 'typical' day!" said the tallest of the three, a boy with what sounded like a Kiwi accent.

"Well, how about today, then?" I asked.

"Today was intense," the blonde one said, clearly American.

The girl of the group nodded and said with a French accent, "We went to the Dharavi slum."

"You went to a *slum*?" I asked slightly alarmed.

"We did. There's an NGO called RealGiving that will take you in," she said.

"Aren't slums dangerous? Like the projects in America?"

The American boy said, "I thought it would be dangerous, but it's not at all."

"It's just people working hard, trying to get by. Make a good life for their family," said the French girl.

"Well, there are parts that are dangerous for the people working," the Kiwi said. "All of the machinery is packed in there, with massive moving parts everywhere."

"There are businesses in the slum?" I asked.

"Yes," the girl said. "There are two parts of Dharavi. One where people live, and the other where people work."

"You should go. It's life-changing," the American said.

The other two nodded.

"We're stopping here," the American continued. "Gotta have some pizza!"

I looked up and saw we were outside a large, modern pizza parlor. It was an odd sight in the heart of Mumbai.

"Don't you eat Indian food while you're living here?" I asked.

They all smiled, and the Kiwi said, "Every day, but you have to have some variety, right?"

I laughed and wished them a good night. Looking inside the window, I saw them go to a long table where some friends had already been seated. They were quite a mix, and by appearances, looked to be from just about every corner of the world. They each wore the same happy smile. Teenagers and pizza seemed to cross borders with ease.

***

I woke up the next day thinking about the phrase the American boy had used: life-changing. It was a description I could apply to each stop I'd made over the past five years, so there was no sense breaking the streak now. I did a search for the NGO on my phone and booked a tour of Dharavi for later that morning.

"One million people live and work in the slum, in an area that is about two square kilometers," my guide, Vivek, explained as we walked down a chipped sidewalk just outside of the slum.

"One million?" I asked.

"Yes. Some of us think the number is actually higher. The government, however, likes the estimate to be lower. Still, it is one of the most densely populated areas in the world."

"But you're here every day, so you would know best."

He nodded and said, "I grew up here."

His English, with a British accent evident amid the rapid, sing-song cadence, was extremely good, and I told him as much.

"I was very fortunate. My parents worked enough jobs to send me to an English school here. I now take classes at university."

"I am impressed. Do all of the children go to an English school?"

"Unfortunately, not every school can teach English, but we understand learning English and how to use computers gives children greater opportunities. I will show you one of the schools in the slum that RealGiving operates at the end of the tour." He slowed his pace and said, "Ok, now we will cross the street and enter."

Dodging small lorries and the ubiquitous black and yellow taxis, we crossed the street and walked into a narrow passage.

Vivek continued his narration. "It is essential for others to understand what a slum is. Most people think slum just means a poor, crowded, and dirty place filled with garbage and homeless people, but a slum is a settlement. A place where people have built illegally on government land or land that no one has claimed. Slums are established during construction efforts. When people come in for a building job, they need a place to live. So, they find an area nearby and build homes for themselves, often with leftover material from the main site. Once the construction effort is over, the people stay and the slums live on. Dharavi is the largest slum in Mumbai and has been here for over one hundred years."

"So this really isn't a giant homeless camp."

"Not at all. Everyone here is working very hard, often in two or three different jobs. In fact, there is a lot of pride here. People here feel fortunate to not sleep in the streets. Fortunate to have work and enough money to have a roof over their heads in the slum."

We'd worked our way into a dark, narrow passage, roughly paved in broken concrete. Wobbly stones barely covered a sewage culvert at my feet. Overhead, tangles of power lines sagged, sometimes down to eye-level. The humid air was heavy with spices and sweat, both occasionally overpowered by sewage in places where pipes were broken or hastily patched together.

"This is the residential area of the slum. You can see how crowded it is," he said, pointing to a small doorway in the alley where someone had left the sheet pulled back. It was a small concrete rectangle, no more than six by eight feet. By the arrangement of blankets and pillows, it appeared that four people lived in the tiny space. There were no windows other than the doorway.

"What about sinks and toilets?" I asked.

"You will see small alcoves where families wash. There is water most days now," he said, pointing to a haphazard set of pipes that ran along the bottom of an exterior wall. Pointing to a rectangular tub area containing a couple of small, plastic stools and buckets, he said, "And people can wash here. Sometimes you will see a small alcove in a home where people wash. Bathing is very important, and you'll find everyone in the slum washes once a day."

"How about toilets?"

"They are a problem. There are not nearly enough here. Some NGOs have installed open toilets where they can, even if it's only an alcove with a drain. There are also toilets across the street, which cost five Rupees. People that cannot afford that, or if it is too crowded, may use some primitive arrangements by the water."

I didn't ask anything further, feeling embarrassed by the clean, flushing toilet I had even at the budget hotel.

The residents seemed to take little notice of us. One or two said hello, but for the most part, we were ignored. As we transitioned into the industrial section of the slum, Vivek explained that RealGiving was the only one to give tours in the slum. The group of elders who informally ran the slum had been very resistant to let them offer tours, as concern for the pride of residents was paramount. As a compromise, visitors were not allowed to take photographs, lest residents be treated like zoo animals. It was a brilliant policy that I completely understood.

The change in environment was mostly visible in the spacing between buildings. Where the residential area was tightly packed with alleys as narrow as two feet, the space between the rows of concrete and corrugated metal structures here was four or five feet, with some passages opening up to small courtyards, mostly used for staging material.

In one space, burlap bags were piled at least twelve feet high.

"What is all of this?" I asked.

"Plastic. Two-thirds of all plastics in Mumbai are brought to the slum for recycling. Dharavi even has a contract with Air India, so all of their plastic waste is recycled here. Let's go inside."

We shuffled around the huge bags into a tall and narrow garage-like space. Four people squatted on the floor, each pulling apart discarded magic markers. Their hands moved like lightning, taking a marker from one bag and dismantling it, then throwing the cap, body, and ink pad each into a different pile. Around them, bags like the ones outside were stacked perilously high. There were literally tens of thousands, if not hundreds of thousands, of markers crammed into the small warehouse.

One of the workers, a young boy, pulled together the corners of a large sheet of burlap under a pile of blue marker caps and tied them into a knot. He hoisted the sack, easily four times his size, onto his shoulder and pushed out the door.

"What happens to the plastic?" I asked.

"It will be crushed into tiny pellets next door and then cleaned in chemicals. After that, it will be melted and turned into something else. Let's go upstairs."

We carefully stepped over the family as they sorted. Vivek pushed a few bags to the side and revealed a small, rusty ladder. We climbed up and through a hole in the floor above where more sacks of plastics waited. Two mattresses were stuffed into a corner, reminding me that the residents used every square inch available.

We took a second ladder up through an opening on the roof. It was covered with trays of plastic pellets drying in the sun. We carefully walked through the maze to the edge of the building. Below us was a sight to behold. Acres of rough metal roofs spread in every direction. Some were covered with tarps for the rain, others were littered with drying plastics, metals, and other little bits that looked suspiciously like peppers. Plumes of dust and fumes and smoke flowed freely across the slum, blurring the tall buildings of the city proper in the distance.

We climbed back down the ladders to see the family still sorting away. Vivek thanked them, and they were kind enough to look up and give me a smile. Their hands never stopped moving.

Our next stop was a metal recycling facility, something that at home would span acres and be surrounded by sturdy fencing and an army of lawyers to handle environmental impact lawsuits. There, it was a shed no larger than a couple of horse stalls built with pitted and sooty brick and cinderblock. Men in shorts and flip flops wore only gloves for protection from the blistering heat. The fumes meant these workers rarely lived far into their forties.

We carried on farther, my mind still trying to process the conditions these men and women worked in every day. At one point, a tray of bread neatly wrapped in plastic popped out next to my knees.

"Bakery," Vivek said, pointing down.

I stooped down and looked through a small passage. Half a dozen people were in a tiny basement surrounded by racks of cooling bread. One man worked a metal pole in a brick oven, the heat continually blasting. I stood up, and Vivek held up one of the loaves that had been passed through.

"Notice the label? Buyers from the markets and restaurants don't want Dharavi written on the packaging out of fear that people won't eat it if it comes from the slum."

"So millions of people don't know their food comes from here, do they?"

He shook his head *no* as a man shouted to him from above. Through a glassless window over the bakery, a man sat at a sewing machine. He and Vivek exchanged a few words, and a shirt was tossed down.

I looked at the label, and it was a brand commonly seen around the world. "Is this real, or an imitation?"

Vivek waggled his head. "Sometimes they are fake, but more often than not, they're real. Plenty of companies know they can have garments made cheaply here."

He bundled up the shirt and tossed it back, thanking his friend. After visiting a leather shop, we found ourselves in a roughly rectangular-shaped patch of dirt. The sewage smell was stronger thanks to an unmoving river next to the open space. The dark water was filled with trash and things I shamefully didn't want to think about. A few young boys played cricket on the dirt using a plank of wood for a bat. A couple of paint cans stood in for the stumps. They ran across the rocky surface in bare feet amid small chunks of discarded concrete.

"The school cricket pitch," Vivek said with pride. "It is also used by the girls for football, what you call soccer."

"I am glad they have the open space to run."

"The residents know that this space is for the kids. It is important to play when you're growing up, isn't it?"

"It is."

"I will show you one of our schools."

We walked around a couple of rough structures before arriving at a surprisingly well-built schoolhouse. Rows of classrooms on the first floor were for primary school children and faced a small dirt courtyard. The second floor, reached from a precarious concrete staircase with the rebar still poking out of some edges, was the secondary school. Two of the rooms contained several computers.

"In secondary school, we continue to focus on English and soft skills, but we also put considerable attention on teaching computer use."

"What do they learn on the computers?"

"Microsoft Office. Our goal is for the students to leave here with basic skills that will allow them to learn more and get jobs outside of the slum."

We proceeded back to the top of the staircase where Vivek wrapped up his tour. Below us, bits of trash blew across the stony courtyard, collecting under the school's outhouse. The teachers and students worked under challenging circumstances, to say the least, but every day, they provided hope. They brought opportunity.

***

I spent days after the tour trying to make sense of everything I was experiencing in Mumbai. Extreme wealth stood side-by-side with severe poverty, beautiful colors blossomed beneath dismally polluted skies, and genuine, peaceful smiles of people stood taller than every disadvantage. I was amazed by every sight, smell, and taste, and ashamed that I'd been scared to come here.

The thought of the people working so hard and living in such severe conditions in the slum was always top of mind, so when I found myself outside a sporting goods store, I knew what I wanted to do for the afternoon.

By the time I reached the edge of the slum, I was drenched in sweat, the two large plastic bags sticking to my shoulder. I had only a rough idea of the direction I needed to follow to find the pitch, but after the first few turns in the dark, narrow paths, I was utterly lost. At one point, I thought I'd reached the industrial area, but one turn later, realized I'd made another wrong turn. In a small, open space, a half dozen women rolled *papadams*, setting them on large wicker umbrellas to dry.

"Excuse me," I said. "Can you point me in the direction of the cricket pitch?"

One of the women looked up at me but said nothing.

I lowered the bags and pulled out one of the cricket bats before miming that I needed to know which way to go. The woman stood up and gestured with her hands, showing me the direction and a couple of turns.

"*Dhanyavaad,*" I said. Thank you.

I followed her instructions, and after a few more wrong turns, finally found it.

The boys on the pitch had no idea who I was, but they certainly knew what I had in the bags. Three became five, and five became eight, then a dozen.

"How are you guys doing?" I asked, lowering the bags off of my shoulder.

"Hello!" the smallest one said, offering a smile.

His friends quickly added their own hellos, repeating the word on and on until I'd said hello a dozen times myself.

"What do you have?" the smallest one asked.

"It looked like you needed some cricket gear, so I thought I would bring some."

"Yes! Yes!" he said, diving into the bag.

I reached down and held it shut. "There's one condition, though."

He gave a broad smile, still trying to open the bag. His feet were doing a little dance.

"You have to teach me how to play, ok?"

"Yes, we will teach you cricket!" he said.

I released the bag, and they dove in, pulling out the two bats, some practice balls, and a package containing two sets of stumps.

"We only need one bat," he said.

"There's an extra just in case the first one is lost. What is your name?"

"Lokesh!" he said with pride.

"Ok, everyone. Lokesh is in charge of the extra bat."

Lokesh took the bat to the side of the pitch. Laying it down next to a short wall, he covered it up with a scrap of wood. "Safe for later," he said.

Some of the boys set up the stumps, hammering them into the hard-packed soil with rocks. Others took turns hitting. One took the plastic packaging and bag and set them off to the side, reminding me that nothing goes to waste.

I spent the afternoon in the heat and dirty air doing my best to understand the game amid the young children, loving every minute. It was chaos, but the smiles on their faces when I did something right made it so worthwhile.

As the sun went down and my soaked shirt began to drip, I thanked the boys and carried the soccer balls over to the RealGiving school. While the students had gone home, a thin young British man remained.

"Looked like you were having fun out there," he said. "I'm Graeme."

"Nice to meet you, Graeme. My name's John."

We shook hands, and I held up the bag. "These are for the girls. I understand they play soccer here."

"They do. Girls here take on a lot of responsibilities in their families, so it takes plenty of encouragement to get them out on the pitch. When they come, they learn teamwork and responsibility. Ultimately, it gives them strength and confidence."

"You are doing great work here."

"Thank you. We love it here. Can I show you around?"

"That's ok. Vivek showed me yesterday."

"Did you take a tour?"

"I did."

"But you came back. Why?"

"Seeing the kids playing with just leftover materials didn't seem right."

"Most people who feel that way send a donation, but you came back and played with them."

"Well, those smiles are pretty inspiring."

He studied me for a few awkward seconds. "How long are you in Mumbai for?"

I raised my hands. "Not sure. My plans tend to be open-ended."

"Know computers?"

"Sadly, yes. I was once an accountant."

"What are you now?"

"Just a traveler. Making my way here and there."

"How long so far?"

"About five years now."

His eyebrows raised. "Good for you. Even the hard case travelers don't make it that long."

I shrugged.

"Want to stay and help for a while? Help the students learn Word and Excel? We could always use a skilled volunteer."

The scuffling of feet echoed from below. Two little girls had come into the courtyard. Graeme shouted hello, and they looked up and replied. With heavy clouds blocking the remaining light, all I could see were their smiles.

"The students here are lovely. I can promise you'll go to sleep each night with a full heart."

I thought a moment. I'm not sure why, because my mind had already been made up.

***

The start of my volunteer work coincided with the beginning of the monsoon season. It would have been easy to dislike the constant, heavy rains. They strained the infrastructure, overflowed drains, and flooded streets and the narrow passages of the slum. Trains and cars were delayed continuously, and the gridlock was horrendous. But to my surprise, a sense of happiness came over the Mumbaikars during the season. Couples huddled closer, and families smiled knowing their relatives' farms were getting much-needed water. And the festivals, oh how the Indians loved to celebrate. It seemed like just as your spirits dropped, the streets would fill with music and color to remind you how precious life there was.

I got to know the staff teachers and meet volunteers from around the world. The students, though, were magical and taught me far more than I returned. In the classroom, they were brilliant, picking up difficult concepts with ease. I became particularly attached to a young boy and his older sister after learning they were the family I'd seen sorting the plastic markers my first day in Dharavi. I'd often stop by their small factory in the morning with *pao* buns from the basement baker and butter or fruit from a local market. Sunil and his wife, Chandini, would make chai and share a story, kindly taking a break from their work. After school, I would walk home with Divya and her eight-year-old brother, Mohit. More often than not, I found myself helping with the family's work for an hour or two before walking back to Bandra.

It was mid-September when the rains finally ended, far later than usual. The island city was more soaked than it had been in years. More than one building in the slum had begun to lean and crack, something that in hindsight should have had us more on edge than we were.

The building just next to Sunil and Chandini's recycling business collapsed just as I was coming by with *dosas* and chutneys. The ground, too saturated to support the weight of the three-story building filled with machinery and barrels of chemicals, simply gave up. A brick wall went first, sagging inwards and buckling the roof and floors like they were made of twigs. This set off a chain reaction, immediately bringing down Sunil's building and the next two structures. Chunks of concrete fell around me. A woman and her baby ducked in the center of the passage, and I quickly pushed them to the side of a stable building, huddling over them until the immediate danger ended.

After making sure they were ok, I looked up to see the path ahead was filled with rubble and dust. Over the screams of men, women, and children, I shoed the mother off, telling her to send people back with as many first aid kits as they could find. I attempted to look for injuries on children running away, but by the screams coming from the piles of rubble, I thought that if these kids could run out, they were likely ok. Or at least in less jeopardy than those trapped inside.

People climbed up the piles, hurriedly tossing pieces of concrete to the side to free those below. Heavy, jagged rocks were rolled down, often hitting someone just below doing much the same thing.

I grabbed the arm of a man next to me and said, "We need to do this carefully."

He ignored me and continued frantically throwing debris behind him.

But another man had heard, and he began yelling instructions. Suddenly, more joined in, and several fireman's chains loosely formed, shuttling rubble across the street to some factory space that was being hastily cleared opposite the site. More men and women joined in, slowing only when we uncovered someone who'd been trapped. Most of the injuries were broken bones and lacerations. Some had severe chemical burns, but as of yet we hadn't come across anyone who had died in the collapse.

"John! John!"

I turned to see Sunil clamoring up the rubble behind me. "Tell me the kids and Chandini are ok," I said.

"The kids are safe. You were late. I sent them off to school and went to the shop for some parts."

"Chandini?"

"Inside," he said, his face grim.

He dove in, digging madly, piece by piece. More men joined us; a few were policemen, which was unsurprising as more than half of the Mumbai police force lived in slums. They were the most official help we would get, I knew, given that fire and rescue vehicles could never make their way through the narrow alleys and passages.

"*Yahaan!*" someone shouted from next to a section of the wall that hadn't collapsed.

We rushed over and saw him pointing at a hand sticking out from beneath a large slab of concrete.

"Chandini!" Sunil shouted. "Chandini"

The fingers moved slightly.

A section of the floor above had fallen. And while one side was on the ground, the other had caught on the last stub of wall. She was trapped in the A-shaped space beneath, but I worried the section of wall wouldn't hold it forever.

We cleared as much rubble as we could around it, hoping she could shimmy out of the opening.

"Chandini, can you hear me?" I said.

"Yes." Her voice was faint and weak.

"Sunil and I are right here, ok? We're going to get you out."

There was no response.

We continued to pull rubble out and make an opening for her. Finally, there was enough space for me to lay down and stick my head through the gap.

She was face-up, pressed against the wall. One arm was free, and she was able to turn and look when I touched her hand. It was too dark to see much beyond her face.

"Can you slide out to me?"

"My leg is trapped."

"Ok, Chandini. I see what we need to do. We're going to get you out, ok?"

I turned to Sunil and said, "Her legs are trapped under this section of floor. We need to lift it up to get her out, but I'm worried about the front portion falling off the wall if we do that."

"Ok," he said.

"It's easier for you to speak Hindi with everyone here, so here's what I want you to do. First, get some men to build a support for the front. Solid wood or bricks. We don't want this falling. Second, send some people to find a jack of some sort. Third, send as many guys up here as you can. We'll try to lift this first, and only use the jack if we have to."

He turned and immediately began issuing orders to the group. A support was quickly built by her head as more men cleared a path around to the other side of the slab. I bent down to Chandini and spoke calmly to her.

"Ok, Chandini, we're working on lifting this off."

"Ok. I am not feeling well, John."

She was likely losing blood. "I understand. Concentrate on me, on our voices, ok?"

"Yes," she replied weakly.

A stretcher had been set next to me, leading me to believe at least someone from the fire brigade had arrived. A group of huge men had come and stationed themselves at the far side of the slab.

One of them, I recognized. A gang enforcer named Harish I'd been warned to avoid.

But disasters don't take sides, so I looked right at him and asked, "You ready to give it a try?"

He nodded.

I checked on the front of the slab, and the men there said they were ready too.

Sunil crouched next to me, and we got as close to Chandini as we could. I put my arms under her shoulders and said, "Now!"

The men grunted, shifting the slab slightly. But it was not enough.

Harish shouted, and more men appeared, squeezing in with the others. Once they were in place, he looked at me and nodded.

"Now!" I shouted again.

The slab made a grinding sound next to the wall, and I knew it was lifting.

"We're going to try now, Chandini," I said, pulling as gently as I could, knowing that the slab could shift at any moment.

Her body moved, and she groaned. She moved an inch, then more. When we had her halfway out, Sunil took my place, and I ducked farther under the concrete.

With my head wedged between the slab and the ground, I worked a hand under her bottom in concert with Sunil. When her entire body was free, I nodded to the men straining opposite. The slab fell violently to the ground and snapped in half, collapsing the pocket that had protected her.

With me supporting her head and shoulders, Sunil carried her to the stretcher and set her down as carefully as possible. One leg was a mess, and judging by the angle and blood, it was an open fracture.

"Chandini," Sunil said. "Can you hear me?"

There was no response. Her pulse was weak, as was her breathing.

"She's passed out from the shock or blood loss. We need to get her to the hospital now."

We grabbed the ends of the stretcher and retreated through the rubble. Harish saw me struggling to walk backward in the debris and crowd, circled around us, and cleared our way through the maze of passages. Groups of firemen began to arrive carrying medical kits and more stretchers. We passed with little acknowledgment, each hoping the other could make it in time.

The courtyard of the hospital had been set up as a triage center where injured slum dwellers were being evaluated. We carried Chandini right to the center of the crowd, and the gangster led a doctor our way before deftly disappearing.

She came to Chandini's side, and I said, "She was trapped beneath a ton of concrete. Open fracture to the leg. Unknown internal injuries."

The doctor felt for a pulse and held her cheek over Chandini's mouth.

"I had a weak pulse and breathing earlier. Now?"

The doctor said, "Yes, both. Let's get her inside."

She shouted to some orderlies who took the stretcher from us.

"You stay with her, Sunil. I will take care of the kids."

"I will."

I held his shoulders. "She's going to be fine, Sunil. You stay with her, ok?"

He blinked twice, then nodded.

"Do you have your phone?"

"Yes," he said, patting his pocket.

"Keep me posted on how she's doing. I will text you when I have the kids. Now go!"

He chased after the orderlies, and I said a quick prayer for Chandini.

Back at the school, emotions were palpable. Some students and staff had left to help with the rescue efforts and check on relatives. Several people had been enlisted as runners, going back and forth with news to keep everyone up-to-date.

Finding Graeme in the upstairs hall, I asked, "Mohit and Divya, are they still here?"

"Yes. Their parents?"

"Father is fine. Mom is in bad shape. Broken leg and unconscious. Sunil, their dad, will keep me updated. What's the update here?"

"So far, almost everyone's parents have been accounted for. At least twenty injuries reported. Two deaths."

"The count will go higher," I said solemnly.

"Judging by the dirt and blood on you, I take it you were there?"

I nodded. "Right around the corner when it happened. It's a miracle that only two people were killed. Where are Mohit and Divya?"

He let me out the door, pointing to the art room. "In there."

I walked to the room and entered. At least a dozen children of different ages were in there. Prisha, one of the teachers, was talking softly to them and stopped as I entered. Everyone's eyes fell on me. I wanted to pull them aside and talk with them alone but had come to understand that privacy here wasn't held to the level it is in other cultures and by the looks on everyone's faces, they were all desperate for any information.

Divya sat next to Mohit, holding his hand. I went over and kneeled next to them. "I was just with your dad. He is fine," I said. "We found your mother together. Her leg is broken, and she's not feeling too well, but she's at the hospital now."

Mohit turned to his sister, his eyes wide, wanting to make sure he understood. Divya, who was fourteen and spoke excellent English, translated for him.

He stood up and grabbed my hand. "We will go to the hospital to see Mama now."

I set him back down gently. "The doctors at the hospital are very busy now, Mohit. The best place for you to be is right here with Prisha."

"But—"

"I know it's hard, Mohit, but we need to let the doctors help."

"Will you stay with us, John?" Divya asked.

I wanted to go back to the site and help with the search effort. Every bone in my body ached to return, but rescuers were arriving as I was leaving and every able-bodied resident would be digging until the last bit of rubble was moved.

And I'd promised Sunil that I would be here for the kids.

"Of course I will, Divya."

***

The teachers and volunteers who stayed at the school did their best to keep the children busy and distracted. We sang, drew, and played football in the courtyard. I heard from Sunil that Chandini's injuries were limited to her leg, and she'd made it through a complicated surgery to repair multiple fractures. The news came in the early evening just as the childrens' aunt and uncle arrived, and the entire family practically collapsed in relief.

They would take Mohit and Divya back to their home and stay with the family until Chandini was well again.

As the last child left, I collapsed in a chair in Graeme's office. He turned his office chair to face me, rubbing his eyes and letting out a long, solemn exhale.

"What's the latest," I asked.

"Three deaths now, and the number of injured is over thirty."

I closed my eyes and sighed. I'd only been volunteering in the slum for two months, but the people I'd met had a special place in my heart. They were kind and welcoming, always offering chai, something to eat, or even just a smile, despite having next to nothing. They were proud, strong, and determined, and a tragedy like this was entirely unfair.

"What can we do?" I asked.

"The office will redirect some funds for clearing debris and rebuilding, but it won't be much. The government will pitch in, but that won't be much either. They never really want to admit to the problems in the slums, much less address them. Hopefully, the Red Cross will engage."

The slum's relationship with the government had never adequately functioned. For a time, there were redevelopment plans. Plans to re-house residents were presented as entirely positive. The reality, though, was that slum businesses would be bulldozed as the land was redeveloped by private companies. No compensation was to be given, likely because the informal economy of the slum had always operated outside of the government tax structure. The people of Dharavi would have ended up far worse than they were. And since that meant they would become an even more significant problem for the government, the plans were eventually scrapped.

"And will it be enough?"

He shrugged. "I imagine enough can be given to rebuild the buildings that collapsed today. Don't forget how things are built here. With materials 'found' around the city or recycled right here, no permits, and a virtually unlimited and entirely motivated labor force. I think if the government and NGOs stayed out of the way, those buildings would be replaced overnight."

I smiled at his accurate appraisal.

"I don't think you're asking about just those buildings, are you?"

"I guess not," I replied, leaning back and looking up to the dirty ceiling.

"You already know the answers. Education and healthcare. The better-educated people here are, the more opportunities they have for a life outside the slum. The better educated they are, the better decisions they can make for themselves and their families, something especially important for the girls here as they grow up to be women. And healthcare…well, you've seen the conditions. It goes without saying."

"Opportunity, then."

"Yes. Handouts, whether they're money or food, are fine for short term problems, but the people here don't want handouts. They want a chance. A chance to do more. And the best we can do is give them the strength and power to go out and do more."

I could tell he was fired up. But I was done. Tired and still in the dusty, blood-stained clothes I'd worn digging earlier in the day. "I think we'll have to solve the world's problems tomorrow, Graeme."

"We can and will," he said optimistically. "Goodnight, John."

I stood up and wished him a good night before leaving. At the last minute, I peeked my head back through the doorway. "That policy you have on the tours. About not taking photographs. Any chance for an exception?"

"You have an idea?"

"Maybe. Could be a way to raise funds for rebuilding. And for schools."

"I'm for it if you're discreet, but the elders here, their enforcers won't like it."

"Think they can be reasoned with?"

He shrugged.

That would have to be enough.

***

"Hungry, are you?" came a booming voice behind me.

I smiled, looking down at my plate. Or plates, as it was. "No breakfast like this at my place, that's for sure."

I was back in one of the restaurants in the Oberoi, indulging in every western delight I could and loving every bite.

"It is so good to see you, John!" Omri appeared to my left, arms wide.

I stood to hug him, saying, "And you too, Omri."

His voice was strong and his smile as warm as ever. But he had aged since I'd last seen him in New Zealand. His hair was more salt than pepper, and the shadows beneath his eyes had deepened.

He ordered coffee, and we caught up. While we messaged one another frequently, getting together in person was a treat. After a second cup of coffee, he ordered yogurt with an assortment of fruit. It was quite unlike him, and I suspected he was following a doctor's orders.

"Are you going to be ok going out in the field old school?" I asked.

"You think I have been spoiled shooting fashion photography?"

"I *know* you have been spoiled," I said, not hiding the smile on my face. "Remember, I've shot on-site with you. Remember Lyon? There must have been eight assistants and who knows how many caterers."

He laughed. "That's not fair. It was Prada, and they weren't going to spare any expense."

"And Nantes, where we needed twenty-some policemen to block off the street."

"The cobblestones there were so perfectly arranged," he said. "But to answer your question, yes, I remember the old days shooting with natural light and having to change my own lenses. Don't forget, I taught you!"

"That you did."

"I also wanted to tell you that I've spoken with a few companies. They are interested in helping, but they need a story with the pictures. We need to make a case for them to focus their philanthropic efforts here."

"You'll see the stories today, Omri. They'll both fill your heart and break it in half."

"We should probably avoid the heart references, John. Mine's not doing so well."

"What is it?"

"Too much wine and cheese. Maybe women and song too."

"In New Zealand, you said you were on some meds and hitting the treadmill."

"Both still, and I had a small procedure to help one of the arteries. But no good news yet."

"I'm sorry, Omri."

"I am still strong, though. What is our plan for today?"

I knew he was changing the subject. "Today will be easy. We'll take a tour of Dharavi to get you oriented. The young man who will show us around is Vivek, and he actually grew up there."

"Are we shooting today?"

"I want you to see it without a lens first."

***

As we sat in the NGO office with Graeme after the tour, Omri said, simply, "Incredible."

"They are, aren't they," I replied.

"They are fighters, John," continued Omri.

"They don't want handouts, but even if they did, it wouldn't last. Wouldn't be right," I said.

Graeme continued the thought. "As John told you, our feeling is that education in addition to decent medical care is what's needed here."

"John told me about your ideas, and I think they are brilliant," Omri said. "The schools, can you scale them easily with more funds?"

"We've set them up so we can. We have the model and the volunteers, and we can secure several more physical spaces in the slum."

"And medical facilities?"

"That's harder. Hospitals need space and doctors need supplies. The best bet is to partner with the Tata Trusts. They're the ones making headway here."

Omri nodded. To me, he said, "We can get the designers on board for this. Let's tell them a story."

We set out the next day to do just that, starting in the Kumbharwada area of the slum known for pottery making techniques that have been handed down for generations.

"Astonishing," Omri said, marveling at the plume of black smoke rising from a kiln.

"Scraps from the textile mills fuel the fire at the bottom of the kiln. The smoke is horrific, which is why the sides of the buildings in this area are black," I explained.

"Nothing goes to waste here, does it?"

I introduced Omri to the elder potter, Lokesh, and they immediately fell into conversation about the techniques used. Before long, they were sitting together drinking chai, chatting like they'd known each other for years.

We spent three days together in the slum, Omri always taking the time to get to know someone before bringing out the camera. I fell into the role of assistant, swapping batteries and lenses and holding a reflector when we needed to highlight the spark in someone's eye.

I'd missed working with Omri. His charm in the world of high fashion was always boisterous, if not a bit cheeky. Much to my surprise, it worked just as well here, and it was beautiful to see how quickly the residents warmed to him.

He selected his shots carefully, delicately juxtaposing dismal conditions with the hope and promise found in the heart of every resident. He captured a man pouring molten aluminum into casts wearing only sandals, breathing toxic fumes that would limit his lifespan to less than forty years. The image was balanced by the beautiful smile of a mother being splashed by her young son as she washed him in a narrow passage. He paid particular attention to the children, like a young boy carrying an impossibly heavy load of fabrics and three little girls dancing in a puddle during a brief sun shower.

He was particularly fond of Mohit and Divya. After meeting Chandini on her crutches and hearing the story of the building collapse from Sunil, he asked the kids to be his assistants, explaining that I really wasn't doing a good enough job. They loved him instantly.

On his last night in Mumbai, I stayed late in the hotel with him, not wanting to see him go.

14

It was four weeks later that Omri returned. Only this time, he arrived with board members from the philanthropic sides of Louis Vuitton, Chanel, and Gucci. Together, they presented a donation check to RealGiving that eclipsed anything they'd ever received before. Graeme and the other directors were stunned by the support.

We took them through the slum, letting them meet families in the residential areas and workers in the small factories. We told stories of the slum, both heartbreaking and inspirational, many of which I'd been there to see, for better or worse. Graeme shared his vision and hopes, along with his plan to realize them.

If I was worried our visitors wouldn't want to be walking the dirty, tight passageways in their shiny thousand dollar shoes, within minutes it was clear that I couldn't have been more wrong. The small entourage from Europe was caring and compassionate, interested and full of questions. At one point, a young girl approached Alessia Ricci, the former creative director of Gucci and now the head of their charitable foundation. The girl reached up and touched Alessia's scarf, admiring what was likely a one-of-a-kind creation. Alessia complimented the girl's own hijab before being led into a tiny home. When they eventually returned, I was touched to see they'd traded scarves and both couldn't have been happier about it.

That night, at dinner in the dark, upscale luxury of Hakkasan, ironically not far from Dharavi, a lively discussion revealed that while fashion had always championed AIDS and breast cancer causes, the industry had grown so much that even more funds were available. As a group, the leaders in fashion wanted to broaden their range of charities and the idea of supporting education in the slums was an ideal place to start.

In the months that followed their visit, more labels joined the effort. Fashion houses in France, Italy, and the UK sent not only funds but volunteers. Graeme was skeptical before the first group arrived, worried they might be only breezing in for a photo op and causing more of a hassle than actually helping. Thankfully, his concern was entirely misplaced.

They came in small groups, perhaps a week at a time. Sometimes they were models, and sometimes they were from marketing, operations, or manufacturing. More often than not, it was a blend of all different types of people who flew down to volunteer for a week. They read to the children, played soccer and cricket on the pitch, or helped us work on the spaces we were refitting as new schools. It was rare that a photographer was sent down with them, but on those few occasions, they were discreet and just as willing to pitch in as everyone else.

A perfect example was Omri, who flew down with Camille and a small group from Hermès. While Camille had come to make a donation of her own and volunteer during a break in her schedule, Omri claimed his role was to photograph the people from Hermès. I smiled when he explained this, knowing the real reason was that he was proud of the work we'd started together and wanted to see the progress. Whatever their excuses, I was happy to have a visit from my friends.

Naturally, Camille was completely at ease with the children in the schools. They made her smile, and she made them smile through the course of the week. She worked with the younger ones on art projects and just as easily played with the older girls out on the soccer pitch. Even the constant requests for selfies were met with a smile as I took her around to share the stories of perseverance I'd learned through my time there.

One evening, we'd talked with Sunil and Chandini over chai for far too long and it had grown dark before we'd realized it. I led our way back to the edge of the slum, holding Camille's hand to be sure she missed the low pipes and dangling wires. I'd always felt completely safe in India, even more so in the slum, but at night it was generally wise to be attentive, especially with a visitor. As we rounded a corner into one of the narrower passageways, I immediately came into eye contact with a good-sized, rough-looking guy. His expression was impassive if not a little stern. I drew Camille a bit closer behind me, excusing myself as I made it obvious we wanted to get around him. Rather than step back, he moved forward, effectively blocking our way as he looked over my shoulder at Camille.

Over the years traveling, I'd picked up a few street smarts. I was far from an expert but had enough practice to be immediately calm. My mind quickly cycled through a number of things I'd come to know about Mumbai and the slum, that it had always been safe for me, that the gang activity I'd heard of usually dealt with misappropriating cargo and things of the like, and the underworld was known to be more giving to slum dwellers. But the fact remained that we were pinned in a tight passage in a country that's no stranger to attacks on women. I took a step toward him, knowing not to escalate but also to confidently stand my ground.

"Evening," I said calmly.

He simply stared. But staring is so prevalent in India that it's not a signal Westerners can decode.

In a clear and non-threatening voice, I said, "Excuse me. Just need to get by." I took another step forward, my face now illuminated by the light coming from a doorway behind him. I could see a few other men now just inside, their backs turned, forming a partial circle. Wonderful. We'd just stumbled upon the gang equivalent of a local union meeting. I edged forward a few more inches, close enough that I could smell his breath.

A flash of recognition passed in his eyes. To my surprise and great relief, he edged backward slightly.

"*Dhanyavaad*," I said, drawing Camille in behind me.

I'd spoken too soon. His hand reached out and pressed on my chest. I went still. But again he surprised me, removing his hand with a brief 'wait' gesture before tapping the back of the man next to him with his other hand. The reinforcement he'd called to action turned. It was Harish, the gangster who had helped Sunil and I pull Chandini from the rubble.

"Hello, Harish," I said keeping my tone neutral, still not knowing where this was going.

I needn't have worried. The big fellow gave me a huge smile. Sure, there were a few gaps in it, but it still put me at ease.

"John!" he said jovially as if we'd been friends for ages. He extended his hand.

I shook it and said, "It's good to see you again."

"It is very nice to see you," he replied. His voice was higher than I would have guessed, and his English startlingly clear.

"The woman you helped us pull out," I said. "We just came from her house. She's doing well now."

"Yes, Chandini," he said matter-of-factly. "I have made sure the family is ok. Her sister is a friend of my cousin's wife." He sounded quite proud of his relationship to her, despite the oddness of the connection. People here just tended to look out for one another.

"That's very nice of you, Harish."

"You want one of the boys to help you back to your hotel?"

Another thing about the people here I'd forgotten is that they always knew everything about everyone. I wasn't surprised he knew that I'd been living in a hotel. He could probably tell me the address, room number, and the last time my towels had been laundered.

"Thank you, Harish, but I can get us back. Just knowing you are looking after Chandini and her family is enough."

He smiled at the compliment before turning to Camille. "I have seen your picture on billboards. You are more beautiful in person."

"Thank you," Camille replied. Her voice was kind as always, but I knew her well enough to hear some tension remained.

"Could we have a picture with you?" he asked.

"We should probably get going," I said.

"We have time for a picture, John," Camille said. The smile she gave was genuine, showing she'd already bounced back.

Harish handed a phone to his colleague for a photo. Before long, the rest of the group had squeezed through the doorway and I was balancing on top of a bucket, getting them all in the frame. After a dozen different shots, I explained we needed to leave.

Harish spoke Hindi to the others before dismissing them. "I told them to keep an eye out for you. If you need anything, put the word out, John."

"Thanks, Harish," I said. "I appreciate that."

Camille said goodbye, and before long, we were outside the train station and hopping into a cab. As we joined the traffic south to the Worli Sea Link, she grabbed my arm with both hands and burst into laughter. "I was terrified, John!" she said.

"Can't say I wasn't a little concerned myself."

"What?" she asked. "But you were very calm. You kept moving *toward* him!"

"Someone once told me that if you're worried about getting kicked by a horse, you get as close to them as possible. That way, the hoof doesn't have the momentum to hurt as much. Harish's friend was about the size of a horse, so I thought the same rule applied."

"You are serious?"

I shrugged and gave her a smile, which only caused another round of laughter.

***

Omri and Camille spent their last day with me in one of the new school rooms, adding a fresh coat of paint to brighten the old, stained walls. A few local residents moved in and out through the day, something that should have provided a distraction. But instead, I found myself bogged down, trying to make sense of something that had been bothering me.

Omri had been unusually quiet during his visit. Typically rather energetic and optimistic, he had been more reserved, spending a little more time with the NGO's staff than I'd expected.

Camille had been different as well. Her authenticity with Mumbaikars was certainly there, her voice the same and her laugh just as quick and heartfelt. But still, there was something. It wasn't apparent in casual interactions, but I knew her well enough to have sensed it more than once during the week. A smile would start from the cheeks instead of the eyes, or the shoulders would lower a fraction as if resignation was trying to sneak up on her resilience. I watched carefully while we worked that afternoon, allowing extended periods of silence to see if either of them would fill the empty space.

It didn't work. I'd forgotten how clever my friends were.

As we finished, a few young girls took our brushes and paint cans outside, dragging Camille with them.

Alone now with Omri, I confronted him. "Tell me what's going on," I said.

"We are painting. Are you critiquing my work? Thought I did pretty well!"

"You know that's not what I mean."

He regarded me carefully for a moment. "It's for her to explain."

"That won't do, Omri."

He picked up a rag and focused on wiping his hands. "She is struggling right now."

"What happened?" I asked with some urgency.

He held the fingers of one hand up, then pinched them together into a cone shape and slowly pulled down. It was the Israeli gesture to be patient. "You know of her boyfriend, the race car driver?"

"Sure. Jorgen. Can't help but see pictures of them together in the news. I've been happy for her and have told her as much several times."

Before he could reply, a laugh from Camille in the doorway silenced us. She came in with one of the girls, both of them smiling.

"You didn't tell me I was covered in paint!" she jokingly admonished, her head down as she wiped spots of white from her arms. After a second, she looked up and instantly read our expressions. The smile evaporated.

Omri watched for a second before holding a hand out to the little girl. "We should leave these two alone for a minute."

She gave him a questioning look as he took her hand and they walked outside.

I gestured for Camille to help me pull the plastic off a desk and sit down. She closed her eyes and sighed. I took a rag and added a dash of bottled water to it, then cleaned a smear of paint from her forehead. When I was done, she took the cloth and wiped a spot on my nose.

"There is a little in your hair too," she said. Her hand moved up and rubbed the top of my head. "You will need to get it out in the shower."

We were stalling.

I put my hand on her arm, slowly pulling down as I sat next to her. "Tell me," I said simply.

She looked down at the rag and picked at the threads with a nail. "It is nothing, John."

"It's something, Camille. Something with Jorgen."

"Omri talks too much."

"To be fair, all I got out of him was Jorgen's name before you came back."

"It is over now, Jorgen and I."

"I am sorry, Camille." I put my arm around her.

She leaned into me, hiding in the crook of my neck.

"What happened?" I asked.

"It does not matter."

"Friends talk about feelings. It helps us sort them out."

She stayed silent, which was troublesome. I hoped she hadn't been hurt in some way.

"Tell me," I said.

"No, John. It is too difficult now."

"It's me, Camille. We share."

She turned away, absently looking across the room, and said, "Do not push." Her voice was low, her tone morose.

I waited a bit before letting it rest. "Ok, then."

She stood and began uncovering the remaining desks.

It was apparent little more would be said, so after a moment, I stood and joined in. Once all the tables were uncovered, we began to set the seats in place.

She moved brusquely, avoiding eye contact. At one point, she argued about where a chair should go. Her tone was slightly rude, which was extremely unusual.

"I know you're upset, Camille, but you don't have to snap at me."

"Argh!" she said, roughly sliding the chair across the room in my direction.

"That's enough," I said, wanting to end this madness. "If you won't tell me what's going on, you don't get to take your frustrations out on me."

She turned to face me and stared for a second. "Fine, John. Do you want to know what happened?"

"I do," I said.

"He asked me to marry him," she said, her voice weak.

"What? But you…"

"I said no."

"Oh, no. Why?"

She crossed her arms, her hands cupping her elbows. "Why? Why do you think, John?"

"I honestly have no idea."

"Think about it," she said, her head tilting down.

I shrugged. "Think about what?"

"Am I going to wait forever?"

"Wait for what?" I asked.

Her arms opened, and she looked up at me. "What do you think, John? You come to Paris, you take me off my feet and then leave! You let me see you sometimes, so strong and caring, but still, I wait!"

My stomach tightened, and the small classroom suddenly felt far too warm. "Me? You're waiting for me?"

Her eyes closed. She turned away to face the door.

We'd always been so close, able to understand one another, even across the years and mountains that had separated us. Of all things, how could I have missed this? Heat rushed to my ears. She'd made a leap that I hadn't. That I couldn't.

"I thought you understood," I said. "That you knew what I was doing, what I am doing." The words came out thready, and I knew as soon as they passed my lips that I was unfairly deflecting back to her.

Her shoulders curled as she began to cry.

"Camille, I'm…I'm not there. I'm sorry. I can't be. There's still…I'm still…"

"I know, John. I have always understood," she said. Her back shook with shallow breaths.

Every muscle in my body wanted to spring forward, to wrap my arms around her and let her know how much I cared for her. But it would be unfair. It would mislead her again, bring her to a place from which I would only cause more pain. I could never do that to her. She was kind and loving, someone gentle and genuine, full of life that she was willing to share unconditionally. It hurt to hear I'd been holding her back, that I'd stolen her chance for happiness.

I had to help her. And to do that, I had to let her go. Let her not be held down waiting for my dents and dings to heal. If they ever would.

"Don't wait for me, Camille," I said.

The movement in her shoulders stopped abruptly.

I hated myself for every second I stood there feeling her anguish.

And even more when she walked out.

***

Late that night, there was a knock at my door. Omri came in silently and sat down on the small, imitation leather couch.

"Why was she waiting, Omri? I'm not much more than a wandering, lost soul. She knows this more than anyone."

"She's been in love with you for years, John, probably since that very first day. She held those feelings in, buried them as much as she could to give you the time you needed."

"That can't be true, Omri. She's had dates. Boyfriends. Just look at the news."

"One boyfriend. Jorgen. That's all. Any others you've seen were only friends."

"Still, there's Jorgen."

"Yes," he said, nodding. "But his pursuit was relentless, and she was growing weary."

"Why is this even coming up? We haven't been on the same continent for ages."

His eyes lowered. "His proposal. It took her back. It would have closed a door she's always left open for you."

"How can someone so intelligent be so difficult?"

"She is full of passion," he said. "And passion beats logic every time."

"This is my fault, isn't it?"

He tried to lighten the moment by giving an Indian head waggle, the local equivalent of an 'almost' yes.

"I'm not ready, Omri. I just can't yet."

"This quest of yours, this search, is going to end someday. What are you going to do then?"

"I have no idea," I replied quite honestly. "But Camille has a whole life in front of her. She shouldn't wait. Goodness knows what shape I'll be in at the end of whatever this is."

"Do you really know what you are doing here, John?" he asked, turning serious.

"No," I admitted. "But I want her to have the life she deserves. She's one of the good people, Omri. She should be happy."

"Don't cut her off."

"I have to. It's not fair to her the way it is now," I said.

"Think about it. Think about how natural you two are with each other. Think about what she's been through letting you go."

"It's the best way," I said. My head fell in shame. "Help her understand, Omri. Please."

"What are you going to do?"

"Put my attention here. It's positive, the most positive thing I've ever done. Hopefully, a little will rub off."

He went silent, watching me. Waiting. Eventually, he stood.

We exchanged a hug in silence before he finally turned and walked out.

***

I threw myself into work, helping with the children, and pitching in where I could rebuilding Sunil and Chandini's business. Week after week, I wore myself to the bone, using exhaustion as my distraction.

Sadly, it didn't work. I remained unsettled, and as a result, the dense madness of Mumbai started to wear on me. I'd come to love the people, especially the children in the slum, but they weren't getting one hundred percent of me. As the next monsoon season loomed, I was honest enough to realize it was time to go.

It was with sadness that I left the friends I'd made. Their sheer determination was as inspiring as their kindness. I'd contributed. I'd made a difference, even if it was at my own small scale, and I was content with my decision to seek a little solitude. I needed to experience the calmness I'd felt in Southeast Asia once again and decided to set off for the mountains of northern Thailand.

I was hiding, I knew. Running away. But I couldn't help it.

Walking through the duty-free shop travelers weave through on their way to the gates in Mumbai's airport, I passed more than one backlit advertisement featuring Camille. In all the airports I'd been through, they'd given me a little laugh and reminded me to send her a message.

This time, they made me sad and ashamed.

15

Chati and Anong, the couple from whom I'd rented a room in Chiang Mai, were absolute models of the tranquility I sought. Their grown children had moved to Bangkok for work, leaving a couple of rooms to rent. I was their only tenant, and they took great care to check on me before and after they went to work at a local tourism office every day.

In the evenings, I walked down to the night market. Strings of light illuminated table after table of goods for sale. If you needed it, you could find it there. Everything from phone cases and trinkets to every type of clothing possible. There were fruit and vegetable stands, every one of them full of vibrant scents and fantastic color. But it was the food vendors that won me over. Curries, grilled meats, quail eggs, mango salad, boiled pork balls, and anything else you could imagine was served on a stick or banana leaf with pride.

Learning that mango with sticky rice was Anong's favorite, I made sure to bring some home each night. They always invited me in, offering tea or homemade rice wine before giving me suggestions for the next day. One night, their idea was for me to be a 'caretaker for a day' at a local elephant sanctuary, and they had made a booking with their favorite reserve.

I'd learned from other tourists in town that this was a favorite activity in Chiang Mai. Elephants had a long history in Thailand. They carried kings and served in battle and were considered holy to the point that they became an integral part of Thailand's identity. As the wars ended and building began, the glorious animals were forced to work as the tractors and bulldozers of the logging industry. They were pushed to their limits, clearing tons of timber day after day, prodded on by the sharp steel of bullhooks, a vicious tool used to puncture the most vulnerable areas of their bodies. After logging became illegal, elephants were brought into towns to perform for tourists. Chained in cities away from their natural habitats and herds, they again suffered a miserable existence.

As more people recognized their tortured conditions, elephant sanctuaries were established in the hills. Through donations, elephants were purchased from loggers, circuses, and street performers and set free in acres and acres of dense, tropical hills to live as they once did.

I was picked up early the next morning by Panit, the owner of the sanctuary. He was thin and more than a little dirty but chatty and happy as could be. We picked up a pair of British backpackers and an American family of four, and as he drove us through the hills to his farm, Panit told us about our plan for the day.

As it turned out, his schedule was off by nearly a year.

It started innocently enough, with Panit and his colleagues bringing us to a young, male elephant to learn about their care. Morning was a time to check their health, making sure there was a little moisture at the base of the toenails, the skin was wrinkly but hydrated, and the 'poops' were moist. Elephant dung, apparently, was essential to inspect, and I was instructed to pull one of the softball-sized gems in half and smell it. So it was with some displeasure and a scrunched up face that I picked one up. I'd carefully selected a sample that was slightly dry on the outside, hoping that it would be less foul after being in the sun for a little while.

"That one old! Get fresh one!" Panit admonished.

Reluctantly, I replaced it. So much for being clever. I was surprised to find it was not unlike a ball of damp grass you'd find clumped in the bottom of the lawnmower. With Panit's impatience growing, I pulled the perfectly round ball in half and sniffed. The odor wasn't foul or offensive and was in fact, slightly sweet. As herbivores that digest only about half their food, elephants produce poop that's not too far off from what they eat to begin with.

After the lesson, we walked to an open space by a small river where a group of elephants had congregated around a shelter that had been built for shade. A group of young Thai men and women were scattered among the elephants, and Panit explained that they were the elephants' caretakers, called mahouts. Each mahout had a close relationship with a couple of elephants and was directly responsible for their care. Panit sent the Brits and Americans off with some of the mahouts and directed me toward a small man in a straw hat and red poncho.

The man greeted me with the Thai wai, placing his palms together before extending his right hand. As I shook it, he introduced himself by placing his left hand on his chest and saying, "Sunti."

"Sunti," I repeated. Apparently, I had the pronunciation correct because he gave me a beaming smile.

I placed a hand on my chest and said, "John."

"Yes!" he replied. "Gohn!"

Close enough.

He directed his attention to our elephant and said, "Madee!"

"Hello, Madee." Turning back to Sunti, I said. "Is Madee male or female?"

"Yes!" he said.

Ok, so Sunti's vocabulary appeared to be somewhat limited, but his smile more than made up for it. Madee towered above the other elephants the guests were meeting, and by size alone, I assumed I was looking at a male. A quick check of the undercarriage indicated that Madee was actually female, and she was staring right at me.

Sunti pointed to a basket of bananas and stalks of sugarcane behind me and said, "Yes!"

I picked up the basket and approached Madee. She raised her trunk in the air and opened her mouth. I grabbed a green banana and held it near her mouth, hoping she would take it from my hand gently and leave most of my fingers attached, but she just stood there, calmly waiting.

Sunti took the banana from my hand and showed the correct procedure, which involved literally placing the banana in her mouth, right on her V-shaped tongue.

"Yes!" he said as Madee very gently moved the banana back toward her teeth and began chewing.

Once she raised her trunk and opened her mouth again, I fed her another banana. More gently and carefully than I would have ever imagined, her lower lip brushed my hand. As she chewed, I put my hand on her cheek. Her skin was thick as armor and prickly with sparse hairs, and I could feel the muscles of her jaw working as she chewed.

"Aren't you beautiful," I said softly to her.

Her trunk reached around me and headed toward the basket.

"Guess I'm not fast enough. What is it you're after?"

I held the basket out and watched as she used the point at the end of her trunk to nudge a piece of sugarcane. I picked it up and fed it to her, utterly amazed with the way she used her trunk to move it to the side and farther back to better chew the thick stalk.

Someone approached, but I couldn't take my eyes off the fantastic animal. She was massive and strong, yet gentle and calm.

"I pick Madee for you, John!" Panit said.

I turned to him and said quite honestly, "She is incredible."

"She is one of first two elephants here. Madee and other one, Lawan, work in bad logging camp, but balance very good because hard to walk on mountain."

"What are these spots?" I asked, pointing to a large pink area on the bridge of her nose between and around her eyes after placing a pair of bananas in her mouth.

"Not spots. Skin color go away there when elephant old. We do not know how old is Madee. Maybe forty years old."

Madee nudged me with her trunk, reminding me to give her the last piece of sugarcane.

"Now she know you, you clean skin. Skincare very important for elephants!" He handed me a group of leafy branches tied together with long grass and showed how I could use it as a small broom to get the dirt off her back.

When I took the brush from him, he said a couple of words in Thai and Madee went down onto her knees and rolled gently to one side.

"This easier," he said now that I was eye-level with her back. "You brush all dirt from sleeping, then we wash in river."

I used the leafy brush to clear off the clumps of dirt, still stunned by her size even as she lay next to me. When I'd finished, Sunti waved his hand and she stood back up. He gave her a gentle rub on her trunk and then walked to a small river a few meters away.

Madee promptly took the little broom from my hand and ate it. I sure hoped I wasn't supposed to hang on to that. As she chewed, she used her trunk to give me a nudge toward the river. I smiled at the fact that she knew exactly where we were going.

The three of us walked into the shallow water, and Madee lay down once again. Sunti handed me a small bucket and a brush and pantomimed that I should scrub her skin. As I washed and rinsed, Panit returned, explaining the scrubbing removed parasites left behind by the dirt and mud. Madee seemed to be enjoying herself, lifting her trunk as I scrubbed behind her ears and down her neck. I let the brush do the work, clearing out the dirt in the wrinkles of her skin, hoping she enjoyed a little spa time after spending years in logging camps. Once I was done, Sunti said something to Madee and then walked up to the bank of the river. Madee stood up, and together we followed him up to the grassy field.

Once everyone was together, we headed into the hills. Panit's sanctuary was several hundred acres of varied terrain, and he explained the elephants could find every food they needed for a healthy life. As we walked, he circulated among us, taking time to explain the benefits of each type of plant and how the elephants' bodies told them what species they needed at any particular time.

The foliage became thicker and more varied, and Madee pulled branches and clumps of leaves with her trunk and placed them in her mouth. At first, it appeared she was just going down the buffet line, taking a big scoop of everything. As we continued on, I began noticing that she would use her trunk to nudge individual plants out of the way to get a specific variety. Her steps were also very calculated, with a slow precision that avoided sloping rocks and always had her feet on a stable section of the path no matter how small.

At one point, she hesitated in her stride, and I realized it was because we were both about to step in the same spot. My foot would have been crushed in a second, but the old girl knew precisely where I was. Despite spending much of her life being beaten and forced into labor by humans, she was going out of her way to make sure she didn't hurt one.

My goodness, Lauren would have loved these beautiful, gentle creatures.

As we made our way up to a pond formed by a small dam in the river, we took a break for water and a quick rest. The elephants continued eating but stayed nearby. Below us was the valley where we'd started, an oval-shaped patch of green surrounded by lumpy foothills and the mountains we were now on. As I admired the perfect bowl shape of the landscape, I could see that almost halfway around the ring of mountains was an open hill, much like the one we were on. An elephant stood there all alone.

I turned to Panit and asked, "Is that one of the bulls?" He'd explained earlier that while elephants moved in a herd, older males would often roam alone.

"That is Lawan. Friend of Madee. She is girl."

"Why is she off by herself?"

"Lawan very sad. She have baby stillborn three years ago. Elephants always sad when another elephant die. When baby die, more sad."

"When will she come back to the herd?"

He shrugged. "Sometimes one year. Her, longer. Don't know why, but she not well. Maybe die soon."

"Can you treat her? Make her healthy again?"

"Veterinarian try long time ago. Not possible to save her, and he think maybe she just old. Now she no let any human come near. No let any elephant near her. She stay alone."

She was so far away that I couldn't tell where she was looking, but something told me she was watching us. I only wished I knew what she was thinking.

I sensed more than heard a presence behind me, then Madee's trunk pushed against my shoulder and moved up and cupped around my face and nose.

Panit laughed. "Madee like you!"

I pushed her trunk down. "Apparently."

"She say time to go."

And so we did, carrying on into the forest with Madee right behind me. After some time, we arrived at the pond formed at the source spring of the river and I watched with fascination as several of the elephants walked straight into the water.

Despite being rather small, the pool was quite deep, and the elephants were quickly submerged. They began to roll and play with only their trunks and the top of their broad heads above the water.

Panit offered the other tourists to swim with them, which they did with great pleasure. I took off my shirt and sandals and jumped in, laughing like the others as the elephants brushed against me, their coarse hair tickling my sides. At one point, Madee's trunk, then face, popped up not an inch from me. Her dark eyes looked straight into mine. Her trunk moved to my side, and I felt her pushing me. Staring at the wrinkles around her eyes, something told me she was smiling. I relaxed and let her gently swing me around to her back.

"She want you swim with her, John!" Panit said.

I stretched out across her back, my hands on her head and my body resting on her tough skin. She turned and swam out to the middle of the pond. Behind the smile, I couldn't stop, my eyes swelled. Of everything I'd experienced on this journey, if I had to remember only one thing, it would be this very moment.

As she rolled and went on to play with the other elephants, I swam to the rocky shore. Panit was fiddling with the camera he'd been using during the day to take pictures of the tourists. I sat next to him and dried off with my T-shirt.

"Camera broken," he said.

"What's wrong?" I asked.

"Everything dark. No picture."

"Let me see."

He passed it over, and I looked through the viewfinder. It was ok, but pressing the shutter only resulted in a black image on the screen. I flicked through the menus and saw the settings had been inadvertently changed, resulting in almost no light hitting the sensor. I made some adjustments, and it worked fine.

Turning to give the camera back to Panit, I saw that he'd left and was presently using a basket on the end of a long bamboo handle to scoop some dung balls out of the water. I didn't want to leave the camera on the rocks and decided to pick up where he'd left off taking pictures. I took a few dozen photos of the tourists and elephants smiling and enjoying themselves before eventually returning the camera.

After a delicious lunch Panit's colleagues had prepared, we set off back down the mountain. During a break on the way down, it was clear that the youngest of the American family's children was out of gas. She was perhaps ten or twelve, and the hike up had worn her out.

A mahout that had been walking with the family took the girl over to one of the elephants. He said something in Thai, and the elephant bent a front leg. The mahout illustrated she should step onto the elephant's heel, then onto its knee and climb up to the elephant's neck.

Panit appeared next to me and said, "You watch. This make girl happy."

The girl climbed up, and the mahout told her to shift forward.

"Is it ok to ride the elephants?" I asked.

"Sometimes," he replied. "Old way to train elephants for ride is very bad. They are trapped in box or hole in ground and beaten. We give food and love, and sometimes they happy to give small ride. If elephant not happy, no ride."

"How do you know if they are ok with it?"

"Boy will want ride soon. You watch, then tell me."

"Are they strong enough to take the weight?"

"Some people say weight bad for elephant spine if ride long time. Children are small, so it is ok. For big man like you, only ok for short time, not long."

"Don't worry, I am fine walking with Madee."

He smiled, pointing to Madee and Sunti who had joined us. "Yes, she happy walk with you."

Just like Panit predicted, as soon as the girl was on top of the elephant with a smile a mile wide, her brother wanted to ride. I asked Panit for his camera and went over to watch. Through the viewfinder, I saw the mahout take hold of the elephant's ear with one hand and place his other hand firmly on the elephant's shoulder. The elephant adjusted position slightly, and then bent the right front leg, just as the girl's elephant had.

After getting a few photos of them both, along with the smiling but nervous parents, I returned the camera to Panit. "If the elephant invites them up by bending a leg, then it's ok," I said.

"Very good, John!" he replied. "Are you photographer?"

Not long ago, I would've said I was an accountant. I didn't really know what I was now, and simply said, "Yes."

He nodded. "I look at pictures in water. Very good. Thank you."

"You're welcome."

Upon returning to the valley, the elephants were all given bundles of tall grasses and plants, indicating the end of our day with them. Panit took pictures as the tourists posed, and I couldn't help but just stand by Madee in admiration. It was with great reluctance that I let Panit pull me away for the drive back to town.

***

As I was leaving the house a few days later, Chati stopped me, holding out his phone for me to take a call. It was Panit, and he asked if I could photograph tourists for him the next day. Apparently, some of them were from one of his charity sponsors and he wanted to give them his full attention. Since I had thought of little more than Madee and the other elephants lately, I jumped at the opportunity.

One thing led to another, and before long, Panit asked if I could join him full time as a photographer. I declined the small amount he offered to pay in exchange for meals and a bed in one of the mahout huts. To say the conditions were primitive would be a vast understatement. There was no electricity other than a solar panel to charge our phones and Panit's computer, no running water other than a series of bamboo tubes set up in a rocky section of the river, and the only toilets were a few outhouses made of thatch and bamboo.

The lack of comfort and not terribly healthy living conditions were inconsequential in comparison to the magic I felt living with the elephants. I came to learn their different personalities and notice their emotions go up and down as our own do. I saw them play with each other, rolling in the dirt on the dry days and sliding in the mud on the rainy days. Their comfort with me grew to the point that as I moved around with the camera each day, they would rub up against me. It was something I thought of like a hug and always returned the gesture.

I would occasionally catch glimpses of Lawan in the hills, digging through the bush for just the right plant or watching us as we marched through the mountains. One evening as we prepared baskets of food for the next day, I decided to take one up the hill for her. I set it down in the middle of a clearing I knew she frequented. The next evening, it remained untouched.

As time went by, I fell into a pattern. Every few days, I would return to Lawan's hill, replacing the basket with fresh fruits and sugarcane. She still wasn't eating anything, but I remained stubborn.

I also fell into a habit of renting my room in town from Chati and Anong one night each week, to give myself a scrub and my clothes a good wash, not to mention have a beautiful night's sleep on a proper mattress in the air conditioning. And with their internet connection far more stable than Panit's, it was nice to post a photo or two and exchange messages with friends.

Camille had removed herself from some of our group chats. Not having her cleverness in the group took some getting used to.

Taking a group of Australians up to the swimming hole one day, Panit brought along a pair of binoculars. "You look," he said, pointing across the valley to Lawan's hill.

Lawan was standing over a basket I'd left, pulling a little bunch of bananas out.

"Great!" I said, thrilled that she'd engaged even in this small way.

I redoubled my efforts, leaving food out for her every other day. Sometimes it was a basket of bananas, other times a considerable bundle of long, leafy grasses or cucumbers I picked up at the market. And while she was never there when I dropped the food off, it was always gone when I returned. It was progress. But still, she remained reclusive, never engaging with the other elephants or staying nearby when I hiked up. It was only from a distance that I could see her. Standing alone. Watching.

Each time we caught sight of her, I studied Lawan through the binoculars. She was massive, larger even than Madee, and showed more pink down her trunk and ears than the others. At times, almost her entire face appeared white against the rich, green landscape. It was her overall build that bothered me most. I'd spent enough time with the other elephants to be familiar with their body shapes. Whereas the body mass of the others surrounded them, it seemed that Lawan's bulk hung lower, resulting in her spine and hips being more pronounced. Even her cheeks sagged, making the distinct shape of the Asian elephant skull more prominent. Her sadness and weakness could be sensed even from hundreds of yards away.

A few times, I lured Madee up Lawan's hill. My thought was that if rejoining the herd was intimidating, seeing an old friend on her own might make it more palatable. Since explaining my plan to an elephant wasn't easy, it took a significant number of bananas to encourage Madee to join me. The first couple of times, she lost interest halfway there, and when we did finally make it, there wasn't much food remaining to leave behind. I had the sense that Lawan was watching from the tropical forest next to the hill, and I wanted her to see that Madee was part of the effort.

Still, we never saw her. When my evening hikes up became daily, and I was even skipping a few weekly breaks in town, I knew I'd become dangerously obsessed. I tried different foods, going at dawn, and also bringing the elephants she'd given birth to with me. Occasionally, I would carry blankets and spend the night on the hill amid the mosquitos, the fear of snakes and nasty insects inconsequential. The mahouts began to think I was crazy. Perhaps they were right, because each time I visited that hill, I could feel her stare from the jungle.

One morning after returning from a night spent on the hill, Panit stopped me on the way to meet the visiting tourists.

"You look bad, John."

"Thanks, Panit. Good morning to you too," I replied not hiding the edge in my voice.

"She dying, John. Sad from baby and old. This how nature works. Ok for her to die."

"I know, Panit, but she shouldn't be alone. Even if she's sick, she should be with the herd. She should be with Madee and her children."

"She see them every day, John. She ok."

"But you know the elephants, Panit. They need the herd, the companionship."

"She no want to make other elephants sad."

Not wanting to make others sad when you're dying. Just like Lauren.

"She's making me sad, Panit."

"Maybe she see that also. But you look bad. Maybe scare tourists. You go to town and rest, ok?"

I felt the stubble on my chin. Seeing the grime that came away on my hand, I suspected I was a bit frightening. "Will you leave something out for her? So she knows we're still here?"

"One of us will leave food every day. You go to town, stay for two or three days. Rest and eat."

He must have called Chati and Anong already, because just as I arrived at the road to hitch my way into town, Anong came on her scooter. Her arm extended and her hand waved in a downward motion, calling me over to join her. With a sympathetic smile, she slid forward to make room for me and carried me into town.

Panit had been right. I'd needed the rest, not to mention the shower. But if he thought the distraction would discourage my effort, he couldn't have been more wrong. I began to bring bamboo up the hill in the evenings, along with some tools. Before long, I'd built a small platform to sleep on that would keep me raised above the snakes and centipedes. After waking up to a horrendous rainstorm in the middle of the night, I added a roof. Each evening after dinner with Panit and the mahouts, I made the hour-long hike up the hill with as much food as I could carry and spent the night. In the mornings, I bathed in the river before joining Panit and the tourists.

As the months went by, I learned more and more about the elephants. Some from books downloaded to the phone, some from Panit and the mahouts, and some from the veterinarians and animal welfare experts who visited. But most I learned from the elephants themselves.

While they couldn't talk, they could tell you plenty. Feelings manifested themselves in the way they walked, played, and even looked at one another. You could hear joy or sadness in their trumpets and chirps or see it in the flick of an ear. You could sense how they felt even through a trunk as it ran over you for a sniff.

After almost a year of living in the hills, Panit even let me lead the small groups of tourists through their first experience with the elephants. I was never tired of their wonder at meeting them for the first time and feeling a connection with the gentle giants.

I felt spoiled that I could spend so much time with them day after day, but never more so than I did waking up one morning in the mist glowing from the morning sun. Visibility couldn't have been more than fifty yards, but I didn't need to see nearly that far, because only five yards away was Lawan. She stood completely still and stared directly at me. I could see every wrinkle, every freckle in the pink splotches on her face and trunk, and every prickly little hair on her head.

Slowly, I folded my blankets back and sat up, thinking she might need to inspect me as well. "Good morning, Lawan," I said.

Her trunk rose slightly and pointed in my direction. Short, steady breaths indicated she was getting my scent.

"Been waiting a while for you."

Her ears flapped.

I looked over to where I'd placed a bundle of food the night before and saw it was gone. "I'll bring some more tonight, ok?"

She gave another snort.

"Everyone down in the valley misses you and would like to say hello."

I received only a bowel movement in reply. I knew it wasn't personal.

"I'm heading down there soon to clean up and have a little breakfast. Want to join me?"

She stared a moment longer before slowly turning and walking into the mist.

My heart filled, happy that my stubbornness had paid off. Glad that in some small way she'd reached out to say hello.

"Panit!" I exclaimed as I arrived in the valley. "You're not going to believe it!"

Pointing to the basket I carried, he said, "I see you bring poops, John. You do not need to bring poops from hill. We have enough poops here."

"They are Lawan's poops!"

"You hunt for her poops?"

"No! When I woke up, she was standing right next to me!"

His eyes went wide, and he smiled. "That is very good, John!" That was a better reaction.

"I know! It's fantastic! She sought out a human. That's pretty unusual, right?"

"Unusual, but you friend. You bring food."

"Her droppings, though. Take a look. They seem pretty loose."

He took one from the basket and studied it. "This ok. She old. Old elephant not digest well. Make poops loose."

He sniffed, and then said, "Smell not good."

"I know. What can we do?"

He shrugged and walked to a faucet. Squeezing some soap out of a cloudy bottle and washing his hands, he said, "Vet needs to be close to see if there is problem. She not like people close."

"How about a tranquilizer? I can put it in her food?"

His brow furrowed. "You know this bad, John. Dose of tranquilizer very hard with elephant. And falling down very, very bad for elephant body."

My shoulders slumped. I knew this but was trying to forget.

"Even with veterinarian, maybe nothing can be done. Elephants hard to make better with medicine. And no medicine to fix being old."

"I know, but…"

"Best medicine in forest. She smart. Eating right plants now."

I looked up at the hills, hoping she was doing just that.

"Best medicine also family," he said. Putting his hand on my arm, he continued. "And you her family now, John. You make Lawan happy, and today, she thank you."

She had thanked me and continued to do so for weeks. Some days it was just a peek through the trees at the edge of the hills. Others, it was a morning wake up like that first day. On a particularly special night, she slept on the pitch next to me after having cleared some grass to make a dirt patch.

One evening, I was late coming up. I'd had a headache for a couple of days and been feeling a little feverish off and on but knew I needed to see her. Sure enough, she was waiting by the shelter when I arrived. Her trunk ran over the carrying pole I'd fashioned like the Vietnamese used and immediately went to the jackfruit I'd brought up. It was a favorite of elephants, and I had to push her trunk away while I used a long knife to quarter it.

"I know what it feels like losing someone you love. It's not easy," I said to her. "It hurts every day, and I don't think you ever truly get past it. But you learn to accept it. The friends I've met helped me see that."

I passed pieces to her as I cut and pulled them off the pointy skin.

"They weren't doing anything specific. They weren't therapists or experts. They were just friends, talking and listening, and giving hugs too. I thought I could—thought I *should*—go through it alone. But really, if I'd done it alone, I would probably still be at home, crying myself to sleep."

I bent down to grab a couple of pieces of sugarcane and noticed that my knees and hips were sore. While I'd grown more fit than ever making the two-and-a-half-mile hike up the hill each night with a load of food, I wrote the aches and pains off to the path being slippery from recent rains. The past few days had been a little tougher on me than usual.

"I don't know why they helped," I said, my mind beginning to wander aimlessly. "I still don't know why Camille, Amélie, and their friends spent so much time trying to cheer me up. Or Omri. Why did he take me in like a son of his own?"

Lawan chewed through the tough sugarcane slowly.

"Mrs. Garland, my neighbor, helped. She'd lost her husband and understood. She tried to tell me about grief, explaining that it wasn't helpful to wish I had died instead of Lauren."

As I pulled apart some bananas, I noticed my back and shoulder were also sore.

"Omri was more the bulldozer type, trying to push me to get on with life. I needed that too. Otherwise, I would have chickened out and gone home years ago." I paused to collect my breath.

Lawan's trunk wandered around my hand.

"And then there's Camille. She didn't try to change me or push me even the slightest. She was a good listener, but mostly, she reminded me to keep things simple. Enjoy the happy times. Enjoy the sun on your shoulders. Smile when you snap off *le quignon*, that pointy end of a baguette, on your way home from the bakery."

Standing and bending wasn't very comfortable, so I sat down in front of Lawan, knowing she could use her trunk to take food from my hands. I pulled out a large chunk of thick bark and held it out for her.

"I think we were good listeners for each other. We got along so well, at least until India. Why did it fall apart there? Why did I *let* it fall apart?"

I wasn't even passing her the food anymore. She was simply grabbing what she wanted right out of the basket.

"Letting her go was wrong, but I was scared. I was confused. It felt like a betrayal. Why did I let her leave like that?"

My mind was wandering, and I felt a little worse. There was a doctor in town who had helped me through a bug I'd picked up in the water a couple of months ago. I figured I should ride into town with Panit tomorrow and see him.

"The point is, Lawan, let your friends help. Let them do whatever they do. Talk, listen, distract, smile. Really doesn't matter. They want to be there for you."

I was feeling flushed, and the thoughts of my friends sent tears down my cheeks. I'd been so lucky to have met them. All of them, from Colin and Klara to Omri. Everyone in between. Perhaps Camille more than anyone. The tears came, and I did nothing to stop them. They didn't come from sadness; they came from thanks. From appreciation for the people who'd just said hello, who'd cared just enough to become a friend.

Suddenly, I felt a slimy mess on my face. With my eyes closed, I hadn't seen Lawan's trunk coming, and it was a bit of a shock. I laughed and kept my eyes shut as she sniffed. Or maybe it was a kiss, and I should add her to my long list of friends too.

Her trunk moved across my chest and shoulders, eventually pushing into my hand. The muscular nub at the end of her trunk flicked between my own fingers and rubbed a few times on my wedding ring.

"Yes, I still wear it. It used to remind me of Lauren. Now? I remember her in my heart. She's part of me. She's what's made me who I am today. This journey she sent me on made me stronger. It's made me happier. She was right, you know. This was the way to accept what happened."

Dizzy, I took a large swig of water. The fever was really getting to me, and I knew I should probably sleep.

"This conversation isn't over, Lawan!" I said dropping the water bottle and stumbling to the shelter. "Your friends and family are ready for you to come home. We all are."

Whoa, I was not feeling good. My head was pounding, and I could tell I was a little delirious. I wished I had an aspirin but kept everything other than blankets and my water bottle down in the mahout huts to minimize my footprint on Lawan's hill. That was feeling like a mistake now. Maybe some water would work, but I seemed to have left the bottle by Lawan. I couldn't go back out to get it as the fatigue overcame me.

I slept fitfully, shivering off and on, having unpleasant dreams, and vomiting a few times. The clouds broke open, drenching the hill. I woke up in the middle of the night, my feet wet where the thatch roof had given up in a few places. I rolled over and felt my water bottle. I couldn't remember how it had gotten there but was happy to drink half of it quickly. As I drifted off, there were sounds of movement just outside of the tent. Perhaps it was the fever.

When dawn finally broke, I opened my eyes only to feel a painful throbbing behind them. Lawan stood just outside the shelter.

"Good morning, darling," I said. "Did you stay there all night?"

She responded by running the end of her trunk across my face.

"Not now," I said, brushing it away. "I feel like absolute shit."

She flicked the water bottle at my side, reminding me to drink.

I did, finishing it. "Thanks. I think I need to get down to the doctor."

I turned and sat, still aching and nauseous, but at least it was light enough for me to make my way down. I just hoped I could. I set my feet in the mud beneath the shelter and slowly tried to stand. I was weak and achy, but if I took it slowly, I could probably make it. A wave of nausea hit, and I vomited all of the water I'd just swallowed.

"Not good," I mumbled, wiping my mouth with a sleeve.

Lawan turned to the side and bent her front leg.

"You sure?" I asked.

I wobbled over to her side, feeling weak but willing to give it a try. I kicked off my shoes, thinking bare feet would be easier on her skin. With my left foot, I stood on her heel, then placed my right foot on her knee. With one hand on her ear and another on her side, I moved my left foot higher, trying to get a purchase on her shoulder. It was slippery, but I felt I had enough of a grip to push up and reach across her withers.

The mud on her leg and my feet had the last word, and I slipped right off, falling straight to the ground. I let out a groan and then quickly moved my feet out of the way. Getting a leg crushed wouldn't help me today. But Lawan still held her foot up, just in case.

"It's ok, girl. I'm out of the way now."

She put her foot back flat on the ground.

I stood up slowly and regained my balance. I put a hand on her ear, ready to try again. Once again, she propped her foot up and I repeated the process, complete with falling flat on my back again. I felt positively awful, the two falls not helping.

"I don't think I have the strength to do it, Lawan." Getting onto my hands and knees in preparation to stand, I said, "I think I can make it walking. Thank you, though."

To my surprise, she gave a little grunt and went down on one front knee, then the other.

I pushed myself up and stood by her. "Aren't you the best friend anyone could have?" I said.

With her a couple of feet lower, I was able to climb up easily. Eventually, I was able to straddle her back and slide up toward her neck. "Ok, I think I'm ready."

She stood up, and I held onto the tops of her ears to steady myself, trying not to grab too hard but not fall off at the same time. When she finally stood, I wasn't sure precisely what to do. I didn't want to kick her, and a 'Giddy up' probably wouldn't help. She'd known I was sick last night and this morning and had wanted to carry me, so I imagined she knew to take me where there were other people and left my fate to her. I wasn't in any condition to tell her otherwise.

Slowly, she led us to the little path I'd worn down the hill. The footing was slick and plenty of the rocks were wet, but just like Panit had told me so long ago, the logging elephants had incredible balance in the hills, and Lawan proved it. I was the weakest link in our pair, with my joints aching, my head spinning, and my balance a mess, but this amazing girl could tell and kept as slow and even a pace as she could, even adjusting her head and neck when she felt me listing to one side.

The walk down took longer than it did when I would walk myself because she was cautious and precise. As the mahout huts, elephant shelter, and herd became visible, I realized the strength she was showing bringing me down. For years, she'd avoided humans and her peers, and she was breaking her solitude for me because she knew I was sick and needed help. I was getting weaker and slouching forward now, but still, I was so proud of her.

"Thank you, Lawan. I couldn't have made it down here myself. I know this is hard, and I want you to know that I love you for being so brave."

I may have mumbled that last part because the exhaustion of just using my core muscles to stay on her back hit me. I slumped forward and rested on the coarse hair at the top of her head. Even with them prickling my skin, nothing felt more peaceful.

I was still in a fog as we came to a stop under the elephant shelter. Large forms moved near us, and more than one trunk rubbed across my back. I vaguely heard some high-pitched voices speaking rapid Thai as I went limp and my vision tunneled to blackness.

16

It was two days later that I was finally coherent enough to understand that I was in the hospital with Dengue Fever. Dehydration along with a low white blood cell count had done me in. The doctors and nurses weren't too excited about how filthy I was, but they were pretty impressed with the fact that a reclusive elephant had brought me out of the hills.

When Panit came over after making the afternoon run to town, he was extremely energetic. "I am glad you are ok, John!" he said.

"Thanks, Panit. I really appreciate you bringing me in. Though I am not quite sure what happened."

"It is incredible! All elephants make trumpet noise. We see Lawan carry you asleep on top! We see you almost fall off, but other elephants hold you up until we come!"

"Lawan, did she stay?"

"She no stay. We get you off, and Lawan smells you, make sure ok. She watches car leave and then goes back to hill."

"Did any other elephants go with her?"

"No, she still sad. Other elephants understand."

The disappointment must have shown on my face.

"John," he said. "It is ok. She help you live! This make her happy elephant!"

I did want Lawan to be happy, but I didn't want her to live the rest of her life alone. "Are you taking food to her?"

"Last night, one man go. He takes veterinarian too."

"Did they see her?"

"No. She does not come out. Maybe she come out only for you. But she knows we still here, thank you to you!"

The doctor arrived to check on me, and Panit took his leave.

"Make sure someone visits her each day, Panit!" I called out as he walked out. "I'll be back as soon as I can."

"You are better soon!"

"Soon" turned out to be over a week spent in the hospital and under the tender care of Chati and Anong at their house. But after that, I was back at Panit's, this time a little more diligent about applying bug spray in the evenings.

The first afternoon I felt strong enough to climb Lawan's hill, I loaded up with jackfruit and cucumbers, her favorite treats. The hot season in Chiang Mai was coming to an end, and a breeze poured down from the mountains as I set my baskets down.

I gave a whistle and called out, "Lawan! Lawan!"

From the dense forest came crashing noises, soon replaced by Lawan peering through the leaves. She hesitated a moment, raising her trunk in the air. Elephants don't have the best eyesight, but they can hear well through their ears and sound vibrations that transmit through their feet.

I stood up and called her once again.

To my surprise, she burst through the bushes and headed straight for me.

There's some debate as to whether or not elephants actually run or simply walk fast. I'd heard a couple of experts discussing it one day, and the issue seemed to be that they always have at least one foot on the ground. So if running means at some point in the motion, all feet are off the ground, then technically, elephants cannot run. At this moment, however, it was apparent the experts had never had an elephant running full steam directly toward them. What I saw was without a doubt running. In a few seconds, I was going to become the world's expert on elephants stopping. Since I didn't want this title posthumously, I sidestepped at the last second to be on the safe side, but the big girl stopped with plenty of time and immediately wrapped her trunk around me.

"It's good to see you again too, Lawan," I said.

She had pushed me right into her chest and was running her trunk across my neck and head.

"I am all better now. Better thanks to you. Thank you for saving me, beautiful girl."

Smushed as I was between her front legs, I could feel her heavy breathing. There was a significant wheeze to each breath that didn't sound good.

"I don't want to comment on your age, Lawan, but how about pacing yourself a little bit?"

She shifted her weight between her front legs, moving her chest side-to-side almost like a little dance. I rubbed her chest and gave one of her legs a hug. There really aren't that many choices on how to hug an elephant, but if anyone deserved a good squeeze, it was her.

The days resumed their usual pace, photographing the tourists as they experienced life with the elephants, taking home memories and an understanding of how these beautiful creatures needed to live as they once did, peacefully roaming the hills. Unfortunately, I'd become part of Panit's lecture on the intelligence of animals. He'd built quite a story around Lawan saving me, which resulted in a barrage of questions. I did my best to make sure my responses praised the elephants and the work

Panit was doing to save them, but still, it felt a little awkward to have cameras pointed at me instead of away.

As the cool season came to an end, I didn't think I had it in me to go through another rainy season. I'd come to think of Chiang Mai as home, with the beautiful people so warm and kind. It had been comforting to learn about Buddhism, which I'd come to think of as the one religion of peace. But after a little more than a year in these hills, it was time to move on.

On the last evening, I climbed Lawan's hill, once again loaded with treats for her. She was slow to come out of the bush but still wanted to feel me push against her broad, wrinkly chest. Actually, it was something we both wanted.

"I'm leaving tomorrow, Lawan," I said. "Panit and the boys will still come up here, though. I want you to visit them when they do and tell them how you're feeling, ok?"

Her trunk went down to the basket and wiggled it before raising up in the air and exposing her open mouth.

I smiled and said, "Ok, here you go," as I gave her a large piece of jackfruit.

"I am going up to Hong Kong for a little bit, and then on to Japan. Panit's going to call me if you need anything, though, ok?"

As I fed her the last of the treats and hugged her goodbye, I felt terrible. Would she expect me tomorrow? How do you tell an elephant that you won't be back? All I could do was tell her I loved her through the tears.

***

For two months I made my way northeast. First Hong Kong and Shanghai, then Japan. I was unsettled, never really embracing the experience of each new city.

One gray afternoon, as I struggled through the crowds in front of the Glico Running Man in Osaka, my phone pinged. It was a message from Pat.

Lawan had weakened to the point of collapse.

The vets were on the hill working on her and some fluids had helped enough to get her up, but he sounded like it wouldn't be long now.

Four hours later, I was on a plane; twelve after that, I was back in Chiang Mai.

I'd arrived too late at night to hike up the hill, so after a brief, restless sleep, I arrived at Panit's door just as the sun illuminated the morning clouds. He came out dressed and ready, and immediately gave me a hug.

"We miss you, John," he said.

"I've missed all of you too," I replied. "How is she?"

"She not good. Vet say not too sick but losing weight. Elephants' teeth—"

"I know. Once their last teeth are done, they can't process the food. How are her poops?"

"Loose. Whole plants coming through. Smell not good."

I held up a large basket of apples and soft fruits I'd grabbed at the market the night before. "Hopefully, she can still enjoy these."

"We see."

"Let's go."

At the top of the hill, Lawan was nowhere to be found, but a line of hollowed-out logs carried a constant flow of water from a stream I knew to be just inside the tree line. They'd dug a small pond for her for water and a way to cool off.

"Thank you for this, Panit. And thank you for calling me."

He nodded, and I could see the sadness in his eyes. "Elephants like to have last time by water. Also by family. Baby that die buried right over there."

He pointed to a spot just off the center of the hill. Some branches, both old and rotting and new, rested there. I'd always wondered why she picked this hill. Knowing only made it sadder.

I whistled loudly and called her name.

We watched the forest for movement, but the trees remained still.

I whistled and called again.

Still nothing.

Again, I tried. Over and over.

"She slower now. We give her time," Panit said.

Defeated, I let Panit lead us back to the shelter where we sat on the edge of the raised floor. A tarp had been added to the top. I wasn't sure if it was because the rains had been terrible or my construction technique had been inadequate.

Panit told me about Lawan collapsing and how the vet had said there was little that could be done for her other than the fluids he'd administered. It had been enough to get her back up and moving, but he couldn't say how long that would last. I asked more questions about her treatment, never getting the answers I wanted to hear. It wasn't Panit's fault, nor the vet's, I knew. It was age and sadness, and all I could do was simply be there for her.

He changed subjects and began to talk about the sanctuary. One of the females had given birth just yesterday, and they'd recently acquired a logging elephant that had been blinded in punishment at some point in its hard life. They were currently watching to see which of the other elephants would bond with it, in hopes that she would pair off for help navigating the new environment.

I listened as much as I could, but my mind wandered, hoping Lawan was ok.

"I know you have to get back down to pick people up in town. I'll walk through the woods, see if I can pick up her track."

"I will send food up for you," he said.

I gave him a hug. "Thank you, Panit, for messaging me. I appreciate it. I just hope I can say goodbye."

"She wait for you, John. You see Lawan soon."

I only hoped he was right as I set off into the forest. I'd planned to establish some sort of grid, walking back and forth or setting out on a half-circle path and gradually widening it, but the thick growth prohibited my systematic approach. Young plants tangled my feet, trees arced in every direction in their quest for light, and moss-covered logs forced constant changes in direction. I resorted to following the game paths forged by Lawan and the other elephants over the years.

I tapped a stick in front of me, hoping to keep any snakes away. I whistled and called until my throat was raw and my lips were dry. There was plenty of evidence of Lawan to be found, from trees that had been rubbed bare or kicked down as she scratched her back to discarded vines she'd uprooted to get to a specific plant or minerals in the soil, but as darkness fell, I still hadn't found her.

I returned to the clearing on the hill just as the last of the light faded. Someone had left a small cooler along with several bottles of water, a thermos of tom yum soup, and fresh blankets in the shelter. They knew I wasn't coming back down tonight.

I set my pack at the foot of the makeshift bed and opened the cooler, not realizing how hungry I was after walking in the thick bush all day. I tore through the spring rolls and cold fried chicken legs, followed by sweet sticky rice wrapped in banana leaf. The soup I saved for later in the night to ward off the chill.

As I tidied up, the rain came, pattering gently on the tarp above. I wrapped myself in a blanket and huddled in for the night, alone. Waiting.

The rain grew heavy as the night wore on. Intermittent downpours pulled me out of fitful sleep, thinking I could hear her walking toward me. When morning finally came, there were no new elephant prints. The sounds I'd heard and hoped for had sadly been my imagination.

I rubbed the sleep from my eyes and ate some of Panit's tom yum soup, now barely warmer than the temperature outside. I laced up my boots, the same ones Anika had given me so long ago, still damp inside from yesterday's search.

"I'm here for you, Lawan," I said, standing up and stepping into the rain, heading for the jungle once again.

The going was harder today. Broad leaves laden with water hung low, drenching me at every turn. The paths were slick, and I fell more than once. A few hours into my search, I was covered in mud and jungle debris enough that if the tourists walked by, they would think I was from a remote hill tribe. Soaked to the bones, I carried on, whistling and calling. I went deeper into the trees and higher than I had the day before, still hoping. Still not finding a trace. At one point, I fell, sliding ten meters until slamming into a rotting log. I stayed there, not wanting to get up and crying that I would never find her again.

Was this the peace Lauren wanted me to find?

I doubted it. This was misery.

"One more time, Lawan!" I screamed into the trees and thick, wet leaves and vines. "I just need to see you once more, ok?"

I rolled onto my hands and knees. A centipede more than eight inches long scurried away. An excellent reminder to stay on my feet.

I brushed off the dead leaves and whatever else had been around the old log and carried on, but having been turned around so many times, I arrived back at the open top of Lawan's hill.

There she was, poking her trunk around inside the shelter.

"Lawan!" I shouted as I ran to her.

She backed up and turned toward me, letting out a series of chirps and squeaks.

I ran straight to her and pushed deep into her shoulder. "There you are, girl! I've been looking for you!"

Her trunk ran through my hair and down across my face before wrapping around my neck.

"Yes, Lawan. I love you too. Come now, let's see how you're doing."

I extricated myself and looked at her. She had thinned some, making her hips more visible and the two bulges on her head more prominent. The staining below her eyes had darkened. I tried to hide my sadness. It was like meeting an old relative in the hospital, where you put on a happy face. You both know it's easily seen through, but that fact is ignored because of the unspoken understanding that you need to be positive.

"I know your chompers aren't doing so well, so I brought you some softer treats." Reaching for the basket in the shelter, I saw she'd already helped herself.

"You cheeky girl," I said. There were still a few things left, so I grabbed a banana and peeled it for her, hoping it would make chewing easier.

I fed everything I had brought to her, hugging her in between every bite. Afterward, I led her over to the pond of water and let her drink. I stood next to her, watching our reflection in the water. I wondered if she could see the two of us together in that image. A sad and lonely wet elephant next to a sad and lonely muddy man, both content only because they were together. Both made a little happier only by the other.

The rain started again, and small circular waves erased our reflection bit by bit. Lawan turned around, and I went to her side. Her trunk wrapped around my arm, and as she took a step, she held me by her side.

I walked right next to her, my hand on her shoulder, as she headed for the pile of branches she'd set over the years where her baby was buried. We stopped a few feet away, and she wrapped her trunk around me and pulled me into her chest. I leaned in, pushing as hard as I could, wanting her to know I was there. We stood in silence, in a mix of sorrow and comfort. In a peace of sorts, a peace that comes from being together in the saddest of times. With our touch, we were giving each other strength. Strength for what was to come.

She took a step back, her trunk making sure I stayed clear, and gently laid down on her side. Once she was settled, I laid down in the crook of her neck, and her trunk wrapped around me. Just like Lauren, she was comforting me until the end.

Through the tears and the rain, a dark form approached. It was Chayan, Lawan's first baby born at the reserve. The fully grown male with long, beautifully white tusks stopped just inches from my legs.

"I think it's time, Chayan," I said, barely choking out the words.

Lawan's trunk lifted from my chest and extended to her son's.

"Look how beautiful and strong he is, Lawan," I said, knowing the two hadn't seen each other for years.

As their trunks twisted about, more of the elephants came. Her two daughters came to her side, letting out low rumbles and covering Lawan with kisses. Others gathered around, and before long, Panit arrived. He pushed his way through and sat opposite me. Lawan reached with her trunk to him before wrapping it around my chest again.

"Isn't she amazing, Panit?" I said through tears.

His sad eyes belied his smile. "She is beautiful. But you beautiful too, John. You make her happy elephant."

"She knows it's time."

"Yes, she know. But she lucky elephant."

"Luck isn't saving her."

"No. She lucky because she will be reborn with good and happy life. You know samsara?"

I nodded. Samsara was the cycle of actions in life leading to a new existence in death. It had always struck me as beautifully optimistic.

"Lawan live happy life because of love you give her. She save you too. These things good for her."

"I hope so, Panit."

"I know this. She come back happy because of you. Maybe you meet her again as happy baby elephant. Or cheeky monkey that eat and play all day. Maybe she pretty bird flying over you."

I tried to smile. "How about an owl. Peaceful and wise. And beautiful."

He nodded vigorously. "Yes! I like this!"

I wrapped my arms around her trunk and looked into her eyes. The notion of death in Thailand was something it had taken me a while to be comfortable with. There was sadness, of course, but there was also pride in the cycle of rebirth. I could see it in Panit's eyes now as he looked at Lawan knowing that he'd taken the best care of her he could and now she would be reborn. Young, healthy, and giving once again.

He put his hand on my arm and with warmth in his voice said, "She go in peace, John. She is happy now. You be happy for her too."

"I will try, Panit," I said, squeezing her trunk.

He stood up and said, "I leave you together."

Her trunk moved across my face, and I wondered if she could sense my tears. Slowly, she lowered her head, relaxing it on the soft, wet ground.

I stayed in the crook of her neck, pleased to feel her breathing relax, telling her how much I loved her. The rain had stopped, and the clouds above were beginning to thin. Laying in the mud with Lawan's trunk wrapped around me and the entire herd circling us, I realized Panit was right. While I couldn't yet convince myself it was a time to be happy, I was warmed by the sense that she would move on to a new, peaceful life. This feeling, this moment of understanding, was the peace Lauren had sent me to find. I closed my eyes and took a deep breath, smiling through the tears. Lawan took a breath in sync with me. And then another, and another, until finally, the only breath was my own.

The change was barely palpable. It was a release, something I sensed in my entire body more than just where we touched. She was free now. Free to move on. The other elephants knew as well, their chirps and bellows full of sorrow as they came closer. As they rubbed her body with their trunks and hind legs, I stayed there in her embrace. If I was crushed by a mourning elephant, so be it. But I knew better. I knew now that they were the most beautifully gentle animals in the world.

I lay with her all afternoon, talking to her herd, her family. After a time, they brought branches down from the forest and put them across her body. Panit and the mahouts joined them, laying *phuang malai*, beautiful garlands of rosebuds and jasmine and marigold. The tribute to her, the love they were showing, was magnificent. Even though she'd left the herd long ago, their love for her had never stopped.

I turned onto my knees and leaned over her, kissing her cheek. The sun cleared its way through the clouds, its warmth spreading across my back. Remembering how Lawan once fondled my wedding ring, I twisted it, turning it freely in the groove it had formed over the years. The skin beneath was pale and soft, smooth and untouched. The rest of my hand was a dramatic contrast. It was rough and dirty, calloused and strong from long, hard days around the world.

I understood now why Lauren had me take this journey. It wasn't to remember her. She had wanted to give me strength, the strength to stand on my own. To see that it was ok to laugh, to love, and to smile again.

"Thank you, Lauren," I whispered.

I twisted the ring off and placed it close to her heart among the branches and flowers, sharing Lauren's love with Lawan. I kissed her goodbye once more and knew that I would see them together someday.

17

That night, I returned to Anong and Chanti's house to find them lovingly calm and gentle with me.

"She peaceful now," Anong said quietly, pulling out her phone and showing some photos Panit had just posted.

One of them was from the day I'd collapsed, with Lawan in the shelter and me being held on her back by the other elephants. Another showed her peeking out of the bush while the mahouts dug her watering hole. The last one had been taken earlier that day when she had laid down that final time. Her trunk was wrapped around me, and I was kissing her cheek.

"See how happy she is?" she asked.

"Thank you, Anong," I said, giving her a hug.

Seeing Anong's phone had reminded me that I hadn't found my own in my pocket or bag when I'd come off the hill. I searched everything before taking a shower, and again afterward, but couldn't find it anywhere. It must have fallen out when I'd slipped and was likely swallowed by the mud now.

My stomach grumbled, reminding me I hadn't eaten much all day. Grabbing my wallet, I headed to the night market to replace the phone and get a bite to eat. Finding a replacement phone was easy enough, and I soon found a small restaurant advertising wifi. While everything on the device was being restored from the cloud, I ordered a curry. By the time I finished, I realized how drained I was, both physically and emotionally. I was yawning and fighting the urge to close my eyes as the downloading pinwheel spun and spun. The best way to stay awake would be to walk, and I was thankful the restaurant owner said it was ok to leave the phone plugged in for a while longer.

Going down the long street of the night market, I mechanically went through the motions, picking up a shirt and replacing some toiletries I'd mistakenly left in Japan.

As I watched the locals sell their goods and the tourists stroll under the lights, for the first time, I felt detached, as if part of me had left with Lawan. The vibrancy of the city at night had paled, and I knew my experience here was complete.

It was time to start over. It was time to go home.

But where was home?

Years ago, the thought of not having a home, of having to choose a place to live, would have terrified me. But that night, standing in the center of the market beneath the strings of light, I was content. My heart was full, and I knew just where to go. Back in the restaurant, I picked up the phone to find a flight.

An avalanche of notifications fell from the top of the screen that crushed my heart completely.

They were all from Paris.

Omri had died of a heart attack early that morning.

Twenty-four hours later, Monique met me at Omri's door, her eyes red and swollen.

I wrapped her in my arms. "What happened?"

"He was at the window, probably opening the curtains to let in the morning light. The doctors tell me it was quick and without pain," she said.

"When I last talked to him, he said the medications were helping. He said he was following the doctor's orders."

"In his own way, but you know Omri. He would have taken the advice he liked and disregarded the rest."

"I am so sorry, Monique."

"We are all sorry for each other, John. He held us together, that wonderful man." She wiped her eyes and stepped back from the door.

"What can I do to help?"

"It is going to be busy here. Come in. You must be exhausted."

The warmth in the stylish rooms at the front of the apartment was missing, and our footsteps were cold and somber. In the kitchen, caterers prepared small sandwiches in silence.

Monique nodded to one of the young men, who set about making coffees for us both. "They will be here for a few days," she said. "With so many people coming in, I thought it would be best to keep the kitchen going."

"He always loved making sure everyone was fed and happy."

She nodded solemnly before saying, "He would be proud to see you now, John."

"I wish I would have been here for him."

"When he came back from India, he couldn't stop talking about you. He reminded us of how much you'd changed when he saw you in New Zealand. How you'd grown, become strong and comfortable with the world around you. When he returned from India, he told us how much you helped those families, how much it warmed his heart to see you with them. And the elephants, oh how he loved your stories about them."

I looked down, embarrassed. "I don't know what I would have become without him."

"You do not have to worry about that. You found each other, and that's what matters."

"What are the plans for tomorrow?" I asked, wanting to steer the conversation away from me.

She understood and said, "The service at the Nazareth Synagogue is at two o'clock. Afterward, a smaller group of us will take him to be buried at Montparnasse Cemetery and then we will return here for dinner."

"What do you need help with?"

"Thankfully, the memorial service is being handled by the staff at the synagogue. The caterers will handle the party here."

"How about the burial?"

"The rabbi's staff are organizing that too. I understand that by tradition, family members will place some dirt on the grave. I think that will be us, John, all of the people he loved having around him."

I thought of Lawan, her children coming to say goodbye, gently covering her just as we would cover Omri. "And Camille?" I said.

"That is where I need your help."

"How is she?" I asked, knowing how hard Omri's death would be for her.

"She came here just as they were taking Omri away. She ran out in tears and has been locked away in her apartment ever since. She won't let any of us in."

I closed my eyes, and my shoulders fell.

"You are the only one who can help her through this."

"We're not exactly on speaking terms, Monique. You know that, I'm sure."

She fixed me with a stern look. "You had a fight, John. This is bigger. He was as close to a father as anyone could be. Her only parent, and now he's gone."

"I doubt she'll even talk to me."

"She will. No matter what misunderstanding you had, you care for her. I know you don't want to see her suffer."

"I don't. Not at all," I said, knowing she was right.

Finishing my coffee, I stood up and hugged her once more. Not in support but to thank her for reminding me that dear friends can overcome anything to support one another.

"I'll go over now," I said.

"Wait. I am sorry to say this," she said with a grin, "but you smell terrible."

I pushed back and smiled, appreciating her attempt to lighten the moment. "You don't like my jungle freshness?"

"I think it is more like jungle rot," she said with a smile. "We kept your room free, so find something to wear in the wardrobe and clean up before you go."

"You are the best, Monique," I said, meaning every word.

***

I pressed the buzzer for Camille's apartment for the tenth time, now leaning on it, but there was still no response.

Like Omri's and many apartments in Paris, I was in a small courtyard separated from the street, thankful for a wall between me and the paparazzi that had camped outside. But still, I wished she'd answer.

If my memory was correct, the building caretaker lived in the unit opposite the panel of buzzers. Going to his door, I hoped that was still the case. After several minutes of knocking, an elderly man opened the door with a scowl.

"*Pardonnez-moi, monsieur,*" I said. "But can you please help me to Mademoiselle Amari's apartment?"

"She is not accepting visitors now," he replied.

"I am an old friend," I explained.

He looked up and eyed me carefully. "You are Monsieur Winter, yes?"

It had been years, and I was surprised he remembered. "Yes. I am sorry to bother you, but Mademoiselle Amari has had a death in her family."

"Yes, yes. Monsieur Uziel. I have read about it in the paper. One minute and I will take you up."

He hobbled away, returning later with a large ring of keys. Together, we slowly ascended the stairs. At her door, he knocked.

There was no response.

"I am worried about her. Please," I urged, pointing to his keys.

He hesitated briefly before finding the correct key and opening the door.

"Thank you."

"Take good care of her, Monsieur Winter," he said.

"I will."

Camille's apartment had always been filled with sunlight and happiness. Bright white walls and cream-colored furniture covered with pillows and blankets in warm, vibrant colors had always amplified the sun, filling the space with cheer. But today, the apartment was hollow and dark. The shutters were closed, leaving only thin daggers of sunlight from the edges trying to cut their way inside. I moved slowly through the foyer and down the hall, gently calling her name. Dirty dishes on the kitchen counter gave a sign of life, but also an indication that the housekeeper had been dismissed. The living room was a mess, with pillows thrown on the floor. A vase lay toppled next to one of the tables, the flowers wilting in a damp circle.

A lump in a mass of blankets on the couch moved slightly. The folds parted, and a pair of sad, emerald eyes connected with my own. Their sides turned up in thanks before closing with a tear. I went to her, and her arms reached out to me. We pulled each other close, holding on to all we had left. Her trembling shoulders loosened tears of my own.

They came not for myself but for Camille. Her anchor, the man who had raised her from a teenager, was gone. I knew the emptiness she felt. I understood not knowing what to do, what it felt like to be a rudderless ship tossed in the waves.

"He was the best man in the world, wasn't he?" I whispered.

"*Mon papa,*" she sputtered, a phrase I'd only heard her use for Omri once before.

"He was. He loved you so much, Camille."

"What will I do, John?"

"You will remember him. You'll remember how loving and vibrant he was. And you will continue on with the life he gave you. You will keep making him proud of the wonderful person you are."

"Will it be better soon?"

"It will, Camille. Not today, and not tomorrow. But yes, it will be better."

"How did you do it, John. How did you get better?"

"I had help from people I loved. From Omri," I said. "From you."

She held me tighter. "I will need you, John."

"And I'll be here for you."

"For now," she said.

I absorbed the bitter punch. Heaven knows I'd said things long ago that I wished I could take back. "I'm here, Camille."

Her eyes met mine, studying.

I gently brushed the hair on the side of her face back and wiped a tear from her cheek. "Let me make you some tea," I said.

"No, John. Please, just hold me."

We stayed there, the slashes of sunlight slowly swinging past us and growing longer. She told me stories of Omri, some happy and some sad. I listened, wanting her to express all of these feelings. Even when she fell silent, lost in her memories, I listened, there for her.

When the sun finally set, her shoulders relaxed. I gently helped her up and told her we were going to Omri's, knowing that being together with the people he loved would help us both. As she showered and dressed, I called her driver.

We drove straight into the courtyard at Omri's, avoiding two paparazzi waiting on their motorbikes nearby.

After the driver let us out of the car, I pulled him aside. "Camille will stay the night here, but we'll need you tomorrow for the day."

"Of course, monsieur," he replied. "What time?"

"One o'clock, please," I said. Thinking Milena would come, and Monique and Gabriel should have a car, I added, "Do you have another car you could send?"

"Yes, of course."

"Wonderful. I think Mrs. Bianci and two other colleagues will need a ride." Hearing voices from the windows above, I added, "Actually, how many cars do you have?"

"Four Range Rovers like this, monsieur."

"That's fine. Let's use them all. It sounds like there may be quite a few of us."

He nodded in reply.

I leaned closer and quietly asked him to have Camille's housekeeper come tidy up her place and let some light in.

"With pleasure, monsieur. All of us like Miss Amari very much. She has always been so kind to us. We hope she will be happy again."

"She will be. It will just take time," I said.

Walking through the outer rooms and into the heart of the apartment, I was happy to feel more life inside. The sounds of voices and the smell of food would have made Omri happy.

Catching sight of Camille as we entered the kitchen, Amélie and Chloe immediately ran to her, their faces open in the genuine care only good friends can express. It was exactly what she needed. Just beyond them were two friends of my own I'd sincerely hoped to see: Ashton and Hailey.

I hugged them both. "I am so happy you two came."

Hailey was still shaken. "I loved that crazy man," she said.

"He wasn't crazy," I said. "He was just all the things we wanted to be but were too scared to try. Expressive, loving, and straightforward."

Ashton raised his glass. "Well said."

One of the catering staff approached and handed me a drink. "Tequila with a splash of lime and simple syrup, if I recall," he said.

"Thank you very much. You are fabulous to remember," I said quite honestly.

As he returned to the kitchen, I said, "Even looking over us now, Omri is the perfect host."

"He was always that," Ashton said.

"Do you remember the day you brought me here?" I asked them. "I was terrified of him."

They laughed.

"I think he was equally terrified of you!" Hailey said. "Such a sad man you were."

"For the rest of my life, I will be thanking you for that moment. To me, Omri will always be magical," I said.

"You two connected," Ashton said. Tilting his head towards Camille, he added, "Or you three, I should say."

"We did. The unlikeliest of friends becoming as close as could be."

"He loved the times the three of you were together, John," Hailey said. "He would talk to us afterward, after your weekends away, and it made us so happy to hear the joy in his voice."

I saw Monique sitting alone on one of the kitchen couches. "It's hard for her as well," I said. "If you'll excuse me, I'd like to check in with her."

Hailey leaned forward and kissed me on the cheek.

I squeezed her hand before taking a seat next to Monique.

She inclined her chin to Camille and said, "It is good to see the life in her again."

"She needs to be with friends now. If there's one thing I learned, it's that hiding alone doesn't help a single bit."

"We're here for her, but I am so glad you came back. And not just for Camille. For Omri, and for the rest of us."

"It was an emotional time when I was here. I was about to give up. On everything, really," I said. "Omri, you, Camille. Everyone here gave me the push I needed to go out and heal."

"That's what friends do," she said.

"That's what *family* does, Monique. And I think of you and everyone here as my family."

There was a bit of commotion in the kitchen, and we looked over to see a young woman rush to Camille. Just as she raised her arms to give a hug, a waiter came around the counter carrying a *barigoule* of vegetables in a large bowl. The timing of her arms swinging up was perfect. She sent the bowl flying, spilling stock and vegetables down the front of the poor man's shirt and across the floor.

Monique laughed and said, "Are you sure *this* is the family you want?"

Everyone burst into laughter and rushed to help clean up. "What better family could there be?" I said.

We all pitched in, picking up bits of artichokes and mushrooms, and more importantly, apologizing to the young man. The poor thing was embarrassed, but the young woman whisked him off to the wardrobe to find a clean shirt and pants.

"Who is she?" I asked.

"Sienna," said a new voice. It was Milena, who I hadn't heard come from behind us.

I stood and greeted her with a hug and two kisses.

"She's an up and comer. She has just the right look, and Camille adores her. She may be the one to take Camille's place on the magazine covers this year," she said.

"Camille isn't modeling any longer?"

Milena shook her head. "You really don't watch the fashion news, do you?"

"Clueless is the word we use for him here," Monique said with a smile.

"It's a world I still don't understand," I admitted.

"Yet here you are, right in the center of it."

I shrugged.

Milena explained. "Camille hasn't worked opposite a camera or walked a runway in quite a while. She's been entirely focused on the business, and we're growing like mad. Even looking at a few acquisitions."

"I heard from Omri a long time ago that you made a great pair."

"I still can't thank you enough for introducing me to her, John."

"You've thanked me plenty. I'm just happy it's worked out so well."

"To be honest, she is brilliant. Her instincts are right on."

I nodded, and we turned to see her talking with Hailey and Ashton.

"How is she today?" Milena asked.

"Better now. She was in a rough place earlier," I said as we watched her.

"I know she will be better with you here."

"With everyone here," I said.

"I've been in Rome the past few days and haven't had the chance to see her yet. If you'll excuse me," Milena said.

As she watched Milena go, Monique quietly asked, "Tell me, John, did you find what you were looking for?"

"I don't think I knew what I was looking for at all. Everyone around me knew, but I was oblivious."

"We understood you needed time to be sad and to be mad. And we knew that afterward, you would need time to decide who you will be next. Omri knew this best of all."

"I think what I found was the confidence to appreciate what I had. I was one of the lucky ones. The love I had is a wonderful part of me, but I need to allow the joy in everything that comes afterward. I understand that now."

She placed her hand gently on my knee. It was like the touch of a favorite aunt, warm and loving, but most importantly, reassuring. "I am so happy," she said. "What do you think is next?"

"I think it's time to go home," I said.

"America?" she asked.

I shrugged. "To be honest, when I've thought of home, it's Paris that comes to mind. It's the place I've wanted to come back to more than anywhere."

Curiously, her expression brightened. "Did Camille have anything to do with that?" she asked.

"All of you had a lot to do with it," I replied.

Across the room, Camille smiled as Hailey shared a story.

Quietly, perhaps more to myself than Monique, I said, "But she's had more to do with it than I've wanted to admit."

Monique smiled. "Omri knew."

"I shouldn't have left it the way I did in India. I shouldn't have cut her off. I didn't realize it until I saw her today. I didn't realize how much she meant to me."

The hand on my knee squeezed. She leaned forward, her voice now little more than a whisper, and said, "You need to tell her."

"The time right now is for Omri. It's about mourning him and helping her through it. It's not a time to bog things down with my feelings."

"Actually, John, the time right now is for all three of you. There's something I need to tell you. When you said Paris might be home for you," she said, spreading her arms, "is this the home you think of?"

"It's where everything started for me."

"As Omri's executor, I am dealing with his papers. He has left the apartment to you and Camille."

I closed my eyes, feeling surprise, confusion, and the smallest bit of happiness, and that I wasn't worthy of such a gift. "It should be Camille's, not mine as well. Why?"

"I don't know, but I remember asking him why he put you in Camille's old bedroom when you first arrived. He said he wasn't sure, but that it just felt right. He saw something, even back then."

"I think you're imagining things," I said jokingly.

She shook her head. "The date on the papers? He made this decision years ago."

I was taken aback. "What about you? Gabriel? You've both known him for ages. This doesn't feel right."

"This is not something to worry about. Omri had quite a large estate, and he's been very generous with all of us."

"That makes me feel better. Camille, does she know?"

Monique shook her head. "I only just found out today when you were gone."

"I'm not sure that she's done being upset with me yet. This might… Well, it might be hard for her since it involves me too. Let's let her grieve first. Is that ok?"

"If it's what you would like," she said carefully.

I nodded.

She waited a moment before asking, "Which are you afraid of, sharing the apartment with her or sharing your feelings?"

An answer wasn't needed.

She fixed me with a frown, her disappointment clear. "You have to tell her, John. The sooner, the better."

"I know, but let's keep tonight and tomorrow for Omri."

I went to stand up, but her hand pressed on my knee.

The thing about a favorite aunt is that they are clever about calling you out. She did this not with words but with a look. An uncomfortable moment passed before she withdrew her hand.

We stood together and reentered our group of loving friends. We told the stories we'd all heard before but that still made us laugh and cry. It was our way to honor the beautiful man who'd brought us all together.

While the caterers finished the last of their cleanup at the end of the night, friends headed off to the various rooms to sleep. I fussed about, tidying up as I used to until realizing I couldn't remember the last time I'd slept. Retreating to my old room, I saw Camille was sound asleep in the center of the bed. I moved the blanket to make sure she would stay warm through the night.

***

The synagogue was completely full. Designers, stars, models, athletes, and politicians filled the seats beneath massive chandeliers. As Camille and I walked arm in arm to the front, we would be stopped periodically as mourners grasped her hand in sympathy.

Following the rabbi's prayers, the French president offered kind and loving words of support. He was followed by Anna Wintour, the editor of *Vogue* and grand dame of fashion. She praised Omri's work in sharing the fashion industry with the world through his photographs. She also spoke of his ability to make anyone feel special, as if they were the only person in the room. It was a trait of his I'd felt every moment we were together.

After the service, Camille and Omri's close friends gathered in one of the rabbi's anterooms while the other guests departed.

The rabbi spoke to us over coffee, explaining how Omri would be brought to his burial site shortly. He shared kind words about Omri and was sincere in his offer to help Camille with whatever she might need. After a time, we loaded into the Range Rovers and drove to Montparnasse. As we walked through the headstones and tombs to the place where he was to be put to rest, Camille's arm was wrapped in mine. She held tighter this time as if holding on to more than just me.

In the beautiful gardens, several rows of chairs had been set up, already filing with mourners. Though still a fair amount of people, it was a smaller group than had attended the service. These would be the people who'd been close to Omri at various points of his life, and I was pleased to see a few soldiers in uniform to honor that part of his history.

Before we entered the clearing, Camille rather emphatically steered me off to the side and took us behind a row of hedges. "I do not want to do this, John." She had planned to speak there, in front of friends rather than at the more public memorial.

"These are Omri's friends. They know how much Omri loved you and would be happy if you just read a nursery rhyme. Don't be nervous. They only want one last chance to be with him."

"No, no, John. I am not nervous about speaking. I…I don't want to say goodbye." She buried her head in my chest.

"I know you don't. Neither do I."

"When they put him in the ground, he will be gone from me forever," she said, mumbling, having difficulty in saying the words.

"He's not gone from you, Camille. He's with you every day. He's part of who you are. He's the reason you and I are here together right now. He's part of who we are."

She stiffened slightly, and her breath paused for the briefest of moments.

I worried I'd said the wrong thing.

She pushed back from my chest and collected her breath. I handed her a handkerchief, and she dabbed below her eyes and nose.

"Let's go say goodbye," I said.

After the rabbi made his blessing, Camille stood. She spoke not to the guests, but to Omri.

"When mama died, you were the father I needed. You didn't spoil me, nor did you leave me to figure out the world by myself. You pushed me when I needed it but protected me when I went too far. You set me on a pedestal when I was most fragile yet put me in my place when confidence exceeded ability. You breathed life into me, gave me joy, and shared more love than anyone in this world possibly could."

She went to continue, but her sadness finally bubbled to the surface. "Thank y—" she began but couldn't finish. When her sobs would not stop, she turned to me and held out her hand.

I went to her, first squeezing her hand in reassurance, then giving up and wrapping my arms around her.

After a moment, she said quietly, "I am sorry, John."

"Don't ever be sorry for crying, Camille."

She smiled sadly at the phrase Omri had used on both of us more than once. It was just enough to give her the courage to turn and finish, saying, "Thank you, Omri, for making me the luckiest girl in the world. I love you. Rest in peace forever, my darling."

As Omri was lowered into his final resting place, the rabbi said a few last words and we were all given a chance to place a handful of dirt in the grave. The guests mingled quietly afterward, speaking with the rabbi or one another before gradually leaving for the apartment. While the cars slowly filled and pulled away, Camille stayed behind, watching the workers finish. I waited by her side, watching until the last shovel of soil was raked smooth.

"I have never felt alone this way," she said.

"You're not alone, Camille. Not at all."

"But you will not be here forever."

"I'd like to stay," I said.

She squeezed my hand solemnly before turning away in silence.

***

The apartment was full, almost like its days as a central gathering spot for the industry. Camille and I went in different directions when we arrived, each taking time with various guests. I spent time with Hailey and Ashton, Gabriel and his boyfriend, and a few of the designers and models I'd met years ago. I spoke with Milena again, and as we noticed the three former Israeli soldiers, we engaged them with others, all of whom loved hearing stories of Omri and his youth. The guests ate and drank and conducted themselves as one does after a funeral, speaking with kind words and respectfully throttling any excess joy. Over time, the crowd thinned, and as I was saying goodbye to one group, Alessia Ricci, the former Gucci creative director I'd met in India, approached.

"I am glad to see you again, John, though I am sorry it is under such sad circumstances," she said.

"Thank you for coming, Alessia," I replied.

"There will always be a place in my heart for Omri," she said.

"He was quite special."

"Where are you off to next?"

"To be honest, I think it's time for me to settle down," I replied, apparently catching her off guard.

"Would you be interested in smaller trips, do you think?"

"Of course. Getting out there helped me so much, but it also left me wanting to see a few more places someday."

"Where would home be? America?" Alessia said.

"It might be right here," I said, meaning it in more ways than one.

"The foundations that participated in India loved your idea there, and they have been very pleased with the results they're seeing."

"Graeme and his team are smart. They're doing good work, and they understood how to scale. My guess is that's not always the case."

"I agree, and you were the one to see they were different."

I wasn't sure how to reply and let her continue.

"Interested in a job offer?"

I laughed. "I'm not much of a hire these days. I'm years out of practice in accounting, and while I've had plenty of time behind a camera, I'm sure not a fashion photographer."

"It's for neither of those," she said with a laugh. Turning more serious, she continued. "We get hundreds of requests a year from charities. All of the foundations within the Kering family do. We'd like you to be our scout. To review the requests, see if they make sense in the real world. To see if they'll help."

"I, ah…"

"We've been following your travels online and through Omri for years. You dig in, you understand the people in these places.

Connecting us with the education project in India was authentic, it was a relationship we were able to develop because of you."

"It was more Omri than I."

"Both of you, I think. But you understand us—the people in this business—and you have strong values, John. Sound principles and a knack for seeing people and their capabilities. There's no one else who would be better suited."

"I'm not sure I am ready for a corporate job just yet."

"It wouldn't be corporate. You'd work independently, advising us and vetting our ideas. You'd work on your own timetable and set your own compensation. And we'd like you to bring your ideas to the table too," she said.

I looked over at Camille talking with some of the remaining guests.

"I would imagine Camille and Milena would like to be a part of it, to participate in the philanthropy too," she said, following my gaze. "If that makes the proposal any more attractive."

"I did see some needs out there. Wells for fresh water and a system for vaccinations would change lives in more than one country."

"See, John? This is natural for you. And I know you've seen more complex problems."

I nodded. "Emergency education in refugee camps. I know it's strange to think of school as a necessity alongside water, food, and medicine, but a lot of refugees will be raised without an education at all. There are half a million children in the Rohingya camps in Bangladesh alone. If they don't get a chance, an entire generation could be lost."

"Would you go there? To understand, to find the right resources?"

"I'd go to the camps in Bangladesh. It's the only way to understand," I said.

Camille had been walking toward us, but immediately detoured and left the room.

Alessia nodded her head.

At the same time, a door slammed loudly down the hall.

"I am very interested in your idea, Alessia. Really, I am. But if you'll please excuse me," I said.

***

"Not now, John," Camille said as I opened the door to the bedroom. She stood at the tall window, her face wet with tears.

Gently, I said, "Camille, please."

"I need to be alone."

I stepped through the door and softly closed it behind me. "I don't want you to be alone now," I said.

"Maybe not now, but you will leave again, I know."

"I left once," I said, my voice calm and slow but deliberate. "It was something I had to do. You knew that."

She nodded, then turned to the window, looking out but seeing nothing.

"I would like to stay. Here, in Paris."

"That will be nice for you," she said, her voice monotone.

"I...I would like to stay for you. For us." I said, stepping toward her.

"Until you leave for Bangladesh," she said turning to me, her eyes dull. "Yes, I heard you talking to Alessia. You are not finished yet, are you?"

"Camille, that was—"

She waved her hand dismissively.

"She wants me to scout charity projects for her. That's all," I said.

The floorboards by the door creaked. We both turned to see a shadow of small feet in the gap below the door.

"I'd like the two of us to go there. Together," I continued.

"When will it end, John? You cannot run away forever."

"I'm done running."

She moved backward and sat on the edge of the bed, bent over slightly, elbows on her knees and hands covering her eyes. "Why, John? Why are you doing this?"

"I am sorry, Camille," I said. My throat tightened as I carefully sat on the bed next to her. "You were a friend, my dearest friend. You cared and listened and made me laugh."

Next to me, she wiped her hands across her eyes, smearing mascara down her cheeks.

"You showed me that I could smile again, enjoy the good moments in life. I needed that to heal, Camille. I needed *you*."

I watched her eyes close. Another tear fell.

"In Thailand, I fell in love with an old elephant. She passed away the other day, and a friend said something. He told me she was happy when she died, happy because we loved each other. He said because of that, she would come back happy in the next life. It was such a positive way to look at things. It made me understand that right now, this is *my* next life."

She took a deep breath and wiped beneath her nose.

"I realized then how much I've missed you, how much I've missed your laugh and your smile." I took a deep breath and said, "I realized how much I love you, Camille."

I worried that saying it out loud might hurt or somehow feel wrong, but the gift Lauren gave was the time not only to heal but to be free to love again. She loved me enough to allow me to be happy when the time was right. It was perhaps the most generous and giving form of love possible. It was something that I hoped to be strong enough to give one day.

"It took me so long. Too long, I know," I said. "But without that time, without the space you gave me, I never would have made it to this point. To this moment right now."

Her eyes turned to mine. Surveying. Reading.

I moved my hands forward and held them open. I waited, giving her the time she needed, the time she deserved, hoping her eyes found whatever they were looking for.

And then, from deep within the crystalline flecks of green and gold, right through the sheen of tears, came a spark. Like a flash from a lighthouse in a storm, it was bright only for the fraction of a second it sweeps by, yet just long enough to guide you home.

The warmth of her hands could be felt before they reached my own. I knew then it was ok. It was ok to be happy again. For both of us to be happy.

In barely a whisper, she said, "It is not too late."

The floor by the door squeaked as someone leaned closer.

A tiny wrinkle appeared in the corner of Camille's eye and turned upward. "You will need to say it again, so Amélie can be sure."

I turned to the door. "I'm sorry, Camille. I love you."

A squeal came in return. Shadows of feet danced before disappearing down the hall.

She leaned forward and said, "Now quietly. Only for me. So *I* can be sure."

I whispered it once more before gently touching her nose.

"I love you too, John." She took hold of my finger and pulled me closer. "I was going to wait how ever long you took."

My lips went to hers.

***

The cozy corner of the kitchen where the rest of my life started so long ago was filled with the friends who meant so much. Hailey stretched across one of the couches, her head on Ashton's thigh. Amélie and Chloe sat closely on the other, sharing a gray cashmere blanket. Milena was on one of the sheepskin chairs, knees bent and feet folded neatly beneath her. Monique was on the other, with Gabriel on the floor in front of her getting his shoulders rubbed. Each of their faces bore a cheeky smile unique to their personalities.

I sat down next to Chloe, who gave me an impromptu kiss on the cheek. Camille looked at the small amount of space left on the couch and decided it would be better to simply sit on my lap. Her arms went around my neck, and mine wrapped her waist.

"Sorry," Camille said to everyone. "Someone is rather stubborn."

"I think we all know how stubborn *both* of you are!" Amélie said to laughter all around.

"What do you say we break into Omri's good Armagnac? I know he'd want to celebrate the two of you coming to your senses," Ashton said.

"Marvelous idea," Gabriel said. "I will help."

When they returned and passed glasses all around, I savored the moment. The friends I'd become so close to at the start of my journey gathered together. Despite all having full lives of their own, they'd each made the time and gone to the effort to help me in some way or another. I couldn't have felt more grateful.

I held my glass and said, "Thank you, Omri, for filling our lives with love and happiness."

Our glasses raised as one in goodbye to our old friend.

"Did you tell her?" Monique asked.

"The important part," I said.

"What is the other part?" Camille asked.

"Omri has left this apartment to you and John," Monique said.

Camille's eyes softened. "Our home," she said. "But it will not be the same with only two of us here."

"I've been thinking about that," I said. "Perhaps Gabriel can still use the studio space? Maybe in partnership with Monique? And everyone else can stay as often as they'd like?"

"I love this idea," Gabriel said, reaching back to Monique.

"Me too," she said.

"It will be alive with all of us, as it has always been!" Camille said.

"*Salut!*" Ashton said as we raised our glasses once more.

Epilogue

"Good morning, John!" came a cheerful voice as I walked into the kitchen.

"Good morning, Adira," I replied, seeing her at the espresso machine. Camille was stretched out on one of the couches, a warm cup in her hands. I gave her a kiss before going to a stool at the counter.

"Café crème?" Adira asked. "I think I have the hang of this monster now."

"I'd love one." Hearing the front door down the hall close, I added, "Better make that two."

Camille had come across the young American at a bistro in the Left Bank a week before. She'd just started a gap year between high school and university when earlier that day, her pack, wallet, and phone were stolen. Desolate, she'd been offering to clean dishes in exchange for a meal when Camille happened by and overheard the conversation. The two had connected immediately, and after buying the wayward traveler dinner, Camille had brought her back to the apartment.

"I think she would enjoy a little help, John. A place to rebuild and start again, like we had," Camille had said. "Just look at her beautiful gold eyes. So big and curious, like *une chouette*...what is the word?"

"Owl," I'd said. "The English word is owl."

The memory still brought a smile, and she'd lived here since.

"Good morning, everyone!" Gabriel said, taking a stool next to me. He threw a kiss to Camille before thanking Adira for the coffee.

"What are you two up to today?" I asked.

"I think Adira is ready for some homework," he said, setting a camera on the counter. "I would like her to tell a story."

Author's Note

After putting the characters in the Jackson Chase adventure novellas into a few places that were special to me, I knew I wanted to write a longer book about traveling someday. While I was lucky enough to first go overseas at thirteen, for years I was a timid traveler, paranoid of every little thing. But as time has passed, those fears have gradually been replaced by curiosity.

With the story of John's journey, I wanted to plant the seeds for new adventures, but also remember past experiences. As a result, some of the scenes and characters are rather close to reality. To that point, I'd like to send my love and thanks to all who took such wonderful care of my grandmother in Shefford Woodlands.

My thanks to everyone who helped in writing this novel, especially my wife Niki, who kindly didn't murder me after reading an early draft. This story wouldn't have been the same without inspiring advice from Ann Huchingson and wonderful input from Demetra George, Carly Turner, Nicole Sterba, Jennifer Raftis, and Nicole Najafi. My sincerest thanks to all of you!

Self-published authors genuinely appreciate the support of readers like you. In fact, without the marketing power of major publishers, we rely completely on your reviews and social media sharing. So if you enjoyed the story and have a minute to spare, please leave a review on Amazon or share a link via Facebook. And if you do, feel free to email connorblackbooks@gmail.com so that I can thank you personally!

About the Author

Connor Black is a UX and UI design consultant and lives with his wife in Northern California. They have two sons, both making the most of life in various parts of the world.

Also by Connor Black

Jackson Chase Series

Exposure – A Jackson Chase Novella

Troubleshooters – Jackson Chase Novella No. 2

Poison Wind – Jackson Chase Novella No. 3

Made in the USA
Columbia, SC
07 July 2021